ENGAGING SIR ISAAC

ENGAGING SIR *Isaac*

A Regency Romance

Inglewood Book Four

SALLY BRITTON

For All Who Give of Themselves for the Safety and Protection of Others,
Including my Husband.

Chapter One

The cream of London Society never played fair. Despite years of trying to adhere to the rules, both those spoken and unspoken, Millicent Wedgwood had given in at last to her mother's demands to stop following the rules.

"Your sister ruined your chances when she ruined her reputation," Mother had snapped angrily only that morning. Lady Mildred—Mrs. Wedgewood to everyone who knew her well—had given her customary lecture to Millie. "It will take drastic measures to restore the family, to find a suitable match. My father was an earl, my mother's father a duke, and you have every right to a title of your own."

Father hadn't said anything, as usual, from his place near the fire. Though Mother never stated it directly, Millie and her father both knew Mother regretted marrying a mere gentleman when she could have had a husband from the nobility. But her family had needed funds, and Father had offered a well-feathered nest.

At least, mostly well-feathered. Things had changed somewhat in the years since Emmeline ran off.

"You have a dowry large enough to tempt any man willing to overlook your sister's unfortunate marriage." Mother never mentioned Emmeline by name anymore. Not since the eldest Wedgwood daughter had absconded with a lowly Welsh barrister on the eve of her betrothal to the grandson of a duke. "Millicent, you have only to form a connection with the right young ladies and they will see you back into Society's good graces. You ought to be grateful Lady Olivia will take the time to meet you in the park."

Millie remembered her mother's words, and the chilly glare with which they were delivered, well enough to shudder as she walked through Hyde Park on a warm May morning.

She held her head high, her bonnet festooned with bright green feathers. The green feathers were meant to distract from her unfashionable shade of auburn hair and lend color to her mud-brown eyes. Best foot forward for one of Lady Olivia's pedigree. She was the daughter of the powerful Marquess of Alderton. Compared to her, Millie was practically a scullery-maid.

At one-and-twenty years of age, she was no longer expected to simper and bat her lashes like a girl in her first season. No, Millicent was sophisticated, self-assured, and ready to do her mother's bidding. *Even if I am not the picture of English beauty.* Not like Emmeline, the golden-haired sister who could do no wrong, who was perfect in every way—until she'd betrayed the family.

Fortunately, Millie had a plan to fix all of the damage dealt by Emmeline's selfish decisions.

"Sarah, are you sure this is the right place?" she asked in a low murmur, waving a fan languidly before her. Despite trying to convey a careless attitude, Millie could hear the tremble in her voice. How had her mother arranged this meeting with one of Society's darlings?

"Yes, miss." Her maid, loyal even if disapproving of their errand, said from a pace behind her. Sarah knew as well as Millie did that Lady Olivia was not a sympathetic soul. "Just over there, I believe."

Millicent kept her chin tilted upward while her eyes swept the walking paths before her. Whatever her mother had done to arrange this meeting on neutral territory, Millie doubted it had been easy.

Everything, all her mother's hopes, hinged on Lady Olivia's perception of Millie. The young, unwed woman controlled half of Society with naught but a few well-placed words in the right ears.

Millie spotted the lady seated upon a bench. Lady Olivia's distinctive height and blonde curls set her apart, as did her willow-thin frame. Accompanying the marquess's daughter was Mrs. Vanderby, the daughter of an earl, not as tall as her friend but certainly as beautiful. The third woman seated with them was unexpected. Lady Sophie, daughter of a duke. The three women together had the ability to cut nearly anyone they chose and still be hailed as women of fashion and distinction.

Taking in a deep breath to fortify her nerves, Millie glided across the grass to the three women. They were in animated conversation with each other, and none of them even bothered looking up when Millie approached.

"...dreadful man. Boorish. I cannot believe he would dare humiliate you," Mrs. Vanderby was saying, patting Lady Olivia's hand consolingly. "He ought to be ousted from Society."

"He is never in Society," Lady Olivia responded, tone as cold as frost. "But I do wish there was some way to make him sorry for it."

"We all have had our share of intolerable experiences with men." Lady Sophie flipped her fan open and waved it sharply, agitation evident in the lines of her posture.

Lady Olivia finally seemed to notice Millie from the corner of her eye. "Which is one of the reasons Miss Wedgewood has been invited to meet with us today." Her words were a slow purr.

Despite the cold uneasiness in her breast, Millie dipped into the lowest, most graceful curtsy of her life. "Good afternoon. I should like to introduce myself. I am Miss Millicent Wedgewood, daughter of Mr. Anthony Wedgewood. Thank you for inviting me to meet with you today, Lady Olivia."

"Common," Lady Sophie muttered, her fan beating the air rapidly.

"Perhaps. But unlikely to draw attention," Lady Olivia countered, her green eyes flashing with interest. "Your mother made quite a plea on your behalf, Miss Wedgewood. She also insisted you would be a worthwhile companion to me, should we suit one another."

Millie had carefully rehearsed simpering speeches of admiration, but given the predatory smile Lady Olivia wore she decided to play the game differently. "My mother admires you greatly, Lady Olivia. Though I confess, I know I am not the most sought-after friend by members of your set."

Mrs. Vanderby chuckled. "That is putting it mildly. Olivia, you cannot be serious. I know you like your pets, but this one is a mouse."

Lady Olivia's eyes narrowed as she studied Millie from head to toe. "That remains to be seen."

Millie looked from Lady Olivia's accessing expression to Mrs. Vanderby. "I will do my best to prove myself to you. Those who know my family's name are aware that we have been relegated to the fringes of the elite. Our family name was rather besmirched by a certain man I do not deign to name." She cast her gaze to the ground, distressed. But Lady Olivia must know, surely, of the stain upon her family. If the marquess's daughter did not, and found out later, it could cause Millie even greater harm.

"Really." Mrs. Vanderby stood from the bench. "That men have all the power and say in such matters is utterly ridiculous. You poor thing." The smile curling her lips was not sympathetic at all. It was calculating.

"Most unfortunate circumstances," Lady Sophie muttered, sounding entirely unconcerned. "I suppose we should give her a test. Olivia?"

"A test?" Millie's eyes widened. Her mother had said nothing of a test.

"Of course." Dry amusement colored Lady Olivia's tone. "Are you under the impression that we befriend fallen women as part of our charity work?" All three women laughed, their voices airy, their noses turned up in haughtiness. They trilled their unkind humor as beautifully as birds.

For a brief moment, panic seized Millie. Though familiar with Society's coldness, she hadn't been openly mocked before. Rather than wilting, as her maid seemed to do, Millie tilted her chin upward. She did not deserve to be laughed at, whatever the case.

"My mother led me to believe you were in search of a companion for the summer, Lady Olivia. If coming into your good graces requires a test, I stand ready to attempt it. Everyone knows your friendship elevates ladies into Society faster than marriage to the right man."

Mrs. Vanderby's gaze swept Millie from the top of her feathered bonnet down to the tip of her walking boots. "Oh, there is a touch of boldness to your mouse, Olivia."

"We are often bold when we are out of other options," Lady Olivia stated. "Very well. Miss Wedgewood. We have a task to set for you. Three tasks, actually. You will earn your place as my companion for the summer, if you can complete the first task."

Though Millie's heart trembled and warned her to walk away, Lady Olivia was right. Millie was out of options. "Name it, my lady."

All three women stopped laughing. In fact, their serious masks were only broken by the gleam in their eyes.

Mrs. Vanderby and Lady Sophie looked to Lady Olivia.

Lady Olivia rose; her place as the leader of the little group was obvious in the way the other two watched her. If Millie won over Lady Olivia and no one else, it would be enough. The woman had a reputation not just for her cold beauty, but for a shrewd mind, not to mention a cutting wit.

"It will not come as a surprise to you, given your history, that there are men in Society who take great pleasure in holding all the power. Even someone such as me, and as my friends here, have been wronged. Your task, Miss Wedgewood, is to gain our revenge on the men who humiliated us." Lady Olivia came closer, her beautiful eyes narrowing dangerously. "What do you think of that, little mouse?"

Millie curled her hands into fists, her mind turning, as it had, to the man who had destroyed her family and tried to crush her in the process. Her sister's former intended. A thousand times, she had thought out how to do to him what he had done to her. A thousand times, she had planned out in her mind how to go about it. But she never would. Never could. He was untouchable, especially since his marriage into an equally powerful family.

But could she even dream of doing for these women what she hadn't the courage or ability to do for herself? And what were they asking, precisely?

"What do you mean, revenge?" The lovely May sunlight dimmed as clouds crept across the sky.

"Humiliate them," Lady Olivia said softly. "Hurt them where it matters most. Each man will prove a different sort of challenge, of course."

Millie cleared her throat. Was she a mouse? Perhaps her mother was right. Millie could not even picture herself doing something so underhanded, so unkind. Then she blinked. Mother had told her to stop playing by the rules. Had she known Lady Olivia would put this challenge to Millie?

"How would I manage that?" She hated the submissiveness in her tone.

Lady Olivia's teeth flashed in her smile. "No one gives someone like you much notice. You are practically invisible. You can go where others would be seen and spoken of, but none will even mark your presence. You will find the weakness in these men. The chink in their armor. You will report to us." Lady Olivia waved a hand to indicate the other two ladies, now silent. "And we will expose their flaws to all of Society. Hurting them. Humiliating them."

"I doubt she can do it." Lady Sophie shrugged, lowering her lashes.

"But a mouse is perfect for this sort of thing. Creeping about."

Lady Olivia's smile warmed, though Millie did not trust it any more than she had a moment ago. If Millie was a mouse, this woman was a cat, toying with her before deigning to pounce.

"I think we ought to give her the first task." Mrs. Vanderby sat upon the bench again.

"I agree. Very well, Miss Wedgewood." Lady Olivia's false-friendliness chilled the air between them. "We will tell you of these men. If you can solve Lady Sophie's difficulty, I will trust you with mine."

"And I with mine," Mrs. Vanderby added.

Millie's heart beat rapidly within her breast. What choice did she have? Her mother had sent her here, had to have known there would be a price to pay for Lady Olivia's favor.

"What are the parameters of this test?" The women would be conniving. Vicious. Clever. No one rose to such importance in the world of fashion and social politics as they did without those traits. No one. And that included Millie now, too.

"Lady Sophie's enemy resides here, in London. The other two will be present in the country, near my family's home." Lady Olivia smiled, languidly, showing her teeth again. "Bring Lady Sophie something she can use to her advantage. Knowledge. Evidence. Whatever you can find that would truly humiliate her Mr. Burton."

Millie nodded rapidly. "I will." Though she did not know how, precisely. It would take some study.

"If you succeed, I will invite you to my family's house party," Lady Olivia continued. "And give you a reintroduction to Society, on a small, manageable level. Should you prove capable, and fulfill your end of the bargain, I will make a pet of you next Season and do all in my power to restore you to popularity. Does this suit you?"

Agreeing to such underhanded schemes did not sit right with Millie. But these women claimed the men they would set her upon had hurt them. Humiliated them. As one on the receiving end of such actions, Millie could easily believe their accusations. She would do as they asked. Do what she could not do for herself.

She raised her chin. "Yes, my lady. It suits me. Point me to your first target, and I will not fail." Mrs. Wedgewood would be so proud of her daughter, of the lack of quaver in her voice.

Lady Olivia's predatory smile preceded her detailed explanations, and by the time Millie left the park, she knew the difficulty of the road before her.

Sarah remained quiet during the long walk home, to a less-fashionable street than Lady Olivia had likely ever visited. The maid's fear and disapproval were obvious, though.

"It is no use looking at me like that," Millie finally said, stopping before the door to her family's town home. She turned slowly, meeting her maid's sorrowful eyes. "I am doing this for my family, and for me. We cannot go on like this. Mother suffers. Father is no longer respected. All because of Emmeline."

The maid lowered her eyes. "Yes, miss."

"We do what we must to get what we want," Millie said under her breath. She would confide everything to her mother. She needed guidance. Her mind had already turned upon several ideas to placate Lady Sophie and impress Lady Olivia, but what did she know of their sort?

"I am hurting no one but those who deserve it," Millie added as she stepped into the house. She lifted her head to a regal angle, removing her hat and gloves. Looking into the mirror that hung above the entry table, she studied her reflection, cringing when she saw nothing but guilt in her eyes.

Millie drew herself up and glared fiercely at her mirror image. Mother was always saying that Millie needed to be stronger. Fiercer. More of just about everything Millie was not. If Millie did not manage it now, her hopes for a better future were dim.

I deserve a chance at happiness. No matter what Emmeline did with her life. I must protect mine.

Chapter Two

JULY 15, 1815

"It will be as I said, Lord Marham. Wellington will rout Napoleon and we will send the Little Corsican directly back to Elba. You will see," Sir Isaac Fox spoke with surety. "Although how they will manage it without me, I have not the faintest idea."

At his ease upon his sister's couch, Isaac leaned against its back while speaking with great animation to his two-month-old nephew. The baby squealed and waved his little fists in the air, a spot of drool on his chin.

"You ought not to argue with your elders." Isaac held his hand near enough for the baby's fingers to grab. "Even if you outrank me, Baron."

The baby's mother, Isaac's younger sister Esther, peeked around the canvas where she worked. "I realize you are both posing and entertaining Little Isaac, but I do wish you would attempt to look my direction every once in a while. Your crooked nose appears to better advantage that way than in profile."

"The baron demands attention," Isaac countered. "See how he threatens us with his fists if we do not heed him?"

The baby cooed and kicked his feet with enough force to

remove the blanket covering his legs. At only two months old, the baby boy had completely won Isaac's heart and devotion. The fact that the child had been named for him only intensified the bond he felt for the little imp.

Esther put her paintbrush down. "The two of you are a pair. However am I to finish this portrait when you are both so difficult?" She came to the couch to sit on the opposite side of the baby, fixing his blanket. The moment the child caught sight of his mother he unloosed a gurgle that had both adults laughing along with him. Esther lifted her son into her lap.

Motherhood became his younger sister, which had surprised Isaac. He never pictured her in the role before discovering her marriage to his lifelong friend, the Earl of Inglewood.

His sister had painted Isaac and Silas a half dozen times each over the years. Isaac was of a height with Silas, though narrower in build. Growing up, they had measured themselves with regularity, a wager between them as to who would reach greater heights. The end result had pleased them both. And apparently pleased Esther's artistic sense, as she was forever speaking of them as fine models.

Isaac stretched his arm over the back of the furniture again, tapping his fingers on the stiff fabric. He let his eyes wander the room, noting that his sister had added new paintings to the walls while others no longer remained displayed. What had once been a proper sitting room she had turned into an artist's study. Canvas, paints, and shelves of supplies lined the walls. Her favorite subjects tended to be brightly colored, which meant the room itself had a cheerful spirit.

"Why am I dressed like a farmer?" Isaac stared at a portrait she had done of their friend, Jacob, in his vicar's smock. "Why not put me in uniform? I am quite dashing in uniform." When Esther had applied to him to come and model for a painting, she had specified he was to wear drab, old clothing.

"I have painted you in uniform once already." She helped her son find his little fist, which he promptly shoved in his mouth and sucked loudly. Esther settled more comfortably into the couch, the baby leaning his head against her chest. "I have never seen you look more dashing, but also never so uncomfortable. You scowled at me all the hours I spent at work." She shuddered. "Most unnerving."

The end result of that particular project hadn't been especially pleasing, either. Though Isaac could say nothing against his sister's talent, his likeness had appeared rather angry. The fact that one of his sleeves had been pinned up to emphasize the loss of his arm hadn't softened the fierceness of the pose either.

"So I am to be what? A tired field hand?"

"No." Esther leaned closer and tweaked the brown cap he wore to complete his strange ensemble. "You are a weary, common man, resting at last after a long day of work. Perhaps a gamekeeper, with those boots." She nodded to his rough footwear.

He made a show of studying the tips of his boots, where they were dull and in need of attention. "What is wrong with my boots?"

"Nothing. You are as I requested. Thoroughly brown, drab, and worn." She eyed the loose blue neckerchief tied in place of a cravat. "I am pleased you still have those old things. Have you used them much?"

Isaac stretched, then removed the cap to scratch at the top of his head, mussing his dark brown hair enough to give his valet fits. "I have not. It is difficult to climb mountains when one has an estate to manage."

His sister shifted, a small line appearing between her drawn down eyebrows. "Silas wished me to remind you of our dinner party Thursday next." Her abrupt change in topic made him groan.

"Dinner party? Another one? Are you two planning to host every family in the county at your table?"

"Silas *is* an important member of Parliament," Esther reminded, lifting her chin in pride. "People wish to speak to him, to know what his thoughts are on the war, trade, and everything else that goes on in the kingdom. He wants to hear their concerns, too."

"You needn't lecture me on your husband's political ambitions." Replacing the cap, Isaac tilted it low over his eyes. He affected the accent of their local fishermen. "Aye, everyone about here knows Lord Inglewood cares for we, the common people."

His sister laughed, as he had intended. "Isaac. Are you coming to dinner this evening?"

A heaviness settled upon his chest, familiar to him now. Every time his sister asked him to be in company, every time he forced himself to have neighbors enter his home, the weight returned. At times it remained light, a gentle pressure reminding him of his brokenness. But there had been instances when the invisible weight crushed his lungs, leaving him gasping for breath.

"Need me to round out the numbers, do you?" If he deflected her long enough, avoided answering, he need not attend at all. Silas did not need him. Isaac held no political clout, no place of importance in their society; his family only invited him because they thought *he* needed to move about more in society.

They pitied him.

"I should like to have my brother, who also happens to be my husband's most trusted friend, join us for dinner," Esther stated firmly, her dark brown eyes challenging him. She appeared rather like their mother when she fixed him with that look, all firm and affectionate disapproval. At least her pity was born of love.

"Fine." The weight pressed against him more insistently. He needed to get out of doors. "I will come. But I might wear these clothes." He pushed himself up from the couch, then pushed the front toggle of the coat through its proper hole with ease. Dressing himself with one arm had been the first thing he had taught himself to do. "I find them most comfortable."

Esther came to her feet, a sparkle back in her eyes. "If you dare, I will let our little Baron Marham here mete out punishment." She cradled her son close and kissed the top of his head where blond wisps of hair covered his soft skin.

It was a shame Isaac did not have her talent with a brush. He would rather have a portrait of his sister and nephew than one of himself in his dull clothing.

"I will take my leave of you both before I trouble you any further, Countess. Baron." He bowed, throwing his hand up in a flourish that made his sister laugh. She walked him as far as the landing, then she waved Little Isaac's hand in a semblance of farewell. He tipped his cap jauntily at them and stepped out of the house, the butler closing the door behind him.

The moment his boots hit the gravel path, his smile faded away. After a few deep breaths, the pressure upon his chest eased. He took up his walk again, compensating for his lack of one arm in the way he held the other. It had never occurred to him, before the amputation, how much he depended upon both arms to keep balanced.

Stubbornness had kept him working at so simple a task as walking after his surgery. Dressing himself. Mounting a horse on his own. He still needed to come up with a way to play billiards, but most card games he had successfully mastered.

Dancing had proved awkward the first time he had attempted it. Not only had he been perilously close to losing his balance, but there were many forms requiring both arms to move through them seamlessly. If only Lord Nelson had thought to write more about living with one arm gone. But in the years since his death, before Isaac had joined the army, the man had turned into an almost mythological being of strength. If he had ever struggled a day in his life without his limb, no stories about such a thing existed.

Making his way northwest, Isaac remained in sight of the beach though his path cut somewhat further inland. His home was only two miles from Silas's door. A short walk, and an even faster run when they had visited each other as boys.

Isaac cut through a farmer's fields, then a bit of wooded area, before finally entering the rear of his property. He skirted ditches, caught his balance once on a tree, then went on. He came to the place where the well-maintained grove of cedar trees separated the wilder woods from his gardens, their familiar aroma strong in the warm summer air.

A horse nickered nearby, causing Isaac to stop short. He

listened for the sound again, his eyes sweeping through the trees and land beyond for a sight of the beast. Some habits persisted, even after military life. Staying alert had kept him alive, and his lack of awareness had cost him almost everything.

Movement from behind a larger tree caught his eye, and he saw the horse's head bend downward as though to taste the grass. The animal was dozens of yards away.

With care, Isaac stepped back, keeping trees between himself and the animal as he tried to find an angle that would reveal the rider. Slowly he went closer, but the trees were planted in a staggering formation that kept whoever was atop the horse out of view. Isaac had to come nearly behind the animal before he at last saw the back of the rider.

The shapely curve of a woman's shoulders, and the deep green gown falling down the horse's side, made him halt his stalking movements.

He did not recognize the rider immediately, but then how many people did he know well enough to recognize from naught but a view of their back? About all he could tell from his vantage point was that she had an excellent seat—her posture was near perfect.

Tipping his cap back, Isaac decided that his sneaking up on a lone woman would not be a story he wished his neighbors to recount. He set up a whistle, a light-hearted tune, and saw woman and beast both twitch at the sound.

The woman turned, one hand at the back of the saddle to support herself. Beneath the shade of the trees as she was, it was difficult for him to ascertain much until he approached. But of one thing he was soon certain. He had never seen her before.

She wore a beaver-style riding hat, and her long riding habit bore military epaulets and bright colored buttons. From beneath the hat, he glimpsed hair the color of a fox's coat.

"You there," the woman called, her voice echoing somewhat against the trees. "Is this the land of Sir Isaac Fox?"

Having never had a lady address him in such a superior tone,

Isaac stopped in surprise. Why did a stranger think she could wander onto his grounds and then start demanding answers?

Then he recalled his clothing. He had dressed as a laborer for Esther's painting. The woman, a stranger to him, did not know she spoke to the baronet. She mistook him for a servant or grounds man.

"This is Sir Isaac's land," he admitted, coming closer. She had a slightly upturned nose, fair skin, and darker eyes than he had expected, given the hue of her curls. He bowed deferentially when only a few feet remained between him and her horse. "Who might you be, miss?"

Her chin came up at the impertinence of his question, and he nearly grinned. "That is none of your concern. I am a guest of the marquess and his family."

That explained the haughtiness in her expression. Lady Olivia Duncan, the marquess's daughter, was an unpleasant person. It made sense that her companions would be cut from a similarly arrogant cloth.

Reminding himself to play the part of a servant, Isaac bowed again. "Beggin' your pardon, miss. It is my job, so to speak, to guard Sir Isaac's lands. Didn't mean any harm by it." Had he made his accent too thick?

She turned away to stare across the grounds again, at the house in the distance. His great-grandfather had overseen the building of Woodsbridge House, during the middle of the previous century. It was a gray-bricked, white-columned building that had been made to mirror estates far greater than a mere baronet should boast.

"I understand your concern," she said without looking at him, her voice softer. That surprised him. Why not continue to order him about? "I promise I mean no harm. As I said, I am a visitor here. I have heard about him—Sir Isaac. I am curious."

Curious? About him? And who had been talking about him? The weight pressed into his chest again, lightly, reminding him of its presence. "Not much people could say about him. He keeps to himself." He studied the woman, noting the intensity of her stare, as though she tried to peer through the brick of the house in the distance.

"Does he?" she asked, her eyes narrowed. "I understand that he is young. Handsome, even. A war hero. Is he shy as well?"

Isaac had been accused of being many things in his life, but *shy*? As though he were a nursery child hiding behind his governess's skirts? "Wouldn't call him shy," he grumbled, scratching at the back of his neck for good measure when she turned to look down at him again. "Private isn't the same as shy, is't?"

Her lips pursed. "I suppose not. Though it does complicate things." She studied him a moment, and he stared back, refusing to lower his gaze. That seemed to amuse her, as one corner of her mouth twitched to the side. "Do you know the family well? I understand his sister is lately married to Lord Inglewood."

"Known the family my whole life," he admitted, lifting both shoulders in a shrug. That simple movement drew her eyes to his empty sleeve, tucked and pinned as it was against his side to keep it from flapping about as he walked. Isaac did not wince, or withdraw, as he had often wished to since the loss of his arm. Instead, he pasted on a roguish grin, daring her to make a comment. He roughened his voice and thickened his accent. "I'd say the baronet ain't any more handsome than I am, though, if that's what ye've come to see."

MILLIE HAD NEVER BEFORE ENCOUNTERED A SERVANT with such a conceited way of speaking. Nor did she entirely know what to make of him, with his charming smile. His hair was dark as the earth, so brown it verged on black, curls of it sticking out from beneath his cap. His eyes flashed, almost contemptuous. Yet for all his impertinence, the man *did* have a fine-looking face. Strong, stubborn jaw, a fair height, and a confidence that finally pulled an answering smile from her.

"If he is half so handsome as you, my good fellow, then it is no wonder he is reclusive. Every miss in the county would set her cap at him." She did not speak flirtatiously. Not precisely. The man was beneath her in every possible way. Goading him on, however, produced the desired result. He stared at her as though she had said something truly shocking, and the hostile gleam left his eyes.

"Mayhap you're right," he said, his strange accent slipping about again, not quite settling correctly.

She bit her lip to keep from continuing the banter. If Mother ever found out she had spent more than a moment in pleasant conversation with a servant, the woman would never forgive Millie. At least Mother hadn't come with her to the marquess's country estate. Millie had enough to worry about without being under her mother's critical eye.

"What else is he like?" If she had caught the man off-balance enough, he may yet give her more helpful information. "Does he ride at any particular time? Does he go about into places I might chance upon him?"

"He comes and goes, as any free man does," the man muttered, almost crossly. She saw from the corner of her eye that he'd turned toward the house, too. And the accent had slipped away again.

Getting anywhere with this strange man kept proving difficult. Yet she could be as stubborn as he. "Sir Isaac is lucky that you protect his privacy as fiercely as he does." She purposefully tipped her nose into the air. If the man was loyal to Sir Isaac, there was another tact to try. "I have heard that his personality is not so attractive as his features. Indeed, some say he is quite rude and far too quick to laugh at the misfortunes of others."

The man's hand curled into a fist and his jaw tightened. "You hear that, do you? Anyone might guess where, too." He cut her a dark look. "Would ye like to know a secret, miss?" The accent was back again, but she smiled pleasantly rather than puzzle over that oddity. "Sir Isaac is somewhat touched." He lifted his one hand and tapped it against his skull. "Not all the time, mind. But on occasion he gets it into his head that he's still defending England against the French. In fact, he patrols the grounds at times, carrying a pistol and sword. If he chances upon someone he does not know, he asks for the password. If they cannot give it—" The man drew up his hand and held it as though looking down the sights of a barrel. "—Sir Isaac fires upon the enemy." He mimicked the sound of a gun firing.

Millie swallowed and looked toward the house peeking up over the trees and shrubberies, hardly separated from the grove by more than a meadow. "I hadn't heard that." Surely the man was lying, trying to be rid of her.

"We don't like to let it slip," the man told her, sighing deeply. "But as you're wanderin' about on Sir Isaac's property, I thought it best to warn you." He tipped his hat to her. "Good day, miss." Then he started whistling and walked directly into the open air of the field.

Watching him go, Millie adjusted the reins in her grip and peered beneath the trees. If Sir Isaac was as crazed as the man claimed, surely Lady Olivia would have warned her.

Not that Lady Olivia seemed concerned for the well-being of others, but one would think the marquess's daughter would share pertinent details such as madness if she wanted her revenge.

A crack in the brush on her left made her startle enough that the horse shifted, then shook its head at her with some irritation. Millie offered the beast a reassuring pat along its neck.

"Quite right, Frances," she murmured to the sweet gelding. "Best we return now, especially since our most unhelpful friend did not share the password." She looked once more to the man walking across the field, his head held high and his whistle drifting back to her.

"What a strange man." Millie turned her horse about and made for the path that had brought her to Woodsbridge Estate.

She hadn't brought a groom with her, as keeping secrets with an audience of any sort would prove impossible. Besides, no one paid much attention to her, no matter where she went. Lady Olivia had been right about that. As someone invisible to the important members of Society, and above the station of everyone else who was not, she moved about with more autonomy than most unwed women enjoyed.

When Millie returned to the rather opulent estate, she took the horse directly to the stables.

The Marquess of Alderton kept grand stables, with horses from the finest lines in Europe. The family had been around since the days of William the Conqueror, and their state of living left no one in doubt of the deepness of their ancient pockets.

After a groom helped her dismount, Millie found a side entrance to the house. A back stair was what she needed, and easily found *after* she asked a footman for help. One could wander about the large estate for hours and never find the correct room.

Eventually, Millie found the bedroom appointed for her use. Since she was without a true chaperone, the marchioness had kept her in the family wing rather than the guest wing. Her door was one down from Lady Olivia's and across the hall from Lady Alderton. Lord Alderton was still in London, along with his eldest son. Where the other two sons were, no one had bothered to tell Millie.

Sarah, Millie's maid, had now had an evening and a morning to do her own snooping and gossiping. Hopefully, Sarah had obtained information that would be of use.

Her tasks would hopefully prove as simple as the first she had performed in London. Mr. Burton had been easy enough to sort out for Lady Sophie. The gentleman not only had enormous gambling debts he had attempted to keep hidden, but he also kept a mistress his wife knew nothing about.

Sharing that information with Lady Sophie hadn't given her so much as a shred of guilt. If a man went about ruining his life, it would only be a matter of time before everyone found out about it. So what if she had been the first to share the information with the general public?

Millie entered her room and rang for Sarah, who was doubtlessly already on her way up if the servants of the household had told her Millie had returned.

Her next two assignments were her focus now. She had to find something in Mr. Weston's character to offer up as blackmail to Mrs. Vanderby, and then find a way for Lady Olivia to humiliate the baronet, Sir Isaac.

If his madness was real, and not generally known, it would be the perfect thing. A whole family could be ruined if madness was found in their family tree.

But that grounds man, or whoever he was, might have made the whole thing up. She nearly smiled again, remembering his jaunty walk and whistle.

Sarah entered the room, starched apron clean, a cap upon her head, and a frown fixed upon her face. "Miss Wedgwood, you have need of me?"

Millie smiled at Sarah through the mirror, allowing herself a moment to relax. "I do. Help me get this habit off, if you will, and tell me how you find your accommodations."

"I can't complain, miss. The maids have a big dormitory in the attics. I've been given a prime place sharing with Mrs. Vanderby's maid."

"That is useful," Millie murmured, stepping out of her dress as Sarah lowered it carefully from her shoulders to the floor. "Perhaps that girl can give you more insight into Mr. Weston's character. I confess, I am not certain how to work upon him when he does not even arrive for another fortnight."

Sarah took the dress away to a closet and clothespress, leaving Millie to pace about in her shift. "I am afraid my foray into Sir Isaac's territory did not go particularly well. I ran into a rather cheeky servant in the baronet's employ." She smirked to herself again, thinking on the way the man had side-stepped her questions and presented himself to her as handsome.

Clucking her tongue, Sarah brought out a gown of pale blue. "That sounds most distressing, miss. I hope you gave him a set down."

"I confess, I did not." Millie laughed when Sarah gaped at her, horrified. "Oh, I know I ought to have, but he was most amusing."

And there was something about that fire in his eyes she had liked. Not many men of nobility had that sort of brightness to them. A fierceness, really, that made her take notice. Gentlemen in Society, the nobility too, prided themselves on acting either as languidly as cats or as brash as fools.

Although Sarah appeared unimpressed, she went on to speak of her own findings. The schedule for the day, the mealtimes, the lay of the house, and when certain guests would arrive for various parties throughout the summer.

"People kept trying to pin down why you were here for such a long time, miss." Sarah sniffed disdainfully. "I only told them you were a particular friend to Lady Olivia, at least so long as you remained interesting."

"They would believe that." Millie went to sit before the mirror once her dress had been laced properly. "Lady Olivia collects people the way others collect artwork. She shows them off for a time, then relegates them to some back room when she finds a new piece to admire."

Sarah put Millie's hair back to rights quickly. "You are ready to face whatever adventures come your way, miss."

"Thank you, Sarah." Though the maid did not approve of Millie's actions, she had an unwavering loyalty that remained a comfort. With a light touch, Millie adjusted one of the large auburn curls that hung just behind her ear. The color of her hair might not be fashionable, but she had learned to make the most of it. If her hair was to attract attention, she might as well do her best to make it appealing.

Millie left her bedroom and went in search of entertainment. Though she doubted Lady Olivia actually wished to socialize with her, playing the part of a recluse in the beautiful house would not be borne. There must be things to keep her amused, rooms where she would be a bother to no one.

Descending to the first floor of the house, Millie searched out rooms meant for entertainment. A few servants, liveried footmen, raised eyebrows when she opened and closed doors to peek inside, but none forbade her curious exploration. She found the music room easily, with its large piano and artwork featuring the muses. The room even had all the curtains drawn back, as though welcoming any who wished to play upon the instruments, which included an elegant harp.

She immediately felt a pang of longing for her own instrument, in their small music room in London.

Millie left that room and kept on her way. Somehow, she did not think Lady Olivia would take kindly to anyone touching her instrument.

She came across a library after a sitting room and a billiard room, and there she walked inside. If she found a book and nothing more, she could be content enough.

The shelves were tall, sturdy, and stained a deep black to make the library austere. The many volumes had all been carefully curated to match, no matter the title. Every book was bound in brown leather with black and gold spines.

Running her fingertips along the books, she read them carefully and recognized a few titles of classic works. Books of philosophy and history. No novels. No volumes of poetry. Not in the grand display of shelves before her. She snorted and lowered her hand.

"I quite agree," a deep voice said from behind.

Millie jumped and spun about, seeing a man lounging on the couch in the room. His hands were behind his head and he stared at her, almost indolently.

"I beg your pardon. I did not realize anyone was in the room." Millie tilted her chin upward, not about to be cowed by the man. His dark blond hair and olive-green eyes easily marked him as Lady Olivia's kin. He must be one of the brothers.

He shrugged and turned his attention back to the ceiling. "The room is big enough for a dozen people. No harm done."

Millie hesitated a moment, trying to determine her best course of action. The family was powerful. Wealthy. Making a bad impression on even one of its members could create trouble for her while she went about Lady Olivia's task, or in the future. "I am Miss

Wedgewood." There. He could do as he wished with her improper introduction.

"Neil Duncan. Third son." He did not glance at her again as he spoke. "Are you Olivia's latest acquisition?"

Her lips twitched. "Of a sort, I suppose."

He frowned at the ceiling, then swung that frown lazily around to her. "Interesting." He sat up abruptly and leaned forward, elbows on his knees, to study her. "They do not usually admit it, you know. Most of the women my sister parades about in Society." His eyebrows pulled together. "Miss Wedgewood. I cannot say I have heard that name before."

"Millicent Wedgewood," she said. "And I do not mind admitting my place here. I am to fulfill a purpose, then I will be gone." Millie gestured to the shelves behind her. "Are there no more books in the house than these?"

"Not on display," he said. "Radcliffe novels would hardly be worthy of this—" He gestured at the shelves. "—monument to education."

Millie made a sound of understanding. "Then I had best look for amusement elsewhere."

"What are you after?" he asked, still studying her as though not sure what to make of her. She felt quite the same about him. He was older than she by at least a decade, yet lolled about like a man of half his age. "Music? Drawing? Flowers?"

"Do you mean to make yourself helpful?" she asked, unable to hide her amusement. "I was given to believe you did not like people, Lord Neil." Olivia had told her that much about her brother, and that he would not be a hindrance to Millie's assignment.

Lord Neil shrugged. "Nothing else to do today." He stood and stretched. "I have the feeling you are not attempting to make a prize out of a third son. Are you?"

She shook her head. "I am afraid not."

"No idle flattery either." He grimaced. "Very well. I am disposed to like you for that alone, Miss Wedgewood." Though his words were said flatly, she sensed a hint of humor to them. Millie studied him thoughtfully.

"Excellent. Then perhaps you could tell me if your family has a place where one might draw, with ready supplies. I much prefer to work with wood and ink, but paper would do just as well."

"There is a room reserved for that sort of thing. Back of the house. Second floor." He held his arm out. "My mother and sister have no talent for drawing, so it is not a well-appointed box."

"That is a shame." She took his arm, her mood lightening somewhat. It seemed her candid attitude had elicited the same from him.

Two strange encounters with two very different sorts of men would give her something to puzzle over, even if she found nothing more for entertainment. Society's description of Lord Neil as a charming, lazy sort fit well enough. But what was she to believe about the mysterious Sir Isaac? Until she met him, the only opinion she had worth any sort of thought was Lady Olivia's. She had made it clear he was a scoundrel, an insulting sort, who would as soon laugh at a person's misfortunes as he would a jest.

Perhaps the man at her side might offer some insight. He would likely be acquainted with the baronet. Yet Lord Neil's small kindness gave her reason to hesitate. If the time came she needed another ally in the house, it would be best to keep him ignorant of the true purpose of her visit.

When he left her in a room with a large window, wide drawing table, and a sheaf of paper, Millie settled in quite comfortably. She would wait until Lady Olivia sent for her. There was no use making herself a nuisance to her hostess. She was not truly a guest, only a means to an end.

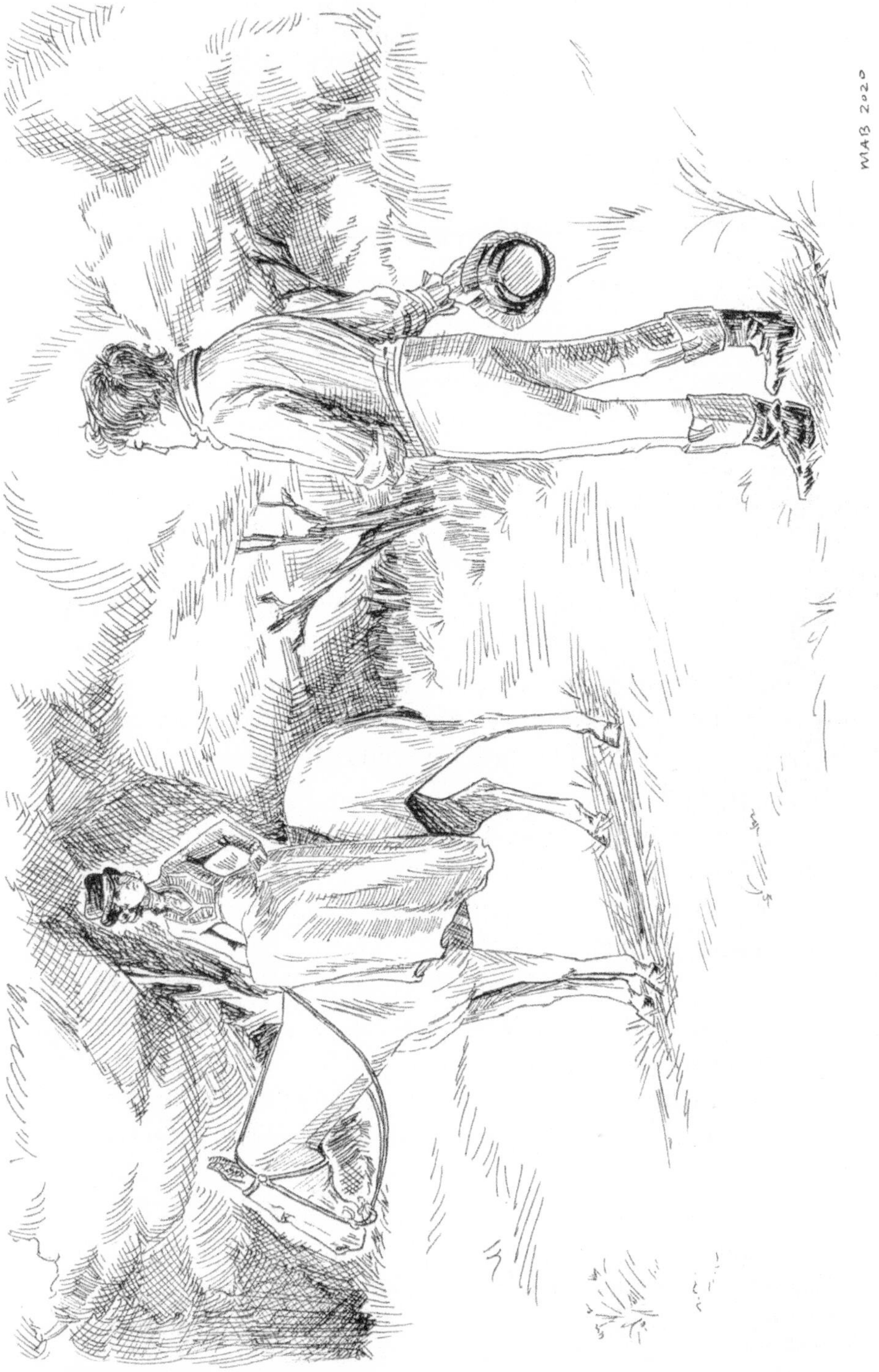
MAB 2020

Chapter Three

One of the worst things about holding a prominent place in the neighborhood, even if it was as insignificant as baronet, was that it meant Isaac had certain duties and responsibilities to perform in the neighborhood. His current duty, though, was only his because his brother-in-law was permitted to bear grudges.

"Thank you for coming with me," Esther said for the third time since he had assisted her into his gig. "Turning down an invitation to dine with the marchioness would have made everyone uncomfortable for months."

Isaac glowered at his sister. "I hardly think it fair that Silas can declare war on the family, and you are still expected to dance attendance upon them."

Esther cut him a look laden with a reprimand. "Silas's little feud with Lord Neil will come to an end eventually. I bear the man no ill will."

"He was flirting with you. A married woman. While your husband was away." Isaac was firmly on the earl's side. And he had his own reasons for wishing to avoid the family.

"Most of the *haute ton* would see that as perfectly normal," she reminded him. "Affairs abound in London among the titled. And everyone knew my marriage to Silas was not a love match. Or at least they suspected, even if it was never said aloud."

"I cannot understand why you are so quick to excuse his behavior," Isaac said, hunkering down in his seat without a care for how it would rumple his clothing or cravat.

Esther shrugged and peered out the window at the darkening sky. "I know what it is to be left on the outside of things. As a third son, I'm certain Lord Neil has had more than his share of lonely moments. Especially as part of the marquess's family. Lord Neil was older than the lot of you, I was younger, and your club left both of us out. When there are not many children of the right sort of families to get on with, it is a trial when the few about refuse your company."

The argument was not a new one, and as Isaac still thought his sister a trifle too sensitive about their childhood play, he let the conversation drop. Lack of friendship as a child should not be seen to justify poor behavior as an adult, especially in the case of one as irritating as Lord Neil.

He pulled his gig to a stop before the large, white marble steps of the Marquess of Alderton's country house. The massive building loomed over the drive with columns, curling ornaments about the windows, and too many chimneys to count. The entry was grand, too, with white and black floors, a sweeping staircase leading to the first floor, and liveried servants at every doorway.

If Isaac had even a tenth of Lord Alderton's wealth, his home would be set up well enough for half a dozen generations. As it was, he only brought in enough revenue to keep from selling off his land.

But as no one knew of Isaac's circumstances, he kept his head high and his smile tight. Silas was assisting him. They would set things to rights soon enough.

The one bright spot to his evening, the only thing he anticipated with any amount of enthusiasm, was the possibility of seeing the woman who had trespassed upon his property two days previous. She had held herself with such poise, even when he gave her insult merely by not acting as submissive as a servant ought to a gentlewoman.

What would her reaction be to seeing him again when she realized he was Sir Isaac, the man she had attempted to spy upon?

"What are you grinning about?" Esther asked in a whisper as they stepped onto the first-floor landing.

"Nothing of great importance." Isaac counted the steps from the landing down the wide hall to the parlor. The activity, simple as it was, kept him calm. Stepping into a room full of people all speaking and moving about, perfume hanging heavily in the summer air, was the very sort of situation he preferred to avoid.

The press of bodies at the last assembly he had attended, seven months previous, had left him physically ill. The weakness of his mind had never made itself manifest until after he had returned from war. Who grew sick in a crowd? Who had to spend days nursing an aching head and endure nightmares as payment for being among their neighbors?

Apparently, Isaac did. He had heard that war left its mark upon men's hearts and bodies in strange ways. But he had hoped losing his arm had been enough of a price to pay.

The fates had other plans for him, it would seem.

Best to stop worrying over it and focus on something he could control. Such as his reaction to the unavoidable shock of that red-headed woman.

Isaac and Esther entered the parlor, and the marchioness stood near the door ready to welcome them. "Sir Isaac, such a pleasure to see you again. We were sorry to miss you in Town this Season. Lady Inglewood, welcome. Such a shame that your husband could not join us this evening." Though Lady Alderton would never be praised for warmth of character, she always presented a picture of the perfect hostess. Her stately bearing reminded one and all of her relationship, distant though it was, to the royal family.

Esther made the appropriate comments. Or at least, Isaac supposed she did, while he allowed his gaze crawl over the room in search of the woman who thought him a servant. He did not want to miss the moment of recollection upon her face. The sudden surprise.

But she was not to be found.

Perhaps she had already left the country?

Disappointment settled upon his shoulders, more heavily than he expected something as simple as a stranger's absence to cause. He had sincerely looked forward to that moment of diversion.

A small squeeze of his arm informed him Esther was ready to move away from Lady Alderton and into the room to greet other neighbors. Only those who held titles or great wealth were in attendance that evening. The Parrs were present, as was Lord Sterling, and the Kimballs. Merriweather Kimball made a show of batting her eyes at every male in the room as was her custom.

Thankfully, Esther turned their path toward some of the least objectionable of their neighbors; Mr. Ashford, his son and two daughters. Their family owned a vast amount of land, and shares in a mine further north. Isaac kept his shoulders squared and his expression as pleasant as possible while they spoke. He was not in the mood for much chatter himself.

More guests arrived. Where there had been a comfortable ten people in the room, now it was nearer twenty. Heat crawled up the back of Isaac's neck and a soft buzzing began in his ears.

He started a mental count to one hundred in his mind, in French. That distraction would see him through until they came to the dinner table, where he could sit and distract himself with food and drink, and focus only on his table companions rather than the room as a whole.

A ringing soprano broke through the din, "...and this is Miss Wedgewood, a particular friend of mine." Lady Olivia, sour in nature, had still somehow managed to cultivate the voice of an angel. At least she had dropped the foolish lisp she had adopted the previous year.

Isaac turned enough to peer over his shoulder, his hope returning that the friend would be his trespasser.

29

A woman dressed in a soft blue gown stood with her back to him, her ginger hair wrapped up in an extravagant twist and augmented by yellow ribbons. She was a head shorter than Lady Olivia, who stood beside her, making her far smaller in stature than he had thought given that during his last encounter with her, she had been on a horse.

Isaac waited for her to notice him.

As though sensing his attention, the woman's head turned. She caught him looking at her from the corner of her eye. Yes. There it was. The confusion. She turned more, meeting his stare with a flash in her eyes, as though affronted by his mere presence. And then she paled, took in his empty coat sleeve, raked her startled gaze across his figure, and ended with a gasp.

Isaac smirked and stepped toward her, away from his sister's conversation with the Ashfords, and bent to speak to her in a low tone. "I told you. Sir Isaac is quite mad."

To her credit, her jaw tightened. Obviously, the woman had words to say but she bit her tongue. Her fan flashed in her hand, coming up to cover the lower half of her face from the people on the other side of her, conversing without any idea what was taking place two feet away from them.

"*You* are Sir Isaac," she accused with a hiss.

"Indeed." He straightened to his full height, amused when her cheeks turned pink. He was far too tall for her to converse easily with him in a whisper. The woman would have to mind her words. "And you are?"

She snapped her fan shut. "I was introduced to the room a moment ago. Miss Wedgewood."

Ah. What a name. It sounded like something a novelist would name a villainess. How fitting for someone of Lady Olivia's ilk. "I cannot say I am familiar with your family." He tried not to sound too smug.

The woman's hackles seemed to rise. Yes, she certainly took his words as an insult. No need to tell *her* he had been out of Society so long, he hardly recognized any names. It simply did not matter to him which families were considered important. It never had.

Esther appeared at his side, her arm slipping through his. He winced, hoping his sister hadn't overheard his last comment. "Esther, allow me to introduce you to Miss Wedgewood. Miss Wedgewood, this is my sister, Lady Inglewood."

"My lady." Miss Wedgewood curtsied prettily, without showing any of the displeasure she had displayed only moments before. "It is a pleasure to meet you. I have had the good fortune of seeing one of your paintings, in London, this last winter."

Isaac blinked, surprised, and looked to his side to see his sister blush.

"Oh, really? I have given several pieces away. You must tell me which you saw, so I may apologize for the lack of skill in its creation." Esther's smile was entirely too self-deprecating.

Miss Wedgewood laughed, the sound unaffected and oddly pleasing. "I understand you perfectly, my lady. I often feel the same about my work. No matter how much attention and love I put into my pieces, I can only see the flaws. I assure you, the painting I saw was lovely. It was of the sea, with gulls in a gray sky, at Mrs. Parr's home. I went to an evening of poetry at her townhouse."

Esther's grip on Silas's arm relaxed. "I did enjoy that one. Did you say you are an artist, too? Do you paint?"

"Not with oils, and rarely with watercolors." Miss Wedgewood did not even glance his way again. She had ruined all his amusement by instantly forming a connection to his sister. Worse still, she spoke with complete sincerity in her compliments. "I prefer other mediums. I do like to work with ink and wood, making over furniture in the ebony and ivory style. And quilling fascinates me as well."

Esther's eyebrows raised. Isaac hadn't the faintest idea what they were speaking of and started to ask when the room's attention was called to order and they were asked to enter the dining room.

The usual shuffle began as women determined who outranked

who. Isaac at least knew his place, escorting his sister. She was the second-highest ranked woman present, after Lady Alderton.

"I wonder how someone such as that came to be acquainted with the family?" Esther murmured to him. "I do not think anyone has ever known me through my painting before." She sounded pleased, and there was a sparkle in her eyes that made him chuckle.

"You do have talent, Essie." He gave her an affectionate smile, then assisted her into her chair. He was then shown to his own place at the table by a footman, closer to the middle than he expected given that most present were gentlemen. It was not as though he minded the slight, though. With the marquess and his heir away, Lord Neil occupied one end of the table and his mother the other. Lady Olivia was near to her mother's right hand. The farther Isaac was from each of them, the more likely he was to enjoy his meal.

And then Miss Wedgewood was seated next to him.

MILLIE'S SHOCK AT SEEING THE IMPERTINENT GROUNDS man at the grand dinner, then realizing he had been her quarry all along, had taken more time to wear off. His sister's art had been a merciful change in topic, allowing her time to regain her mental balance. At least she could compliment Lady Inglewood's artwork sincerely, though Lady Olivia disliked the woman as much as she did the baronet.

Lady Olivia had contrived to put Millie and Sir Isaac next to each other at dinner. Perhaps Millie could make up for her earlier tart behavior during the course of the meal. After all, nothing truly unpleasant had passed between them. He may only think her an overly curious sort.

Once their first course was before them, a broth-like concoction the color of cream, Millie sent her seatmate a tentative smile. A flirtatious, innocent character would likely be the best to play. "Sir Isaac, you ought not have teased me so when we first met."

One of his eyebrows rose, but he did not even turn to face her when he answered. "Did I tease you? I am not certain I would call the tone of our conversation teasing."

"Perhaps not entirely." She allowed herself a spoonful of soup before continuing. "I did spend most of my day wondering about you, though."

"About me?" he asked, his tone still lacking interest. "Do you mean the supposedly mad baronet you were warned about or the rude grounds man?"

Millie pushed an airy laugh from her lungs. "Both, of course. Your deception was quite clever, sir."

His eyebrow tilted upward again, then lowered into a frown. She hadn't impressed him, it would seem. He did not succumb to flattery easily. "I hope your curiosity on the matter has been satisfied." He spoke dryly, without so much as a smile.

"I am afraid not," she said, sighing dramatically. "I only have more questions about you, and I will not rest until they are all answered." Surely that flirtatious comment, accompanied by one of her prettiest smiles, ought to draw him in. Most men delighted in speaking of themselves, bragging about their accomplishments, puffing up as a prized rooster in a hen yard when paid the least bit of attention.

But Isaac Fox was not a rooster, nor did he take her sweetly baited offer of conversation. "You will have to find your answers elsewhere, Miss Wedgewood. I am afraid I am not nearly so interesting as you seem to believe."

He pointedly turned away, toward the gentleman on his other side, and began a conversation on the topic of growing hay.

The man would rather speak of farming grass than to her.

Millie winced and put her soup spoon down, ready to try something else, even if it was merely the second course.

Chapter Four

Millie sat in the little art room of the second floor, staring out the window without really seeing the gray clouds rolling in for a summer storm. A sheet of paper lay before her, filled with intricate ink drawings of flowers and birds and ivy, twisting about each other in elegant swirls. She had completed the work that morning and intended to use it as a pattern for her next project, likely a box for her father's pipes. She only needed to decide what to put in the center of the lid. Usually she put a larger scene, such as a couple dancing, or a ship upon water, in the middle of whatever object she worked upon.

Sarah sat in the corner of the room, mending one of Millie's dresses they hadn't realized had a torn hem until she had put it on. A soft knock at the door made Millie hastily correct her posture. "You may come inside," she said, rising from her chair to face the door.

Lord Neil entered, the same confident laziness in his posture as the day before. "Miss Wedgewood. I am glad I found you here. I have a question to put to you."

She clasped her hands before her, relaxed and smiling. "I hope I have the answer you seek, my lord."

He folded his arms over his chest and took her in, but not in a lewd way. His attitude was calculating, much as his sister's had been on their first meeting. Yet he lacked the predatory mask his sister wore with such ease. "Olivia has put you up to something, has she not?"

Millie's eyebrows shot upward. "Put me up to something? Whatever do you mean, my lord?"

"It is obvious she does not consider you a friend. Last evening, before dinner, she made a point of introducing you, yet the two of you have spent no time in each other's company in the three days you have been here."

Millie did not so much as blink at his observation. The man was cleverer than he let on. Yet she could not admit anything to him without betraying her promises to Lady Olivia.

"It has something to do with Sir Isaac. The deliberate way you two were put next to each other at the table was obvious to anyone paying attention. Sir Isaac could not help but see the slight against him was intentional, to seat so many gentlemen in more favored places. What, precisely, are you doing for my sister? And why are you allowing her to dictate to you? I am dreadfully curious."

There was that word again. Curious.

"My lord, I am not at liberty to discuss this with you. Whatever it is you have perceived, you ought to speak with your sister."

He waved that comment away. "I tried. She denied everything, as though I am foolish enough to believe her word on anything." That hardly spoke well of their relationship as siblings. "Olivia is up to something, and you are playing along. I will agree to stay out of it, but only if you promise me a favor at a later time."

This did not bode well. A favor, to a man known for acting the part of a charming rake? She had heard rumors of the way he flitted about society, from one lady to another, never settling into his place, a profession, or a marriage. Unsteady, some called him. A lay about, said others.

Yet all he had shown her, since the first moment of their meeting, was a begrudging sort of kindness.

"Why would you want a favor from me?" She did not see a way around it. Not really. But agreeing blindly would hardly be wise.

He shrugged, almost carelessly. "You seem to be an industrious sort of person. One day you might be in a position that I find useful, though you certainly are not in a favorable place now."

Millie swallowed. "I will owe you a favor, my lord." She did not want or need another person poking about while she attempted to fulfill the task given her by Lady Olivia. "But there must be conditions. I will do nothing that will harm my reputation," she said quickly.

"What reputation?" he asked, one corner of his mouth going upward. He glanced at the maid in the corner, then back to her. "I think we both know you haven't much of one to ruin."

Millie felt the heat rushing into her cheeks. "Perhaps not. But it is a condition. I will do nothing disreputable."

"Agreed. Anything else?" One corner of his mouth turned upward. Despite their conversation, she sensed no malice in him. Amusement, perhaps, but not even directed at her. The man was a puzzle, yet something about him eased her concern.

If only she could think of something else to ask of him. Then it came to her. "You know Sir Isaac better than I do. My other condition is that you must tell me how best one would get past his defenses. He is not eager to befriend me, and I would know how to change that."

"Befriend him?" Lord Neil's eyebrows rose, and he dropped his hands to his side, as though genuinely astonished. "Olivia does have something strange planned. I can agree to this condition. I could tell from watching last night that he had little enough interest in you. But you were going about it all wrong. Sir Isaac is a military man. If you wish to break through his defenses, attacking head on will get you nowhere." He directed a grin at her that reminded her of a wolfhound. "Does that help you, Miss Wedgewood?"

She was sure it would. In time. "I believe we have reached an accord, my lord."

He bowed. "So it would seem. Good luck, Miss Wedgewood. Whatever my sister has put you up to, I am certain you will need it."

Lord Neil left without another word.

Millie turned to her maid; Sarah had her sewing at rest in her lap and was staring wide-eyed at her. "Was that a good idea, miss? Seems to me you just made a deal with a devil."

"I do not think him a devil. His sister, perhaps." Millie lowered herself into her chair again and rolled the pen upon the table, watching the nib twirl across the wood. "He said I should not attack Sir Isaac head-on. What do you suppose that means?"

"It's like in battle, isn't it?" the maid said, lowering her head back to her work. "You've got to sneak up behind him, find some way to infiltrate the ranks." Sarah had three brothers in various branches of the military. All three had been called back to action when Napoleon had escaped Elba and began his war anew.

"Infiltrate the ranks." Millie turned the idea over in her head, her eyes upon her artwork again. "Of course." She stood abruptly. "Sarah, tomorrow morning we must pay a call on the Countess of Inglewood." If she could ingratiate herself with Lady Inglewood, infiltrating the ranks of the family, she might have a better chance against Sir Isaac.

Somehow, everything would come together. This would be her way back into Society, the way to return her mother to the world she loved, and undo everything Emmeline had ruined by running off and jilting the grandson of a duke.

Chapter Five

C alling on a titled lady without notice was hardly good manners, but Millie had a purpose. Multiple purposes, in truth. Though she had searched the house high and low, nothing in the Alderton home would suit for her project. There were no suitable boxes, and no suitable ink for working upon wood. With Lady Olivia ignoring Millie for the most part, and no one else in the house but the marchioness and Lord Neil, Millie passed the hours with difficulty.

The art room had become her haven, more so than the bedroom assigned to her during her stay.

After Lord Neil's visit, and his hint at how best to get around Sir Isaac's defenses, she had hit upon the perfect place to begin.

If she could befriend Lady Inglewood, or at least form an acquaintance based upon their mutual enjoyment of artistry, she may find a way into Sir Isaac's trust.

Sarah came with her on the short walk to the Inglewood estate and went around to the servant's entrance once Millie's admittance by the butler was assured. Thank goodness for the maid's cheerful presence. Though not many would admit to such a thing, Millie counted Sarah as a friend. Perhaps her only friend, since Emmeline's betrayal.

The butler showed Millie to a sitting room on the ground floor. The room's stark furnishings and windows looking out to the front walk made it a formal room, not graced with the family's presence on a regular basis. The furniture was of the latest style, with elegant curves and stylish fabrics, but nary a personal touch graced the room, not even a single embroidered cushion upon a seat.

A painting over the hearth did capture her attention. The scene called her forward, so she stood directly below the artwork before even realizing she had taken a step.

It was magnificent. In oils, artfully rendered, was a stretch of beach with the ocean extending into the background, the sun peeking out of the clouds and bathing everything beneath in the soft light of morning. Children played upon the beach, racing behind a boy with a kite. The perspective the painter employed kept the children at enough of a distance that one could not see their expressions in great detail, but their figures were bounding across the sand with unabashed joy and delight.

"Do you like it?" a voice asked from behind, soft and somewhat uncertain.

Millie turned, startled, to see the countess standing in the doorway. She looked back to the painting. "Is it one of yours, my lady?"

"Yes." The countess came to stand beside Millie, staring up at the painting herself. She pushed back a strand of her deep brown hair, and eyes similar to her brother's studied the painting most critically. "I still cannot quite accept my work here." She pointed to one of the children trailing behind the others, a little girl smaller than the others. "This painting tells the story of a memory."

With that piece of information, Millie took several steps back and looked at the work again, tilting her head to the side as she studied it. "The other children are similar distances apart, but that little girl is twice as far from them as they are from each other. Is it you, in the painting?"

The countess blushed, but she nodded once. "I do not feel like that anymore. As though I am behind. But the memory..." She shrugged.

"You keep the painting in this room, where you do not have to see it so often." Millie nodded her understanding and looked again. "I think it must be a good place for it, though. When you have visitors, this painting reminds you how far you have come. You are not a little girl at the rear of the group, but a countess who commands a great deal of respect. I imagine you are the one people trail behind now."

The woman's eyebrows rose, and she took in Millie's words in quiet for a moment. "I wonder if you are right. Certainly, seeing it hanging here when I welcome someone new into my home has an effect. It reminds me to stand a little taller, as it were." She lifted her chin and her lips formed a gentle smile. "Forgive me for the rather abrupt conversation. But before, when we spoke of art, you seemed to be a kindred spirit."

Millie relaxed and nearly forgot Lady Olivia's off-hand remark that involved taking this woman's pride down a peg. Given Lady Inglewood's humility in regard to her own artwork, it was difficult to imagine her ever acting anything other than gracious.

"I cannot boast of such talent as you, my lady, but I do enjoy creating things of beauty. There is a thoughtfulness in painting that makes me take notice, but my own work does not seek to tell stories so much as it does to delight the person who sees it."

"Oh? I believe you said you enjoyed quilling and ebony painting." The countess gestured to a seat in the room, which Millie took gratefully.

"I do. And that is what has brought me here today, my lady." Millie folded her hands in her lap. "I understand that Aldersy is several miles away, and that the apothecary there has supplies for painting, but I wondered whether you knew if he also had the things necessary for my preferred pursuit. I am in need of ink, and a box or two on which to work. Lady Olivia does not intend to venture into the village for several days, and her supplies lack what I need."

The request was genuine enough. Millie had no wish to disturb the marchioness, or any other member of that family, to ask for the use of a carriage. She well knew her place among them was more tolerated than it was welcomed, even with Lady Olivia as the only person who knew of the true reason behind Millie's invitation.

"And it would be a shame to make the trip into the village and find they did not have what you needed. Worse still, to send to Ipswich if everything you had need of could be had cheaply and more swiftly." The countess nodded her understanding, her gaze moving to the window as her expression twisted thoughtfully. "I cannot recall at the moment what is available in Aldersy. I am afraid most of my supplies are ordered from London. I am quite particular, and my husband indulges me."

"Oh." Millie let her shoulders fall. Drawing would have to continue to entertain her, then.

"But I might have what you need here," Lady Inglewood said with a brighter smile. "Come upstairs with me. We will raid my supplies."

Millie could not help but return the countess's ready smile. "Are you certain? I do not wish to impose—"

"One artist to another, I do not mind in the least. Come." Lady Inglewood led the way from the room, talking all the while. "I spend hours in my studio." They went up the staircase to the first floor, then down a long, wide hallway. While their home was not so grandiose as the marquess's, it certainly was one of the finest Millie had ever entered. "There is a very large closet, and shelves and shelves of my supplies. Perhaps I have what you need."

Then she opened a door, and Millie followed the countess into a room filled with sunlight. The windows took up most of the wall, nearly stretching to the ceiling from the floor, and most were open to allow a breeze to circulate sea-salted air into the room. Millie took a deep breath, as much to enjoy the sensation as in awe.

The room was bright and airy, full of light and life. A couch and two chairs were the only places to sit, and they were near the door; the rest of the floor was littered with easels and narrow tables filled with books and art supplies, while the walls were lined with shelves and canvases alike.

"I have never seen a room like this," Millie whispered in awe. Most grand houses had a room dedicated to a woman's artistic pursuits, but they were generally small, and served also as a sitting room, or sometimes a sewing room.

There was no doubt that this room served only one purpose for its mistress—it was her place to create.

Despite her years of planning, of hoping for an elevated station in society, Millie had never pictured such a room for herself. She had the vaguest idea of being mistress of a large house, of commanding legions of servants, setting the fashionable world on its ear with her choices of dress and decor, but she had never thought of what it would mean to have a single room so perfectly situated for her own particular use.

The countess bustled about, unaware of Millie's state of mind. "It might seem a little strange, to convert a sitting room into a studio. Lord Inglewood has offered to build me a room on the ground floor, with a glass ceiling. If we ever decide upon the design, perhaps it would be better, but I confess the idea of giving up my sea view holds little appeal."

Millie swallowed and nodded, though the countess hadn't glanced back at her.

"Here we are." The countess opened a cabinet, and Millie tore her eyes from the beautiful, practical room and went to stand near her hostess. "I did order a substantial amount of things from Ackermann's this spring when *The Repository* featured some clever penwork designs. I am not certain what you would need. I am afraid once the materials arrived, I was quite busy with the birth of my son." Her eyes glowed when she turned to Millie, a secretive sort of smile upon her lips that Millie could not understand.

"I will fetch a box for you to carry home your supplies." The countess disappeared before Millie could protest, leaving her to stand before the little cupboard.

She took a deep breath and began sorting through the materials. Though her mother had allowed Millie to practice penwork, it had been with reluctance.

"Such a terrible, dirty pursuit. You will smudge every sleeve and dress with ink," Mrs. Wedgewood had declared more than once. She frequently commanded her daughter to "get that dreadful mess out of my best room." Every room had somehow become the best room when Millie settled in with ink and pens.

Yet she kept working at the art, whenever she had opportunity. It fascinated her, to fully transform a box, a fan, even a picture frame, into a work of art with nothing more than simple tools.

The countess had everything Millie could want. Sharp quill pens, thin brushes, and black Indian ink. The ink was the most important part, of course. If it was the wrong mixture, it would smear and smudge rather than stain. The brush would be useful for broader swaths of black. Using Lady Olivia's watercolor brushes for such a task would ruin them, but these new brushes were quite perfect.

But did the countess have—yes, there it was. A jar of isinglass, to seal the wood before she began her work.

Millie placed her selection upon a table near the small cupboard, chewing her bottom lip as she thought over how much ink her design would require. Of course, she needed a box first.

The door opened and Millie turned to see the countess float inside, holding a baby instead of a box. But a maid came in behind her, wooden box in hand. A box the perfect size for a gentleman's desk. "Set the box just over there, Mary," the countess instructed. "Thank you."

The maid put the box down, curtsied, and left.

Millie's attention was arrested by the child in the countess's arms. "I see you brought someone for me to meet," she said, a little warmth creeping into her heart.

The only thing she ever wondered about her sister, the only

43

thing she ever permitted herself to wonder, was if Emmeline had given birth to any children yet. If only her sister would write to Millie, she might know at once, but Emmeline had remained silent.

But to have a niece, or a nephew—

Millie closed her mind to that way of thinking and concentrated on the present moment.

"This is my son, the little Baron Marham, Isaac Riley."

At that, Millie's eyebrows rose, and she came forward to better see the baby waving his arms about. "Named after his uncle?"

"Of course. I am quite fortunate that my brother and husband are dear friends. It did not take much to convince either of them of my choice." The countess lowered herself to the couch and gestured with a hand for Millie to sit on the other end. "I do hope you do not mind him joining our party."

Millie grinned and held her gloved hand out to the baby, allowing him to take a finger in his grip. "Not at all. I suspect he is a fine gentleman in company."

"The very best." The countess seemed to relax, holding her infant so his back was supported by her chest, one arm wrapped loosely about his middle. "I quite adore him. I know I ought to leave him in the nursery more often, but he is a dear boy. He hardly ever makes a fuss. I am afraid that makes him the subject of quite a few paintings." She tipped her head toward a corner of the room.

Turning that way, Millie could not hold back a laugh. Three canvases leaned against the wall upon the floor, and several drawings had been tacked to the wall, all featuring a tiny baby with large brown eyes. "I do not blame you at all. Who could resist capturing such innocent beauty?"

The countess kept her smile upon her face, but her expression softened into something more curious than polite. "If you do not mind my asking, Miss Wedgewood, how long will you be a guest of the marquess's family?"

That was not the easiest question to answer. "As long as Lady

Olivia wishes, I suppose," Millie said, keeping as close to the truth as possible. She could not leave until Lady Olivia was satisfied with her work upon both Sir Isaac and Mr. Weston. The second gentleman would not even be in her orbit until the house party in ten days' time.

"Does your family not expect you home at a certain date?" The countess's smile had faded, her brows knit in concern.

"My mother is quite pleased with where I am, at present." Millie kept her eyes upon the baby, gently wiggling her finger in his grip when he tried to put it and his fist into his mouth. "She likes the connection to the Marquess of Alderton. I think she believes it will help my cause next Season." Again, all the truth, even if she kept the reasoning behind it concealed. Mother knew all about Millie's bargain with Lady Olivia, and hoped, as Millie did, that upon the completion of her tasks, Millie would have her pick of a husband once more.

Mother insisted Millie find a man with a title. "Nothing less than a future baron," she had said with a gleam of hope in her eyes. One sister jilting the grandson of a duke was enough to keep anyone that lofty from proposing to the other sister. But a common gentleman? Her mother would never have it.

The countess said nothing for a moment, though Millie felt her scrutiny. Finally, the woman took up the baby in her hands and offered him to Millie. "Would you like to hold him? I can put your supplies into the box."

"Thank you, my lady." Millie accepted the small, warm infant and held him close to her heart a moment. He put his fists against her chest and pushed himself slightly away, looking up at her with his large round eyes, his perfect lips parted. He frowned at her, as though puzzling out why a stranger held him instead of his mother.

Whatever was wrong with the relationship between Lady Olivia and the baronet, Millie could not imagine doing harm of any kind to Lady Inglewood. The countess's warmth and kindness, her immediate generosity, made her the sort of person Millie had always wished to befriend.

Unfortunately, as a social climber, a woman with her mind set upon her path in Society, Millie could ill-afford to disappoint Lady Olivia. But nor did she wish to make an enemy of Lady Inglewood.

The baby cooed at Millie, coaxing a smile from her despite her troubling thoughts. Somehow, she would do what she must to ensure her place in Society, as her mother demanded.

THE LATE-MORNING SUNLIGHT CAME INTO THE STUDY AT an angle through the Earl of Inglewood's window, yet hardly any dust motes could be found dancing in the air. Isaac wondered how his friend managed to have one of the cleanest studies he had ever seen. The poor maids of his household surely had to work harder than any servant he knew to keep the room so spotless.

"We have yet to settle upon the position of the new dam," Silas said, shuffling a paper from one hand to another. "I truly think it would improve things for your farmers if you kept more water here." He pointed to a sketched map of their two properties. "And since the stream flows out to sea, we would be hurting no one, only improving our own water collection."

Isaac hummed his agreement. "You know better than I where it ought to go. The surveyor gave you his full report, did he not?"

"He did." Silas opened a drawer in his desk and removed a large sheaf of papers, along with a folded map. "He had curious things to say about that ridge, here. He thought we should have an expert in geology out to look it over."

"There is nothing in all of Suffolk to mine." Isaac knew this better than anyone. His father had sought out experts in mining to look over the land years before. "That is not the route for me to make my lands wealthy again, Silas, though I appreciate the thought."

Silas dropped the papers and leaned back in his chair. "You have good land, Isaac. There are ways to make it more than self-sustaining."

"Of course there are. I simply have not happened upon them yet." He grimaced and turned his attention back to the window, longing for a breath of fresh air rather than the closed-in warmth of the study. "Esther does not know?"

"I have kept my word and said nothing, to anyone, of the difficulties you face." Silas sounded tired. It must wear on him to be unable to solve all of Isaac's problems. But Silas needed to understand that a man must stand upon his own two feet.

With his own list of items to see to on his estate, Isaac rose from his chair, ready to bid his friend and brother-in-law good afternoon.

"You cannot leave without seeing Esther," Silas said suddenly, before Isaac could do more than open his mouth. "You know she will wonder why you did not wish her a good day before disappearing. She likely even has our Isaac with her, and you must say hello to your namesake." Silas was not fooling Isaac. Though he kept his tone jovial, the worried look in his eyes remained.

Silas, Esther, Jacob, and Grace all looked at him like that. As though they still waited for some sign that he had returned from war the same person as he had been when he left.

They waited in vain. The loss of Isaac's arm was just the most obvious of the changes in him.

"I will make certain to greet Esther. Where might she be at this time of day?"

"Where else? Painting." Silas chuckled and walked Isaac to the door of the study. "Nothing gives her so much happiness as her artwork and our son."

Esther had always loved to paint. It seemed to cure her of most of life's ills, too. If she was melancholic, or anxious, a paintbrush in hand had usually been enough to soothe her troubled heart.

Perhaps Isaac ought to find something to take up his time, too. Something that would help him as his sister's painting had helped her.

With weary steps, he went down the hall to his sister's domain. Her room was not far from Silas's study. His hand was upon the handle of the door when he heard an unfamiliar voice from within, along with baby laughter. Isaac hesitated.

"He is absolutely darling. Just look at his handsome little eyes," a woman's voice cooed. "And his charming smile."

"It is always gratifying to hear someone outside the family say such things," Esther said, sounding amused.

Outside the family? Who would Esther have allowed into her domain if it was not their friends, whom they all considered family? No one entered her art room on a whim.

Curious enough to push aside his discomfort, Isaac rapped his knuckles on the door before pushing it open. Esther stood on one side of the room, a plain wooden box in her hands, and upon the couch a head full of red swirling curls turned, a pair of brown eyes meeting his.

Miss Wedgewood held his nephew in her arms, and she stood when she saw Isaac. She adjusted the baby against her shoulder and dropped a curtsy in polite greeting.

Isaac mechanically returned the bow. "I beg your pardon. I was not aware—" But he had stood and listened at the door. He cleared his throat and turned his attention to Esther. "I merely came to wish you a good day before going about my business."

"Are you and Silas finished with your discussion already? I had hoped you would stay and take tea with us." Esther brought her box and put it on the table near the couch. "Miss Wedgewood is staying—"

The other woman laughed, though the sound was without good humor. "Oh, no. I could not possibly impose upon you any further, my lady. I thank you for supplying me with the necessary equipment for my project, but I had better be on my way." She glanced briefly at Isaac, almost guiltily, before handing the baby to his mother.

She scooped up the box and held it tightly against her chest. "I will collect my maid. Thank you for your time. Good day, Lady

Inglewood. Sir Isaac." She dipped her final curtsy and left the room, not making eye contact with Isaac though she had to press herself against the door to avoid brushing his left shoulder.

Before she had even made it out of his sight, as he watched her retreat down the hall, Esther was berating him. "What did you do to that poor girl at dinner two evenings ago?" Esther asked. "We were having a perfectly charming time until you came in, and suddenly she could not escape fast enough."

Isaac turned to take in his sister's deep frown, and he offered a one-armed shrug. "I cannot say I did anything that would give cause for that sort of offense. She kept trying to flirt with me. And you know Lady Olivia well enough to guess at what sort of friends she would bring home with her." He stepped further into the room and shut the door behind him. "What was she doing here? That is my greater concern."

Esther turned her son in her arms so Isaac might see the baby's cheerful face, charming smile and all. "Miss Wedgewood came to ask about art supplies. She wanted to find out if the Aldersy shops had what she needed or if she ought to send to London. She is a creative sort, and she requires something to keep herself busy." Esther's frown deepened, though it was no longer directed at Isaac. "I have to say, I do not think she is very happy to be Lady Olivia's guest."

"I cannot imagine what gave you that impression. Lady Olivia made it a point to note how dear a friend Miss Wedgewood is to her." Isaac went to the window as he spoke, looking out over the gardens to the stretch of sea. The dark blue line was steady and still, no clouds above it that day.

His sister came up beside him, standing near enough for the baby in her arms to reach out and pat at his sleeve. "I think she is quite lonely in that house. Lady Olivia is not a warm or kind person. From our conversation, I think Miss Wedgewood might be a reluctant guest. I am under the impression her mother worked out the arrangement."

Isaac tried to shrug off the doubt, and the accompanying guilt, that his sister's theory inspired. "You think the best of people, Essie. I love that about you, but I cannot say I am inspired to think as well of Miss Wedgewood as you do." He watched a gull pass outside the window on its way to the beach.

"She will be here all of summer," Esther told him. "Perhaps you will have time enough to form your own opinion of her. An opinion that has less to do with what you think of Lady Olivia and more to do with Miss Wedgewood's merits." She stood on her toes and placed a kiss upon his cheek. "Come to dinner at the vicarage tomorrow, Isaac. I miss you."

"You see me nearly every day," he protested, a corner of his mouth pulling back despite himself. He had received an invitation from Jacob and Grace Barnes, two of his dearest friends, but had yet to decide on whether to attend.

That worried look came into his sister's eyes again. The same one Silas had laid upon him minutes before. "I am grateful for that."

He needed to leave before she tried to pry his thoughts from him again.

Isaac bowed, made his excuses, and slipped from the room after promising to come to dinner. The moment he stepped out of doors, he drew in a deep breath of the warm summer air, closing his eyes against the breeze.

It should not be difficult to visit with his closest friend and his sister. It should be the easiest thing in the world to sit with them, passing hours in their company and conversation, but sitting still for any amount of time had become more and more difficult of late.

Idleness did not sit well with Isaac. He itched to move. To do something constructive. There were hours of quiet in the war, but they had been filled with expectation for the next battle, the next set of orders.

Orders did not come anymore. Isaac had to set his own battle plans, had to see to himself.

A phantom itch on his left hand made his right hand twitch.

But he did not reach to scratch the hand that no longer existed. It had taken some time, but he at last trained the response out of himself. Someday, that ghostly sensation would pass all together. As too would his restlessness.

At least, that was his hope.

Chapter Six

When the invitation arrived from a Mr. and Mrs. Barnes to join them for dinner, Millie held it in her hands with absolute puzzlement. She sat at the breakfast table, Lady Olivia opposite her and Lord Neil several chairs down. The marchioness took breakfast in her bedroom, as she had every day since Millie's arrival.

No one looked up from their own correspondence to even notice that the butler had handed her a note upon her own silver tray. Millie turned the invitation over, looking for some hint as to who these people were and why they might wish her company for that same evening.

"Pardon me," she said at last, drawing Lord Neil's attention while Lady Olivia's glance barely flicked up from a letter she read with a smirk. "Are either of you acquainted with a Mr. and Mrs. Barnes?"

Lord Neil's chin came up, and he glanced to Olivia. His sister, for her part, finally put down the paper in her hands. "Barnes? He is our vicar."

"And a friend to Fox," Lord Neil added, folding his arms over his chest. "What are you about, Livvy?"

She slanted a glare in his direction. "Do not call me that." Then the elegant woman turned to Millie, her perfectly rouged lips pressing together as she thought. "Is that an invitation from the vicarage? I recognize the stationary." She sniffed. "Cheaply made paper."

Millie hadn't noticed that the quality of the paper wanted any in quality, but she said nothing to this. "They have invited me to dinner this evening, but I have never met them."

"Curious." Lord Neil's expression remained thoughtful, but not unkind. Lady Olivia appeared almost gloating. "If you have not met them, I imagine one of their other guests for the evening asked for the invitation on your behalf."

"You are making progress," Olivia said a little too brightly. "Mr. and Mrs. Barnes make up part of that little club. How did you go about entering their circle with such speed? I am impressed."

As Millie had done nothing to secure the invitation in her hands, her insides squirmed. She glanced at Lord Neil, who only raised an eyebrow at her, and then lowered her eyes back to the neat handwriting upon the paper. "I will accept the invitation. If it is from a vicar and his wife, there can be no harm in attending a dinner with them."

"No harm?" Lord Neil asked, retrieving his cup of coffee from the table. He did not look at his sister again, but Millie instinctively felt he spoke to her with his next words. "It remains to be seen, but meddling with that group of people cannot end well." He put his cup down after no more than a sip, then stood. "Good morning to you both, Olivia, Miss Wedgewood." He left the room at a leisurely pace, as though he had nowhere in particular to go.

"I am impressed, Miss Wedgewood." Lady Olivia's deep green eyes gleamed like a cat's, ready to set upon some small, helpless creature. "You will have to tell me all about this dinner party." Then she stood from the table, gathering her letters in her hands. "Good day to you." She left without so much as a curtsy or another word, without giving Millie leave to join her later, or any sort of invitation to spend time with her.

Alone at the table, with only footmen standing along the edge of the wall to fill the silence with their quiet breathing, Millie took one last bite of cold toast. A swallow of tea washed it down.

She left the dining room, making for her quarters. Sarah would need to be told about the invitation; they would pick out a dress together. And then Millie would pass the hours until she left in the art room, inking out the design she had drawn upon the plain box Lady Inglewood had given her. It was the perfect size to hold a gentleman's pens, pipes, or letters.

If she did not go mad from the quiet, from the near-loneliness of being ignored, it would be a pleasant day indeed.

WORD CAME AN HOUR BEFORE THE APPOINTED TIME FOR dinner that the Earl of Inglewood had generously offered his carriage to take Millie to dinner. That explained her invitation. If the countess and earl were friends to the vicar and his wife, they likely orchestrated the entire evening. The generosity in her inclusion surprised Millie.

What could the countess possibly hope to gain by inviting Millie to an evening among friends? No one ever did such a thing without reason, without their own motivation or scheme. Millie had learned that well enough in her time on the outside of Society, observing all she could as she tried to find her own way back inside those well-guarded circles of the elite.

The carriage arrived at the appointed time. Sarah helped Millie put on her cloak, but the maid did not accompany her this evening.

Millie did not wait to be collected at the door, which startled the earl's groom who came halfway up the steps before realizing she was already on her way down. He did an abrupt turn and ran back down the steps to open the carriage door, bowing.

With a deep breath, Millie stepped inside the equipage. Inside already, Lady Inglewood smiled her welcome. Across from her ladyship was the earl, a man Millie had never laid eyes upon before. As she took her seat next to the countess, her cheeks warmed. There was not a man she could think of as handsome as Lord Inglewood. Not many, at any rate. His hair was nearly black, his eyes a bold green, and if he ever showed his smile, she guessed it would cause women to swoon. As it was, his visage was stern, stony. As though he had never smiled a day in his life.

"My lord," she said deferentially, "my lady. Thank you for having me."

The earl inclined his head slightly. "My wife has taken a liking to you, Miss Wedgewood. She does not often find someone with whom she feels such swift kinship."

Lady Inglewood laughed, the sound at odds with her husband's stern expression. "Stop, Silas. You are going to frighten her. Miss Wedgewood, please forgive him. He has his House of Lords mask upon him at the moment." She raised her eyebrows imperiously as she teased her husband.

He sighed and crossed his arms. "I haven't the least idea what you mean." Yet a spark in one eye indicated those words might be a falsehood.

Millie tried to make herself smaller and tucked her gloved hands tightly in her lap. Was banter such as theirs common among younger married couples? With her own parents and few others as an example of matrimonial life, she'd always thought marriage to be a necessary arrangement rather than a pleasant one. Thus far, her idea had been well supported.

"I am glad you could accept the invitation this evening. I hope you do not mind that I suggested you as a guest to our friends. Mr. and Mrs. Barnes are quite dear to us, almost like family." The countess continued her chatter, most pleasantly describing the vicar and his wife. They had been married shortly after the earl and countess and were expecting a child of their own before Autumn. "So there will not be many more dinners at their cottage after this one."

A cottage was their final destination? How interesting. The

highborn rarely deigned to call upon those of lesser rank, let alone eat at their tables.

When the carriage came to a stop, the earl stepped out and then handed out first his wife, then Millie. She followed the couple as they walked arm-in-arm down a small pebbled path lined with strawberry plants and daisies.

The cottage, as they called it, was a small house of two floors. There were two large windows on the first floor, set apart from the door in the middle, and three windows above. There could not be more than six or seven rooms in the whole building, yet the fine couple before her appeared as pleased with their arrival here as Millie's mother would at arriving at a palace.

The door opened before they knocked, a gentleman near the earl's age standing in the doorway with a broad smile. "It is about time you arrived. We have been waiting and waiting for you."

The earl tipped his head back. "The way we waited and waited for your sermonizing to come to an end last week?"

Millie's mouth popped open in her surprise while the men glared at each other, only to burst out laughing. She could not decide which was more shocking, someone addressing a peer in such a familiar manner or the peer mocking a man of the cloth.

The countess caught sight of Millie from the corner of her eye and appeared to take pity on her. "Do not mind them, Miss Wedgewood. They have spoken to each other with such irreverence for twenty years. It is also unlikely any amount of respectability or old age will keep them from it in the future."

The vicar did not precisely turn sober, but his smile did turn politer as he bowed. "Welcome to our home, Miss Wedgewood. Forgive the familiarity between myself and his lordship. We still do not take ourselves as seriously as we ought." He gestured for her to enter the house as the nobleman and his wife passed inside.

"I thank you for the invitation," Millie said, unable to think of anything better to say.

"Any friend of Esther's is most welcome." He held his hand out

for her cloak, which she shed most gratefully. "I am afraid you will
have to forgive the informality of the evening, too. We are all old
friends here, and we do not stand on ceremony when we gather
together."

It sounded as though Millie was in for an odd evening. She
followed their host, along with the countess and earl, through a
short hallway and into a comfortable parlor overlooking the front
garden. A woman waited for them; she was nearly of a size with
Millie, though had a few inches greater height to claim.

"Good evening, everyone." The woman curtsied, then came
directly to Millie with hands outstretched. "It is such a pleasure to
meet you, Miss Wedgewood. I am delighted you could make it on
such short notice. Esther said she thought you the very sort of
person to enjoy our rather uncommon company."

Millie's lips twitched into a smile. It was not the first time
someone had told her she might expect a strange evening. "I am
pleased to be here, Mrs. Barnes."

"Isaac has not arrived yet?" the countess asked, taking her place
on a chair near the window. "He promised he would come."

Millie's ears perked up at that. She hadn't been informed there
would be another guest; certainly the countess hadn't mentioned
her brother's attendance that evening. Had Millie's invitation been
extended in order to make the table even? With such old friends
spending time together, that was an unlikely reason.

The vicar and his wife took the couch, leaving two chairs
remaining, and a rather large footstool. The earl took up a position
near the hearth. Millie claimed the chair nearest the door, her back
to it.

"He sent word he would be here," the vicar said, extending his
hand along the back of the couch near his wife's shoulders. They
were all at such ease in each other's company, a thing immediately
apparent to Millie. Each of the four in the room wore smiles. Even
the earl's stern expression from the carriage ride had relaxed.

"Until Isaac arrives," Mrs. Barnes said, turning with purpose in

Millie's direction, "I would enjoy learning more about our guest. Esther tells me you have not been in our part of the country long. How do you find Suffolk, Miss Wedgewood?"

"It is quite beautiful." Polite topics she could entertain well enough. She had been raised for an elevated place in society, after all. "The lands are inspiring in their loveliness, especially at this time of year. I rather hope to spend some time upon the beaches soon, when I can find an escort." The marquess's family hadn't seemed inclined to visit the sea. Lady Olivia had proclaimed the sand "dirty and most inconvenient to slippers." But perhaps once the house party began, Millie could find someone willing to accompany her.

"Oh, had I known, I would have taken you when you came to visit at Inglewood," the countess proclaimed. "Our gardens at the house have a path leading directly to the sea."

The vicar's wife perked up. "We have access to the beach from here, too. If we were not all in our evening finery, I would suggest a walk after dinner."

Millie experienced a strange twinge to her conscience. These women were quick to include her in their doings. Very unlike Lady Olivia, or any of the women of Society she had attempted to befriend in the past. But perhaps, if they knew her background, they would not welcome her without hesitation. Her place as a guest to Lady Olivia likely gave them no reason to suspect her anything other than a welcome member of Society.

Still. The invitations were kind and gratifying. "I would be happy to take a walk, even in my finery." Sarah might not appreciate the sand in her slippers, but a walk at sunset would be marvelous. It was still early enough in the evening, with dinner occurring at seven o'clock as country hours dictated, that it would be near sunset when they finished. Though the beach faced eastward, it would be lovely to walk along the shore at dusk.

A door opened and closed, then a familiar voice shouted through the house. "If you have started dinner without me, I will take it as a grave insult."

The men in the room exchanged grins, then the vicar went to the parlor door and opened it, raising his voice as he spoke. "We would never dare consume so much as a crumb without you, for we would never hear the end of it."

"Good."

The vicar stepped back, opening the door wider, and Millie felt the skin on the back of her neck prickle the instant Sir Isaac entered the room. Her pulse sped up, though with anxiety or enthusiasm even she could not be certain. Did he expect to see her, or would he be as surprised by her inclusion as she had been regarding his?

She rose and turned to the door, keeping her eyes lowered as she dropped her curtsy. Everyone else might be on familiar terms, but she was a newcomer and hadn't been invited to drop any of her formal behavior yet. When she raised her eyes, her gaze immediately clashed with Sir Isaac's. His eyes were dark, the corners of his mouth turned down in a frown, and no sooner had their eyes met than he turned his stare to his sister.

"Miss Wedgewood," he said, none of the prior warmth from his shouts in the hall evident. He bowed to her, quite stiffly. "I did not know you would be a guest here this evening."

Heat filled her cheeks, though she knew she ought not to let the baronet have such an effect upon her. His tone implied she had no right to her invitation. If he knew her true purpose in being present, how much more disapproving and cross would he become? She cleared her throat, staving off the guilty thoughts. The man had proven himself unpleasant to all but his friends thus far. Lady Olivia's description of his character fit better and better with every meeting between Millie and Sir Isaac.

"I could not resist inviting her," Mrs. Barnes said, her tone cheerful. "There are not nearly enough pleasant ladies about with whom to pass an evening, and I knew from Esther's account that Miss Wedgewood must make a fine addition to our conversation." She started to stand, and her husband hurried to assist her, as her large midsection seemed to put the small woman off balance.

"Men never understand a woman's need for female companionship," the countess added with a superior tilt to her head, as though she hadn't noticed the glare her brother sent in her direction.

A woman in a clean apron appeared at the door and curtsied. "Dinner is ready, Mr. Barnes."

"Excellent." The vicar took his wife's arm, and Millie caught his murmured, "Not a moment too soon."

She lowered her eyes to the floor, attempting to regain her sense of balance. She had every right to her invitation, to her place as a guest. When she raised her eyes, ready to follow the group into the next room for dinner, her heart leaped somewhat alarmingly to find Sir Isaac standing beside her with his arm extended. He meant to escort her to the table, despite his obvious disapproval of her?

But there was no one else. The earl and his wife had taken the vicar's escort of his own wife as their guide, apparently. The married couples were exiting the room.

Hesitantly, Millie put her gloved hand upon the baronet's arm. "It is a pleasure to see you again, Sir Isaac," she said softly. He hadn't liked her flirtation, and Lord Neil had said not to attack him head on. Perhaps humility would achieve more than flattery.

Sir Isaac tipped his head forward, acknowledging her words without returning the nicety. Disagreeable man. Could he not even pretend it was pleasant to lay eyes upon her again? Granted, she had given him little cause to like her thus far. Spying, proving an annoying dinner companion, and showing up where he did not want her.

What would a captain in the British army appreciate most? If not a direct assault, perhaps at least a direct conversation.

"I did not know you would be here," she whispered as they entered the dining room with its large window facing a hill and the distant graying sea.

His gaze slid to hers, but barely from the corner of his eyes.

"Nor was I informed of your invitation, Miss Wedgewood." He spoke her surname with such distaste. It was not as though she could help what her ancestors had been called.

The table had six chairs about it, and the whole thing was *round*. No head or foot. A round table. Mr. and Mrs. Barnes took seats beside each other, the earl and his wife to the right of Mrs. Barnes, leaving a chair next to the vicar for Millie and the remaining seat to her reluctant escort.

What an odd seating arrangement.

The baronet held her chair out for her before taking his seat directly to her left. Before there was so much as a moment of silence, Mrs. Barnes and Lady Inglewood took up the topic of a summer gathering hosted at the Inglewood estate.

"There must be activities for everyone. Horseshoes, bowling, battledore, and a cricket game," the countess said, her eyes sparkling brightly. "I thought I would speak to Lady Alderton, to make certain our plans do not spoil any aspects of her house party. But I do desire some sort of entertainment."

"I dare say people are always looking for a good time," her husband said, less solemn than before, giving his wife an affectionate glance even Millie could not help but observe. "What does it matter if they play cricket at our estate one week and then at Alderton Meadows the next?"

Mrs. Barnes lowered her spoon into her soup with a delicate air. "Men do not understand the planning that goes into these activities."

"We do not want Lady Alderton to feel as though we are attempting to usurp her plans." Lady Inglewood flipped a stray brown curl back behind her ear, then turned her cheery expression toward Millie. "Have you any knowledge of the schedule for the house party? It begins in less than a fortnight now."

"In nine days." Millie had counted each one carefully, hoping to have sorted out Sir Isaac before the next gentleman quarry came into view. "I am afraid I have not been given any details." No one had told her anything, except the date on which other guests would arrive. At least that meant no one could expect her to take part in any of the planning, either.

"I imagine they will have all the usual sorts of activities." Sir Isaac, at her left, spoke dryly. "Picnics, riding parties, visits to the abbey ruins, and evening entertainments at the house."

Millie dared to turn a cheerful expression in his direction. "You sound as though you do not particularly care for those entertainments, Sir Isaac. Are they so terribly boring?" It was a shame a man of his bearing, someone with obvious confidence and good looks, would prove himself against the idea of diversion.

"You used to love parties," his sister, the countess, said before taking a sip of wine. "And you know that you and I will be invited to a great many of the events, given our status in the neighborhood. You cannot avoid them."

Sir Isaac dropped his spoon in his soup and gestured sharply to the earl. "But Silas can? I fail to see why it falls to me to wait upon the whims of *that* particular family. Or their guests."

A blush rose in Millie's cheeks and she lowered her eyes to her bowl, determined to empty it quickly. Sir Isaac included *her* in the distasteful group of guests. The man had absolutely no tact, and if he would insult her so easily she had no choice but to rethink her plan in regard to Lady Olivia's revenge. How did one convince a hedgehog to cease his prickliness?

The earl answered the outburst after a moment of discomfiting silence. "I have my reasons for avoiding any event where Lord Neil is present. But I will not and cannot avoid all association with the family, or their guests. It would be social and political ruin."

Mrs. Barnes cleared her throat. "Jacob will probably attend anything to which we are invited. I am afraid my excuse is quite a valid one." She gave the bit of her midsection above the table a gentle pat. Her husband's posture changed, as he somehow managed to appear taller and lean toward his wife at the same time. The affection with which he regarded his wife said a great deal about their relationship. He did not mind her reason for keeping away from Society in the least.

The conversation turned, rather expertly by Lady Inglewood, to other neighborhood matters.

Remaining silent, Millie did her best to not so much as glance at Sir Isaac. If he resented her presence, she would not give him greater reason to note it.

Why did his resentment affect her so?

WHEN THE DESSERT COURSE WAS LAID BEFORE HIM, Isaac perked up. The cake with strawberries and cream atop it was one of his favorites. Had Grace arranged for it on his account? He turned to where she sat, nearly across from him, and prepared to express his gratitude.

Grace glared at him, most pointedly.

As kind and gentle a soul as she was, the glare was disconcerting. He raised his eyebrows, waiting for a reprimand, or a hint at what he had done to earn her displeasure. She looked purposefully to his right, then back at him.

Isaac peeked at Miss Wedgewood from the corner of his eye. The woman was calmly selecting a strawberry to spear with her fork. Clearly, nothing wrong there. After making eye contact with Grace again, he shrugged and raised his eyebrows. Then turned to ask his sister a question, but Isaac found Esther glaring at him, too.

What had he done wrong?

He studied Miss Wedgewood again, this time noting the tension in her shoulders, and along her jaw. Perhaps she was upset. What the other women at the table expected him to do about it, however, was a mystery.

"Miss Wedgewood?" he asked.

She jumped in her chair rather like an abruptly loosed spring, stabbing her plate rather than the strawberry she had meant to eat. The copper-haired woman put her fork down and gave him her full attention for all of a second before she lowered her eyes to his cravat. At least he thought that was where she stared.

"Yes, Sir Isaac?"

As he hadn't prepared what to say and could not precisely remember what the rest of the table had conversed upon up until that moment, Isaac mentally groped for an acceptable question. "Where did you say your family spends their summers?"

The color in her cheeks faded abruptly, leaving her white. "Usually we remain in London. But my father has a house in Bedfordshire. We live near Woburn."

"Ah." Isaac hazarded another glance at Grace and Esther, but neither of them seemed mollified by his first attempt. As Miss Wedgewood's dinner partner, he supposed he hadn't been attentive. Yet what did they expect from him? Inviting a stranger, even if she was lovely, among them? He cleared his throat. "And what of your family? You are visiting by yourself. Where are the rest of your people?"

The smile the woman forced appeared uncomfortable. "My parents are yet in London, Sir Isaac. My mother quite prefers it to our country home." No mention of any other family followed, and when she lifted her fork again Isaac relaxed. She did not wish to speak to him any more than he did to her.

After dinner, when the ladies rose to go to the parlor, Isaac remained with Silas and Jacob for coffee.

"Isaac," Silas said the moment the ladies were safely away, "do you have a desire to be drawn and quartered?" His tone remained dry, and a lift of one eyebrow suggested he had no intention of amusing anyone.

"You cannot quarter a man who is already missing one arm." Isaac leaned back in his chair. "What have I done to offend you that you would threaten me so?"

Silas and Jacob exchanged a glance before the earl answered. "I am not threatening you. Merely informing you of what Esther and

Grace have planned if you do not repair the damage you have done this evening. Esther has taken a great interest in Miss Wedgewood, and Grace prides herself on setting people at ease."

"I fail to see what I have done to upset either of them, then." Isaac tapped one finger on the arm of his chair, considering the situation. "I have been polite all evening."

"Polite?" Jacob asked, then snorted. "One of the first things you did when we sat down at dinner was to say you had no wish to entertain the guests of the marquess. You do realize that included the woman in our company, did you not?"

The memory of that comment came back, and Isaac winced. "I did say that. But I did not mean Miss Wedgewood. Not precisely. Though she has not done anything to merit my leaving her out of that classification of person, either."

Jacob groaned and rubbed his forehead, while Silas shook his head slowly.

"You cannot be so dense," Silas said, folding his arms upon the table and leaning forward. "Miss Wedgewood hardly said two words after that, though all of us tried to include her in the conversation. All of us except you. Of course, you did not say very much either."

"My hope is that the ladies are salvaging the evening in the next room," Jacob said lightly, wrapping one hand around his cup of coffee. "Otherwise, your fate will be settled."

Isaac squeezed his eyes shut as he spoke. "I have done absolutely nothing wrong. A man can be quiet at dinner without giving insult."

"Not if he made another guest uncomfortable by his conduct." Silas used his lordly tone, the same one he employed when speaking to political groups. "We all interpreted your remark about guests to include Miss Wedgewood, so it follows she did the same. Then you remained silent, unpleasantly so, all evening. That curtailed her desire to speak. You have amends to make and asking the woman about her family will not suffice."

"I agree," Jacob put in. "You are going to have to do a great deal more to fix the situation, or none of us will hear the end of it."

A pulse began behind Isaac's eyes, thrumming at a steady tempo. A headache would soon follow. A dismal one, if he were to guess, that would leave him in pain for some hours. All because of a woman he barely knew.

Yet he saw Silas and Jacob's point. "I would not upset Grace or Esther," he admitted at last. "I will do what I can to set Miss Wedgewood at ease."

The door to the dining room opened and Esther stepped inside. All three men rose, and Isaac's heart sank. Esther was already sending a poisonous look. "Silas, I am afraid we need to be on our way. Miss Wedgewood has told me she is not feeling well. We must return her to the Alderton house at once."

"Of course." Silas did not argue, but as he went around the table, he made certain to meet Isaac's eyes. "Good evening, gentlemen."

Esther did not immediately follow her husband from the room. He likely went to inform a servant of their need of the carriage.

Esther came another step inside the room, fixing her brother with a sharp-eyed stare. "Isaac Fox, I have come to accept that you are not the man you once were, and that is understandable. But I am absolutely appalled by your behavior this evening. I have every reason to believe that Miss Wedgewood finds her situation in the Alderton house awkward and unpleasant. I had hoped to make her feel welcome among us, so she has a place of refuge while she is visiting. But your cold reception and lack of gentility served to show her she is unwanted here, too. It is most unkind of you."

"I have hardly said a word to the woman," Isaac argued, keeping his voice low. "If she wishes to be overly dramatic about the situation—"

"Overly dramatic?" Esther asked, voice pitched to match his. "It is not dramatic to find oneself friendless, Isaac. To feel alone. I thought you would understand that." She shook her head, her disappointment in him settling like a weight upon his chest. "Good evening, Jacob," she said to the vicar. "I am sorry we must leave early."

"Quite all right, Esther. Good evening." Jacob bowed, then cut into Isaac with his own disapproving frown.

"I haven't any idea what you want me to do about the situation," Isaac said when his sister left. "What any of you want me to do. I did not attempt to befriend Miss Wedgewood—I have no wish to befriend her. That was all Esther and Grace's idea."

The door opened again, this time allowing Grace inside. She sighed, hand at her back as though to support her large middle. "I have never had a guest leave with such speed."

Isaac's bravado faded. "Was it really my fault?"

Grace winced and came back to the table, retaking her seat there. "I am under the impression that Miss Wedgewood has a great deal to trouble her but being an unwanted guest has certainly dampened her spirits. I will not cast the blame on you, Isaac." Then she offered him a tired smile. "Not the entirety of the blame."

He dropped back into his chair. "Esther seems to think I was meant to somehow set everything to rights for Miss Wedgewood during her stay here."

"Esther is in a rather unique position. I think she sees a great deal of herself in our new friend." Grace raised her hand for Jacob to catch in his. He raised her knuckles to his lips and brushed a kiss upon them. Isaac lowered his eyes rather than see the intimate glance which passed between his friends.

He was happy for them. Happy for Esther and Silas, too. And Hope with her new husband, the two of them away in Spain for half a year now. Each of his dearest friends had found their other halves. Leaving him the odd man in the group. The lone bachelor.

While he might not understand Miss Wedgewood's predicament, or her supposed discomfort with the marquess's family, he could well appreciate what it meant when excluded from certain situations.

"I cannot like her," he muttered aloud.

"Why ever not?" Grace asked, and Jacob appeared surprised, too. "You like everyone."

"Not everyone," he said at once. "Not people like the Marquess of Alderton."

Jacob started to nod. "And Miss Wedgewood's association with their family would give you pause. Understandably so. But we are not always like our friends, are we?"

"I found her trespassing on my land," Isaac reminded them. "Asking impertinent questions about me."

"Perhaps she needs another chance." Jacob, as vicar, would have to suggest such a thing. Second-chances, opportunities to prove oneself changed, prodigal sons returning, and every other unlikely redemptive state of a mortal. Isaac had once reminded Jacob of a person's need to both forgive and seek forgiveness. As Isaac disliked hypocrisy more than any other human fault, he had no choice but to follow the counsel he had once given to his friend.

"A second chance." He rubbed at his temple again, the headache pulsing now against the backs of his eyes. There would be no sleep for him that night. All due to Miss Wedgewood's appearance in his life. "Very well. When next I see Miss Wedge-wood, I will attempt to forget my initial thoughts and impressions about her. Does that suffice?"

The married couple exchanged a glance heavy with meaning. It was as though they held a full conversation in no more than a single look.

"I think that would be perfect," Jacob said. Grace nodded her approval.

With the party already broken up, Isaac did not feel the least bit guilty for leaving immediately after his surrender. The ride home in the dusk, as the sun had only just begun to set, proved refreshing. The sea breeze drifted inland, and he took in deep draughts of the briny air.

Miss Wedgewood had intruded upon his land and somehow found a place among his friends, all while the guest of a woman he could not help but despise. Lady Olivia's conduct, her morals, and everything about her character caused him to doubt anyone who claimed a relationship with the marquess's daughter. But if he had misjudged the situation, and Miss Wedgewood, he would admit his fault.

To know for certain, Isaac had no alternative but to attempt to further the acquaintance with the young woman.

Chapter Seven

After answering all of Lady Olivia's intrusive questions the night before, Millie hoped to avoid another encounter with the rather upset noblewoman for the rest of the day. She hadn't meant for her visit with the baronet and his friends to end sourly, but given his complete animosity toward her, Millie had no desire to remain near him until she formed a new plan.

The humiliation she felt, sitting next to him while he had scoffed at her, truly made her ill at ease. Not to mention his questions regarding her family. Always it came back to her family, to their reputation, to *Emmeline* and her mistake.

Thinking on it that morning, sitting at her art table with Sarah in the corner reading a book, Millie's hand trembled too much for her to do the delicate ink work on the little wooden box. So, she had taken to preparing scraps of paper for quilling instead. Twisting the colored paper into tight circles required little elegance, though the placing of the paper would eventually mean regaining control over her emotions.

It is not as though you can befriend any of them. Not the countess, the vicar's wife, or anyone else with a relationship to Sir Isaac. It was her duty to expose him to Society, after all. To find the means to humiliate him. Hurt his reputation. None of his friends would thank her for that.

Her enjoyment at their welcome was foolish. A mistake. One she could not repeat. If the earl and his wife knew of what Emmeline had done when she ran off with her ridiculous solicitor, they would shun Millie as everyone else had shunned her family.

They were not her friends, nor could they ever be so. But she had to earn their trust to get close to Sir Isaac.

It was not as though he had shown any interest in spending time in her company, however.

A knock at the door startled Millie from her thoughts. She stood and smoothed the skirt of her gown. "Come in." No one but the servants knocked, she had learned. Lady Olivia and her brother came and went from every room with the full confidence of those who owned the house and everything in it.

The door opened, and a footman stepped inside. He bowed. "Sir Isaac Fox to see you, Miss Wedgewood."

Her honest shock kept her from doing more than opening her mouth to reply. But the footman withdrew, leaving the door open, and Sir Isaac stepped inside the little art room.

"Miss Wedgewood." He said her name with less distaste than the evening before. Almost politely. Then he bowed, his dark eyes barely meeting her gaze before looking away.

Belatedly, she curtsied. What had brought him to her? The night before, everything he had said, how he'd acted, had spoken loudly of his dislike for her.

"What is this room?" he asked, his brows drawing down.

She looked about, knowing he saw what she had the first time she entered it. The room was small. Not at all well-appointed. At the rear of the house, away from all the important rooms. The window let in some usable light, but she had taken to keeping a lamp lit upon the table when she worked. The chairs were not even very comfortable, but straight-backed and wooden.

"It is a room for pursuing artistic endeavors," she said at last, lowering her eyes to her twists of paper upon the table. She hadn't even been working upon something impressive. He would think her such a simpleton—not that she cared what he thought so long as she accomplished her goals.

"Oh. My sister would say it is unsuitable for such pursuits." One side of his mouth went upward, as though he meant to smile but forgot how to manage such an action.

"I would agree with her," she admitted with honesty. Then Millie remembered her manners. "Will you sit down, Sir Isaac? I could send for refreshment—"

He raised his hand to wave the offer aside. "That will not be necessary. I have come merely to look in on you, Miss Wedgewood. You left quickly last night, and my sister told me you were unwell."

Millie stared at him, shocked. Likely his sister had put him up to the visit, too. "Thank you, Sir Isaac. I am much better today."

His head jerked downward in what might have passed for a nod of approval. "Excellent. I am glad to hear it." He cleared his throat. "I hope you remain well." He appeared as uncomfortable in the situation as she had been the previous evening. Perhaps she ought to extend an olive branch. There was something almost endearing about the way he stood, tall and straight, but with the air of a boy who had been caught in mischief.

"That is most kind of you, Sir Isaac. Thank you. Please, if you see your sister before I do, give her my compliments. She was most gracious when she brought me home, and I am sorry I broke up the dinner party earlier than what was expected." There. If he would not apologize for his behavior, she could at least make certain to do so.

Sir Isaac finally met her gaze with his, puzzlement appearing in his warm brown eyes. Heavens, but the man was attractive. Perhaps that was where his arrogance stemmed from, knowing that he was handsome. Though one might think the loss of his arm would humble him, that unfortunate result of war did nothing to detract from his appearance.

"No one worried over the early evening," he said at last. "But there was a great deal of worry in regard to you. My sister and Mrs.

Barnes, they have gentle hearts. I know they both hope to count you as a friend. They were distressed that you could not remain." He lowered his eyes and cleared his throat. "In fact, if there was anything that I did to hasten your departure, I must apologize for it. I am not the best of company of late. I do not always think before I speak, and—"

An actual *apology*. A moment before, she never would have expected such a thing. She hastened to interrupt him, wishing to put him at ease. "Not at all, Sir Isaac. Please, think no more of it."

There. She had given him permission to forget the whole evening, if he wished. "I can understand how difficult it is to have a stranger in the middle of familiar friends." Millie attempted to smile, but he appeared no more at ease in her company than before. "Thank you for coming to inquire after my health."

Sir Isaac gave another distracted sort of nod. "Of course, Miss Wedgewood. I had best take my leave now. Good day." He bowed, turned stiffly on his heel, and left the room. She took a few steps after him, stopping in the doorway to watch his retreating back. When he came to the turn in the corridor, he glanced over his shoulder and saw her there. Swiftly, he snapped his head forward again and disappeared from sight.

How odd.

But promising.

"He is a strange one, miss," Sarah said from her corner, where she had silently stood during the whole of the exchange.

"I quite agree with you." Millie closed the door slowly. Her thoughts began spinning again. As she tried to put them in order, a new plan formed. She smiled to herself. "Perhaps things are not as dire as I thought. I may yet fulfill Lady Olivia's demands."

Sarah frowned, but pressed her lips together rather than give voice to whatever unpleasant thought had occurred to her. The maid had given up trying to talk Millie out of her course of action, which proved a relief. Every time Sarah had tried, Millie had faltered, had wondered if there was another way to regain her family's place in Society. She could not afford to be swayed. Not now.

Sir Isaac was her quarry, the fox she meant to trap. If she did not, her mother would never let Millie forget ruining their chances. Everything depended upon her success.

❦

THE HOUSE STIFLED ISAAC. HE WOKE UP EVERY morning with the desperate need to simply get out of his own home. That morning was no different. The comfortable bed he had enjoyed prior to his time in the military had yet to give him a full night's rest. He would have slept better in a mud puddle out in the fields.

Despite the stone house's generous size, and the fact that Isaac and the servants alone lived there, an oppressive weight hung in the air. Perhaps it was merely the disapproval of all his ancestors, staring down at him from their portraits. At least one antiquated painting hung in each room of the old house.

After he deftly put his coat on, something he had practiced many times until getting it precisely right, Isaac tucked the mostly empty sleeve up and pinned it into place. His valet stood behind him, waiting for permission to adjust Isaac's cravat. "Will you be going far this morning, sir?" Matthews asked, adjusting a fold in the white cloth at Isaac's neck.

"Not too far, I should think." His morning walks had become a habit. He took a small breakfast in his room, then rambled about on his estate or by the seashore before returning to the house to see to his daily affairs. In the afternoons, he went riding. The routine had become both blessing and curse. He knew precisely when he might escape the confines of the house and company, but he had tired of the sameness of every day some time previous. The hours spent out of doors cleared his head and relaxed him, but he could not very well set up a canvas tent and camp in his own gardens.

People might think him as mad as he had tried to lead Miss Wedgewood to believe.

Miss Wedgewood.

Isaac trotted down the front steps of his house, walking stick tucked under one arm. This time, he did not smirk to himself over the memory of Miss Wedgewood's expression when he had described the baronet as touched in the head. Not since the night at Jacob and Grace's dinner table had he been entertained by that particular memory. It would not do to paint Miss Wedgewood with the same brush as Lady Olivia merely because the two of them kept each other company.

He did not adhere to the usual paths that day, but marched directly through the estate's meadow, making for the lane. Leaving the confines of the house was not enough. He needed to escape his lands entirely, if only for a few minutes. So he tromped across the grasses, pushed through the hedge, and came to the road. Anyone else who traversed the lane might see him and think his exercise unusual, but he hardly cared.

Most of the neighborhood seemed uninterested in his doings. When Miss Wedgewood had said, during their very first meeting when she had no idea of his identity, that women would flock to a man with his looks, it had taken him by surprise. True, he was still a decent enough catch for women of the gentry class. At least those who did not mind an old title with little prestige.

But Miss Wedgewood had called him handsome. She hadn't stared at the place his missing arm ought to be, nor had she asked wide-eyed questions about it the way some of the misses in the neighborhood had in an attempt to pretend they understood his difficulties.

Actually. He had almost enjoyed their first meeting. Only the recollection of whose house she occupied bothered him.

He really hadn't been fair to her at all.

Isaac walked, as though with a purpose, but with no destination in mind. He breathed deeply. Marched in time to an imaginary drummer.

A little more than a year before, he had been presumed dead in one of the last skirmishes between French and British forces. His family had mourned him, and he had arrived barely in time for them to cease preparations for his memorial service. A plaque still graced the church's wall, actually, though his death date had thoughtfully been removed after Jacob Barnes became vicar.

A man ought to maintain gratitude in his heart to go from dead to living as he had. Yet sometimes, in the loneliness of night, in the midst of his dreams, Isaac wondered why he had lived while so many others, men under his command, his superior officers, his *friends*, had never come home to England again.

But he could not go on blaming the past for his foul moods or rudeness. Especially to a young woman who had done nothing wrong, save show a bit of curiosity.

His jaw tensed and he used his walking stick to lash out at a branch that dared hang too near the road.

"Dear me," a voice said from his left, across the dirt track. "Whatever did that bush do to earn your wrath?"

Isaac jerked around, startled. Standing parallel to him was none other than the distracting Miss Wedgewood. "How long have you been there?" he asked, then swallowed when he heard the offensive tone he had used. He had to do better.

She turned and pointed at a break in the trees. "I stepped through there a moment ago and saw you walking. I hadn't made my mind up whether to call out to you until I saw you mistreating the flora." Miss Wedgewood faced him again, her expression clear and bright as the morning, one corner of her mouth higher than the other. "Someone must come to the defense of our native plants."

Whatever did she mean, jesting with him in such a familiar way? He narrowed his eyes at her, attempting to categorize her behavior in a way that made sense. She had been cowed by him at the vicar's dinner party, generous when he apologized, and now acted as though they were on good terms. No one was that quick to forgive and forget.

Miss Wedgewood did not cross the road to his side, but she took up her walk again. He gave her one glance before doing the same. Eight feet of road divided them.

"You look as though you wish to pick a fight with me again," she observed, tone amused. "I wish you would tell me how I have offended you, so I might make things right between us. I thought, after your visit, we might be on more friendly terms."

"That does surprise me. Many in your place would hold me in contempt." He gave her a swift glance, noting the way her dark auburn hair peeked from the back of her bonnet. In profile, she was quite lovely. Though one might mistake her for a much younger woman, given her stature. "I appreciate the direct approach in your conversation today."

"Interesting. I was told being direct with you would be a waste of time." Her lips pursed prettily, and Isaac nearly walked into a branch. He barely stepped around it in time to avoid choking on a mouthful of leaves. "Given your apparent distaste for the family hosting my time in Aldersy, I should not be surprised the advice was ill-conceived."

Isaac kept his eyes trained upon the path ahead of him, determined not to allow her to distract him again. "I much prefer direct and honest conversation to jests. Anyone who knows me well should know that. I imagine it was Lady Olivia who told you otherwise."

"Lord Neil, actually. Though I think some of his counsel may have been sound." She made a thoughtful humming noise, keeping pace with him on her side of the lane. "As you say you prefer directness, might I assume you give the same to others?"

He almost smiled and darted a look at her, finding her expression almost peaceful. "That would be a safe conclusion to draw."

"Wonderful. Then I hope you will answer my earlier question. What have I done to offend you?" She stopped walking, turning to face him. Her posture was stiff, her chin tilted at precisely the same angle as that of a soldier awaiting inspection. But that peaceful look remained in her eyes, watching him, studying his response with care.

He tucked his walking stick beneath what remained of his left arm as *he* studied *her*. Directness. That was what she wanted. What they both wanted. "Your trespass upon my lands, accompanied by your blatant curiosity, followed upon by what you clearly meant as a flirtation at the marchioness's dinner party sowed the first seeds of distrust. Finding you suddenly turning up near my sister, my friends, deepened my suspicions."

Even from his distance, he easily saw the way her eyes gleamed at him. While he shared his surname with a creature known for its cunning, he had the sudden thought that Miss Wedgewood appeared more the fox than he did. The shade of her hair contributed greatly to the intelligence reflected in her eyes.

"Your suspicions of what, Sir Isaac?" That corner of her mouth moved upward again, revealing a dimple in her cheek. Did she have another, on the opposite side of her heart-shaped face, to match?

"That you are up to something." Isaac winced as soon as the words escaped from him. He had no proof. Only a feeling that Miss Millicent Wedgewood had a purpose, a story, she would not be quick to share with him or anyone else.

Quiet laid between them, stretching across several seconds. Her amusement did not fade, but her posture did not relax, either. Finally, she brought her arms up to cross them over her middle while she tipped her head to the side. "I will tell you what I am up to, Sir Isaac. I am here at the home of the marquess to appease my mother."

He tipped his head back and crossed his single arm over his middle, taking hold of the stick tucked under his war-shortened arm. It was his best way to approximate her guarded stance. "How so, Miss Wedgewood?"

"My family is out of favor with the fashionable set," she said, and a muscle in her jaw twitched. "We have been for some time, due to circumstances outside of our control. My mother finds the situation deplorable. Unsuitable. When Lady Olivia offered a path back into the good graces of the elite, I was given my orders to make myself useful in whatever way possible."

She spoke plainly enough, yet Isaac wondered at how she cast her eyes downward at the end of her speech. Miss Wedgewood did not reveal all. Though he hardly blamed her for it. Despite his preference for honesty, he rarely expected to receive it from those outside of his more intimate friends. English Society was built upon the keeping up of appearances, after all, and the forming of alliances. Not from stating the truth baldly and boldly.

Miss Wedgewood continued before he could voice his observations, which he fully intended to do. "Lady Olivia is not overly fond of my company. I think she finds me dull. But I am here, waiting upon her pleasure, until after the marquess's house party." Her tone changed, becoming almost indifferent, which made him focus his attention on those words. The indifference was feigned. The way she cut her eyes to one side, the disappearance of the dimple, indicated a deeper emotion than she expressed.

"Does it trouble you to be unwanted?" he asked, his usual blunt speech easily slipping from his tongue. He closed his mouth over the question, knowing Essie would take him to task for his lack of gallantry.

But Miss Wedgewood's shoulders drooped, and she met his gaze squarely again. "Yes. It leaves me quite lonely. And I did flirt with you," she added, further surprising him. "Because that is what a woman does to gain attention from a man. I also trespassed upon your land to ask questions about you, because what your neighbors said of you intrigued me." She lowered her eyes and uncrossed her arms, giving her attention to adjusting her gloves. "And I rather like your sister, so the last several times we met had little to do with you and more to do with seeking out *her* company."

Her tone undoubtedly indicated a wish to deflate his vanity. Strange, he hadn't thought he still possessed any of that particular vice. Losing one's arm tended to keep a man from thinking too highly of himself.

Isaac peered down one end of the road and then the other. No one was about. He crossed to her, tired of keeping the distance between them for no reason other than stubbornness. She watched him come, her eyes widening, but she did not retreat. Instead, she took up that soldier-like posture again, waiting for him to decree whether she passed muster or not.

"Miss Wedgewood, what is it you want?" he demanded, voice lowered as he stared down at her. He did not break eye contact. Did not allow her to look away, either. He watched for the telltale sign of a lie, a truth concealed. Isaac trusted his observations of people more often than he did their words. Even before his military career, he depended upon what his friends had called an ability to discern a person's true character. The ability came naturally and served him well.

Her clear toffee-colored eyes studied his, as though she practiced her own version of his unique talent. "I want a place in Society. I want people to care whether I exist. I want friends."

All true. Every word.

He stepped away, removing his walking stick from beneath what remained of his left arm. "I want to be left alone. Most of the time."

"Pity." Her cheeks lost some of their color. He started walking again, this time near her, and she fell into step beside him. He shortened his longer gait to make the experience less troublesome for her. "I rather hoped you would not mind my presence. What if I promise not to flirt with you anymore?"

He started, nearly dropping the stick. "I beg your pardon."

"I thought you preferred direct speech?" Her eyebrows shot up and a grin spread across her face, revealing she did—in fact—have a matching dimple on the other side of her cheek. "I have already confessed that I am lonely, my hosts having no need of my companionship, and I find your conversation intriguing. If I promise not to flirt with you, will you tolerate my company?"

Isaac spoke stiffly, disapprovingly enough to make any general proud. "You are a very odd sort of young lady, Miss Wedgewood."

The woman at his side laughed, the sound almost joyful. "I thank you for your directness, Sir Isaac." She sounded far more amused than she ought, yet a pleasant sort of warmth spread through Isaac's chest at the easiness of the sound and her smile.

"No flirting," he said, capitulating to her terms merely out of curiosity. Who was this woman with her vibrant laugh, crooked smile, and clever eyes? Whatever had her family done to put her on the outskirts of Society, necessitating she give so much time to the whims of someone such as Lady Olivia? "I suppose if Esther likes you, that ought to be testament enough to your character."

The woman wore her lively expression comfortably. "You both have such odd names. I cannot think I have heard Esther as a given name very often. Everyone seems to prefer having a dozen Marys in the family to anything more original."

"Our mother felt the same." Isaac offered the explanation with a shrug. "She used to say that people preferred New Testament names to Old, which she liked better. More drama in the Old."

"A sensible woman." Miss Wedgewood tucked her hands behind her back, adopting a lofty tone. "My mother named me after her, at least in part. She is Mildred, I am Millicent."

"Those are not the same name," he noted dryly.

"No. But both of us had papas to call us Millie." A softer look stole over her, which he would not have seen had he not been studying her from the corner of his eye. The light in her eye dimmed, her smile changing from a broad grin to a gentle pressing of the lips.

A bittersweet expression. In fact, when her eyes settled upon the ground, she fully appeared as lonely as she had proclaimed herself. Whatever feelings she had in regard to her situation, she did not strike him as a bad sort. There was a cleverness in her eyes, but nothing cruel.

"Millie," he repeated, quite without thinking.

Her eyes darted up to his. "Now Sir Isaac, if I am not permitted to flirt, neither are you."

His chin jerked upward. "Me? *Flirt?*"

"Speaking a woman's Christian name without leave is most certainly flirtatious." She grinned at him, then pointed at a turn in the lane. "I must go this way to return to the marquess's home. Good day to you, Sir Isaac."

He merely gaped after her retreating form, but after she had gone a dozen steps he could not help but chuckle. "Good day to you, Miss Wedgewood," he called. She turned enough to look over her shoulder at him, a saucy smile upon her face. She raised her hand in a brief wave, then continued on with a light step.

Flirt. As if he would ever contemplate such a thing.

A smile tugged at his lips all the rest of his walk home.

Chapter Eight

"I have an invitation to spend the afternoon and evening with Lady Inglewood." Though Millie hadn't expected Lady Olivia's praise for obtaining the countess's interest, the marquess's daughter's sneer was something of a surprise. Especially when the lady had appeared almost statuesque while playing the harp.

"You are off to have tea parties with Esther Riley? How does that accomplish anything at all?" Lady Olivia kept plucking at the strings of the instrument as she spoke. "Amusing yourself in that woman's house is not precisely what I expected when we settled upon this arrangement."

Millie came further into the music room and sat upon a chaise near the harpist's chair. She folded her hands primly in her lap, resolved to explain things. "You tasked me with humiliating Sir Isaac. I cannot complete the task without coming to know the two of them better. The first task set for me was accomplished easily by spying, where no one expected to find a spy. But this is different. I must gain their trust if I am ever to learn their secrets."

It was a thing her mother had taught her, years before, and taught Emmeline, too. Knowing the secrets of others gave a woman power, and in a world ruled by men, every scrap of advantage must be taken. At least, that is what Mrs. Wedgewood had said.

Lady Olivia's hands stilled the vibrating strings as she appeared to contemplate that idea. "What makes you think you can win their trust? Sir Isaac has been famously stand-offish since his return from war and Esther Riley is nearly as closed off as her brother."

Although reluctant to admit that most of what she had already learned had come by sheer luck, Millie had to make some sort of answer. "I have similar interests to the countess, as you pointed out before. That much has captured her curiosity. Sir Isaac is a different matter. I am attempting to find the crack in his wall as of yet."

That did not appear to impress Lady Olivia at all. She plucked at her harp again, gentle notes slipping from the strings into the rest of the room. "I suppose I do not care how long it takes you, so long as I am assured satisfaction. Sir Isaac's humiliation will be difficult, there is no doubt. But his sister—I will be most pleased when Lady Inglewood is an unknowing instrument to bringing her brother low."

Millie cleared her throat, a trifle nervously. "Lady Olivia, perhaps if you told me *why* you wish the baronet harm—"

"That is not your business," the woman snapped, her eyes hardening as her shout echoed through the room.

After a long moment of silence, Millie at last spoke, her voice soft in the quiet. "Of course, Lady Olivia. As you say."

Lady Olivia rested her cheek upon the curve of her instrument. "We will not expect you for dinner."

The clear dismissal left Millie no choice but to stand and curtsy. She took her leave of Lady Olivia and walked out the door, feeling as though she fled a tiger's lair. As she stepped from the room, her eye caught sight of a man leaning against the wall beside the open doorway. Millie started, then realized Lord Neil stood there, appearing as indolent as she had ever seen him.

Yet his eyes glittered in the shadows of the hallway. "What are you and my sister planning?" he asked abruptly, the slyness absent from his tone making him sound entirely too serious, too knowing.

Millie shut the door to the music room behind her before meeting his eyes again. "Nothing of importance, my lord."

He stayed leaning there, one ankle crossed over the other, arms folded on his chest. "It did not sound like nothing. I suspected your business with Livvy might have something to do with Fox. But not with the countess."

"I have no idea what you mean, Lord Neil." Millie's feigned innocence did nothing to soften his expression, nor to remove his suspicion.

"Miss Wedgewood." He pushed away from the wall and offered her his arm. She took it, though his cordiality was clearly naught but a tool meant to get his way. "Did you know that I have been banished from all Inglewood lands?"

What on earth could such a confession mean? Millie shook her head. "I hadn't heard such a thing, my lord. Is there a particular reason for that unlucky fate?"

They walked slowly down the corridor, lit by windows along one side, the other lined with closed doors.

"I insulted Lord Inglewood by flirting with his countess."

Millie startled and pulled them to a stop. "You did what?" She took in the nobleman's warm eyes, a mix of brown and green, and the wave of his dark blond hair. He certainly was handsome, and dressed with an obvious sense of fashion, yet she hadn't thought him a great flirt or a scoundrel. To admit to such a thing, to such an intent upon a married woman, marked him as both.

And yet. There was still something about him. Something that made his character, the outward manifestation of vanity and self-ishness, feel false. His sister was as she presented herself. But there was something different about Lord Neil.

"You need not appear so shocked, Miss Wedgewood." His sly grin returned, yet the merriment did not reach his eyes. "The upper-classes are full of people who not only flirt but also bed those married to others. I thought to try my luck with Lady Inglewood." He shrugged and continued their walk, pulling her gently along beside him.

His confession did nothing to raise him, or the rest of Society, in her estimation. Though not naïve, Millie preferred not to think of what the upper echelons of Society deemed appropriate behavior. Everyone with wit enough to read a newspaper knew the Crown Prince himself had mistresses and that fidelity was often sniffed at; those with titles and money and the favor of their peers never suffered overlong for their indiscretions.

That was not a part of society Millie had any interest in joining.

"Not only did the countess rebuff my every advance, with a fierce loyalty to her husband's good name, but she carried herself with graciousness throughout my ill-conceived plans. Nor has she treated me with anything other than neighborly kindness since her husband's proclamation." Lord Neil's grin was part predatory, part admiration. "I rather like her. Which brings me back to my point." He released her arm and stepped away, looking down upon Millie with that same expression on his face. "Whatever my sister has done to persuade you to her side, whatever plans the two of you have made, leave Lady Inglewood out of it or you will suffer the wrath of many a person who esteems her."

He bowed while Millie's mouth fell open in her surprise. "But when you knew about Sir Isaac—"

He waved a hand to interrupt her. "I care not at all for Fox. Olivia and you can have your way with him." He turned his back on her and walked back the way he had come, saying over his shoulder, "But you have been warned regarding Lady Inglewood."

Interesting of him to come to the defense of a woman who had rejected his advances.

Millie stared after him, trying to puzzle out Lady Olivia and her brother. They were a strange pair. If she did not need Lady Olivia's influence, her sponsorship back into the bosom of Society, Millie would pack her trunks that instant and return home.

But her mother might not allow Millie to return. The acceptance of the nobility, the repair of their family's status, was all that mattered to Mildred Wedgewood, formerly Lady Mildred, daughter of a viscount, granddaughter to an earl and duke. If Millie ruined their last chance to rise once more into an exalted sphere of titles and wealth, fashion and sophistication, her banishment from her mother's life would leave her quite alone in the world.

Why had Emmeline ruined everything by running off with that horrid Welsh barrister?

Returning to her room, Millie rang for her maid. Not only did she need to dress for an afternoon of quiet, but her maid would have to accompany her, and they would need to bring a dress for her to change into for dinner. Lady Inglewood had even instructed Millie to bring "something to work upon."

Despite Lord Neil's warning and Lady Olivia's temper, Millie anticipated the time with the countess almost happily.

The image she inked on her box had begun to take shape the previous afternoon, while she'd puzzled over her chance encounter with Sir Isaac. She could easily pack up the things she needed to continue that work within the box itself. No matter what Lady Olivia wished, or Lord Neil warned, Millie would permit herself to enjoy an afternoon with someone who hadn't sneered at her favorite artistic pursuit.

Although Lord Neil's warning meant reevaluation of her plans, yet again. No flirting with Sir Isaac, no betrayal of Lady Inglewood, yet she must satisfy Lady Olivia's demands.

If she knew why Lady Olivia wished ill on the baronet, perhaps it would help matters.

As she slipped a gown the color of her favorite pansies over her head, Sarah helping, Millie found herself looking forward to the afternoon immensely. Lord Neil's warning had come as a relief. She had no wish to hurt Lady Inglewood. Not when the woman had been kind.

Sarah packed a small bundle of Millie's things for the evening, then accompanied Millie down to the ground floor of the large house to wait for the promised Inglewood carriage. That was another thing; the countess did not expect Millie to walk in order to wait upon her. Lady Inglewood was thoughtful.

If only the countess had the same connections as Lady Olivia. The sort of connections that would make Millie's mother happy. Then Millie might prevail upon Lady Inglewood to help her.

As the carriage bearing the Inglewood crest of red birds on a yellow field appeared, Millie brushed away those ideas. Most likely, if Lady Inglewood knew of the Wedgewood family's shame, she would turn up her nose at Millie. Many members of the nobility and aristocracy as kind and gracious as Lady Inglewood had already done so.

She stepped up into the carriage and the groom handed Sarah up behind her. Sarah, one of the few who knew how terribly Emmeline's betrayal had cost all of them. Thank goodness for Sarah and her loyalty.

"This promises to be a lovely afternoon, miss," Sarah said, her eyes on the window and not on her troubled mistress. "The Inglewood servants are most accommodating. Last time we visited, they let me sit about drinking tea like I was a fine guest myself."

Millie sighed deeply, reflecting with gratitude how much Sarah meant to her. "I am glad to hear it. I hope you pass as pleasant an afternoon as I shall."

When Emmeline had left in the night, it was Millie who had gone to tell her betrothed. Lord Carning, the spoiled grandson of a duke, third in line for the title, hadn't been pleased. He *had* been inebriated. And he also had made highly inappropriate remarks and advances upon Millie. Only Sarah's quick-thinking had kept Millie from being another reason for her family to hang their heads in shame.

But that was in the past. The day was fine and golden. She rode in the carriage of an earl. Sarah hummed a simple, reassuring tune.

In a very short time, Millie could restore her family's honor and make everyone forget all about what Emmeline had done, and what Lord Carning had tried to do.

⁕

THE NIGHT HAD PASSED HORRIFICALLY. NO OTHER WORD came to mind when Isaac attempted to understand what had gone wrong, why his dreams had been littered with the gasps and moans of the dying soldiers. He had taken something for sleep, at the advice of the apothecary, and sleep had come, but with more vivid nightmares than he had experienced in months.

So he found himself out walking most of the day, ignoring his responsibilities, and trying to fill his mind with light rather than the darkness of his memories.

He trudged about his lands, counting trees, inspecting the location for the proposed dam to keep his tenants' farms from flooding, and then he'd made for the beaches of Inglewood. His property did not border the sea anywhere, but it was an easy thing to cross into Silas's estate. He wandered for a time beneath the birch trees, reflecting on the happy afternoons of his childhood.

The shadows withdrew with each passing hour he spent away from the emptiness of his home.

Though he disdained the company of others, Isaac equally hated being alone. Before the war, social gatherings had filled him with energy, and he had looked forward to every opportunity to be among friends and neighbors.

But of late he wished to keep out of sight. People looked at him, expecting him to be as before. More than his arm had gone missing in battle, though. He had lost the desire to laugh at the oddities of life. He did not care for vapid conversation, for insignificant topics, for doing *nothing*, and being proud of an indolent state.

Isaac settled upon a large rock overlooking the beach. The rock marked the beginning of the earl's gardens, sitting beside the path that led up the hill and into the manicured hedges and flowerbeds where Esther spent many a morning painting. With his back to his friend's house, Isaac breathed deeply of the sea air. The waves rolled gently up to the beach, then tucked themselves back again. They were a comforting sight, their soft roars soothing.

Not at all like his nightmares.

Perhaps he ought to sleep on the beach one night and see if it cured him better than the apothecary's powders.

There was little of late to provide him joy in his life. Isaac needed to take a greater swath of the darkness out of his soul, cast more of it away. There was purpose in making his estate financially stable once again, and Silas had helped with many ideas that would see Isaac successful in that pursuit. But there must be more. Must be something he could do that would fill the shadows of his heart with life and the will to move forward again.

A thought came to him—the memory of Miss Wedgewood's laughter. It had surprised him, when she had laughed the day before, as though her heart knew the happiness his lacked. Yet she'd admitted, quite freely, that her circumstances were not ideal.

It was a shame, really. A woman with such intelligence, with that endearing set of dimples, trapped with a spiteful Lady Olivia. It still pained him that he had stolen her enjoyment of the Barnes' dinner party with a few ill-conceived words. He used to speak so well. Used to guard his tongue. Of late, he said whatever thought came into his head, almost without realizing it.

Thinking on Miss Wedgewood would not get him anywhere that afternoon. He needed to help himself first. But where might he find something—someone—that brought a sense of belonging?

When the answer came, Isaac allowed himself a smile. Though he did not wish to discuss business with Silas, or have Essie fuss over him, there was a member of his family he knew would lift his spirits. His nephew, Little Isaac. And Essie had said the nursery door was always open to Isaac for visits.

Why not pay a call on the baby? Some might think him daft, wishing as he did to see an infant that was not his own, but the title of uncle far outpaced that of baronet in his favor. His small nephew was also his godson, and the infant had no expectations of Isaac except that he make amusing faces on occasion. Really, it was perfect. A baby's smiles had a magical ability to cheer up anyone.

Isaac walked through the gardens, making his way to one of the rear doors of Inglewood Keep.

Laughter in the garden drew his attention away from his purpose. Familiar laughter.

Miss Millicent Wedgewood. Isaac pivoted to face the direction where the sound of merriment had originated. What was she doing at Inglewood? Again?

Esther had a soft heart. Her adoption of a lonely soul should not surprise him.

If his sister lingered in the gardens with Miss Wedgewood then Isaac needed to stop and say hello. It would not do to enter his nephew's domain without at least greeting one of the lad's parents.

Making his way through the hedges, Isaac went to the fountain at the center of the more ornamental gardens. Another bright laugh confirmed that he had taken the correct path. Rounding the last of the flowering shrubs, Isaac stopped abruptly. He hadn't fully expected the scene before him.

Miss Wedgewood sat upon the ground, knees angled so that his nephew could be propped against them in a reclined position. A thin blanket was all that was between the two of them and the soft grasses surrounding the fountain. The baby held the woman's fingers in his fists, swinging them about and grinning toothlessly at his captive.

Esther was nowhere in sight. Had she so much trust in the near stranger already, to leave her husband's heir in the woman's care? Not that Isaac suspected the woman to have any nefarious purpose in regard to the baby, but—

She looked up at him and her posture stiffened with surprise. But the startled look faded into a welcoming smile. "Sir Isaac. Your nephew and I were just speaking of you." She wore a gown of a vivid purplish color that brought springtime to mind, with a bonnet upon her head and a shawl lying upon the ground next to her. The woman appeared quite at her ease in the countess's gardens.

"That explains the laughter." Where the quip came from, he could not say, but he was rewarded for it. Miss Wedgewood laughed again, softer this time, and turned her attention back to his nephew.

"Do you hear that, little one? Your uncle thinks we are laughing at him." She slanted her eyes toward him and lowered her voice to a stage whisper. "We must not tell him the truth." The baby cooed and waved his tiny fists, still holding tightly to Millie's fingers.

Millie. The shortened version of her name suited her better than the mouthful of her given name, especially when she made such a pretty picture with an infant under her care. Millicent Wedgewood sounded like a Shakespearian villainess. The name was far too weighty to settle upon someone of her delicate stature, too.

"I find myself curious what you would say about me outside of my hearing," he admitted, making his way to the fountain to sit upon its edge. "Especially to my entirely impressionable nephew."

She peered up at him from beneath her wide-brimmed bonnet. "Impressionable?" The auburn-haired woman wrinkled her nose and stuck her tongue out at his nephew, who squealed a happy response. "You see, he is not at all impressionable. He knows I am a silly woman. He will not take me seriously at all."

Isaac chuckled and folded his arm across his chest, tucking it beneath what remained of his other arm. "You are adept at teasing my curiosity, Miss Wedgewood."

"Do you hear your uncle?" she asked the baby with an animated expression. "He will not let us alone until we have shared all our secrets. Really. The man has no sense of decorum." She extracted one hand from the baby and used it to introduce the ribbon from her bonnet to him, dangling it just out of reach. Little Isaac's focus immediately went to the brightly colored ribbon, and he released her fingers completely in order to grasp the satin instead.

"That may not have been wise," Isaac noted, thinking of the state of his cravat any time he held his nephew near. His valet always sighed rather hopelessly when Isaac returned from a visit with the child.

Millie shrugged, not the least bit bothered when Little Isaac put the end of the ribbon in his mouth. "I neglected to bring any toys with me. Your sister had an unfortunate accident with a large pot of paints. This wee one was in the room with us, and most upset by the lack of attention. I brought him outside while his mama went to change and clean up. The outdoors always puts me on the mend when I am out of sorts."

Isaac studied her face, the slight upturn of her nose, the freckles dotting her cheeks. How old was she? Over the age most ladies of rank or means came out into Society. "I feel the same. I have been walking about all morning trying to regain my balance, actually."

Why had he made that confession?

The woman's head tilted, but whether from curiosity or the way his nephew tugged at the ribbon, Isaac could not tell.

"Are you off balance often?" she asked.

"No." He lied. But it was the only acceptable answer a man in his position could make. "Are you?"

She lowered his nephew to the blanket and tugged off her bonnet, putting it on the ground next to the baby so he could more easily entertain himself with the ribbons.

"I would never admit to being anything other than perfectly poised." She flashed him a smile, granting him a brief glimpse of her dimple again. His breath caught for a moment, startled by how attractive that expression made her.

He needed to move about in Society more. Never in his life had he been attracted to a woman with her coloring, or her petite frame. He much preferred women with golden curls and tall, willowy forms. Before the war, that was the sort of woman who had turned his head. Not that he had paid much attention to women at all since his return. A fact his sister constantly brought up in conversation.

"Is something the matter?" she asked, and Isaac blinked, realizing she had caught him staring at her.

"Not at all. Merely thinking." He nodded to the blanket. "Might I join you down there? I actually came up to the house to pay a call on Isaac."

"That might be confusing someday. The shared name." She smiled and moved aside, creating a larger spot for him to sit. "I think that is why I am not precisely named for my mother. She wished to avoid any difficulty a shared name would bring."

Isaac left the fountain for the blanket, settling upon it and leaning forward to gain the baby's notice. The child's eyes narrowed at him a moment, then the baby squealed and started kicking his legs in excitement.

Isaac could not hold back his smile when his namesake recognized him. "Good afternoon to you, too," he said. "I hope you have conducted yourself as a gentleman in Miss Wedgewood's company."

"Quite so," Millie answered while the baby kicked and made contented baby sounds. "He is the perfect companion, and an expert at listening without interrupting." She leaned back, resting her weight on her hands, and turned her face up to the sunlight. "I fully expect he keeps confidences, too." She closed her eyes, and he heard the deep breath she drew in.

Isaac rescued her hat's ribbon from the baby. He tugged off the glove he wore using his teeth and then dangled that above Little Isaac until the baby caught the soft leather in his hands.

Without his permission, his eyes went back to Millie. He traced her profile, the softness in her face. But there was no peace in her expression, gentle or not. He could see tension in the curve of her neck, the slight downturn of her lips. Though someone else might think her repose was one of contentment, Isaac sensed something else entirely.

"You perplex me, Miss Wedgewood." The observation slipped out before he knew he wished to speak it aloud.

A tight smile appeared on her lips. "I believe that is what ladies are supposed to do to gentlemen, sir." She tipped her head to the side and opened her eyes, meeting his gaze directly. "You have but to ask it, and I will tell you whatever you wish to know."

"You said you are with the marquess's family due to your mother's wishes. Mothers wishing to better their social standing, and that of their children, are no unusual thing. But why do you bear the burden of your whole family? And why the Marquess of Alderton?"

A line appeared in her forehead briefly but smoothed away again as she adopted a more ladylike posture. Which was impressive, considering they both sat upon the ground. "Lady Olivia presented an opportunity, and an acceptable rung of Society. My mother is not used to where we have settled. My family, until only a few years ago, held a much more respected place."

The baby started to fuss, likely upset about the lack of attention upon him. Isaac carefully turned the little one over, giving him the amusement of pushing himself up on his chubby arms. The boy would be crawling about on all fours soon, if his nursemaid was to be believed.

"What happened to lower your family's esteem?" he asked, watching his nephew. "I have been out of Society myself for many years, with the war, so I cannot say I am at all aware of your family or their circumstances."

"That is a very direct question," she murmured. "But as you would learn the answer soon enough if you asked the right people, I suppose there is no harm in telling you our history." Her voice had softened, almost to a whisper. Then the silence stretched long enough that Isaac looked up again, eyebrows raised. He knew the question was impertinent. Most would find it bordering on rudeness.

Her face had paled, and her lips pressed together so tightly they were bloodless. But she did not appear ready to cry. Rather, a flame of hostility danced in her eyes. The tilt of her chin was fierce, almost daring. She was not, he realized in that moment, a woman one wished to cross. There was fire beneath her skin, burning in anger.

"My family was ruined when we gave insult to a duke's grandson, and he took it upon himself to remove us from Society." She stated the truth without embellishment of tone or words.

Isaac had nothing to say. Not immediately. He stared at her, uncertain. Most would mumble an apology, try to end the moment of discomfort. He had witnessed it many times himself, when people asked about the loss of his arm and he told them without pride or bravado it had been blown off because he was not where he was supposed to be at the moment the loss occurred. He only treated the loss lightly when with his friends, the people who knew him. Strangers had no business asking such questions.

Yet he had asked this woman to answer a similar inquiry.

"Forgive me for asking, Miss Wedgewood. My sister says the war made me forget my manners. Perhaps she is right." That was the right thing to say this time.

She shrugged, lowering her eyes and lifting her bonnet. She smoothed the ribbon Little Isaac had gummed and drooled upon. "I did not have to answer. You said you preferred directness. I offered it to you. But now you owe me an answer, sir."

That seemed fair. "You have but to ask the question."

"Might we be friends now?"

Of all the things she might have asked, he hadn't expected that. "Friends?"

"I have few enough of them." She put the bonnet back upon her head, leaving the ribbons to dangle loosely down her shoulders. She tilted her head down, the bonnet's brim obscuring her expression somewhat. "Never mind. It was a foolish thought. I will not be in the neighborhood long." She spoke dismissively, but there was a hint, the barest touch, of vulnerability in her voice.

Why would a woman such as herself, an outcast of Society or

not, wish to befriend him? He had been nothing but rude to her since their first meeting.

He hadn't made it easy on anyone, not even his sister and Silas, to act as friends. Truly, the only reason his morose moods and unsociable behavior was tolerated by those he counted as friends was due to the longevity of their relationships. They were patient with him, because they loved him. He hadn't allowed anyone new to come close to a relationship with him.

Strangers generally saw only the social mask he wore that lied to the world about the state of his mind. Yet the unfortunate Millie Wedgewood hadn't even seen that pleasant falsehood.

"Then perhaps we can make it a temporary arrangement." Isaac watched as she raised her head, her eyes widening. "I will be your friend for as long as you are in the neighborhood. Does that suit you?"

Her posture relaxed and a hint of her playful smile returned. "It does. Thank you."

"Here you are," Essie's voice said from the break in the hedges. "I am terribly sorry, but it took much longer than expected to put myself to rights." She came across the grass, fixing Isaac with a serious frown. "I hope you have behaved yourself, Isaac."

"Me?" he asked, feigning innocence. "I always behave myself."

His sister's expression well told how much credence she gave that remark. "Has my son caused as much trouble as his uncle?"

Millie laughed while Isaac started to splutter a protest. "I assure you, my lady, both Isaacs have put me completely at ease."

Essie bent and swooped up her baby in her arms, causing the little one to squeal happily. "That is exactly what I wish to hear. Come now. Let us all go inside for some refreshment. Isaac, I assume you will wish to keep us company for a time?"

Isaac came to his feet without difficulty and with enough speed he was able to offer his hand to Miss Wedgewood to help her stand. He had forgotten his glove on the ground, so when her bare hand landed in his, soft and small, it surprised him enough that warmth bloomed in his chest.

Assisting her to stand, Isaac did not immediately relinquish her hand. She raised her gaze to his and offered him a tentative smile, a blush appearing upon her cheeks. "Thank you, Sir Isaac."

He tilted his head forward. "Miss Wedgewood." When she released her hold on him, following after Essie to the house, Isaac curled his hand into a fist. How strange. Between their discussion and that simple touch, something had shifted. He had pledged himself her friend. That had to account for the sudden feeling, the awareness of her size, and the strange urge to keep her hand tucked in his.

He scooped the glove up from the ground and gathered the forgotten shawl and blanket at the same time. Then he followed after the ladies, his earlier somberness tucked away. Hope that the afternoon might prove more pleasant than his morning made Isaac's step lighter.

Chapter Nine

S pending an afternoon in the company of Lady Inglewood and her brother did more to damage Millie's confidence than anything had before. They were good people. Of course, Sir Isaac had been a bit grumpy at first, but given the man's protective nature, she understood why he had viewed her with suspicion. One had but to see him with his infant nephew to glimpse a gentler side of him. And nothing about Lady Inglewood indicated she was the prideful peacock Lady Olivia had claimed.

Millie sat in the music room with the family, between the countess and baronet, before dinner. They had arranged a short row of chairs facing the pianoforte where the earl himself entertained them with a new piece of music from Austria. He played quite well, and apparently his performance was not the first of its kind.

Not a single member of the marquess's family had welcomed Millie. Nor had anyone been as kind to her as the people in the room at that very moment. Yet she had agreed to earn their trust only to betray it. Lady Olivia would settle for nothing else, and Millie's mother expected her to perform her part to put them back at the top of Society.

When the earl finished the lively piece, his countess applauded him, and Millie did as well. Sir Isaac, with only the one hand, clapped it heartily against his thigh.

"That was most entertaining, Silas," said the baronet. He had let his guard down enough that he wore an actual smile. The warmth in his countenance, now fully relaxed, set her much more at ease.

The countess rose gracefully from her chair and went to her husband, looking over the music with him to choose another piece. Millie folded her hands in her lap and turned to Isaac, again wondering what he had done to earn the enmity of Lady Olivia.

"I had no idea he enjoyed playing," Isaac said, catching her glance. "Not until after he and my sister were married. We have been friends nearly all our lives, and still he managed to keep that a secret."

Millie turned her attention back to the couple at the instrument when Lady Inglewood laughed, her husband's deep chuckle joining hers. They appeared perfectly content in each other's company and shared such a joyful look between them that it seemed they had forgotten they were not alone in the room.

"They care very much for each other, I think," she said softly.

Sir Isaac shifted in his chair, leaning closer to her. "I am afraid it is more than that. The two are in love. The circumstance makes it quite difficult to be near them. Only see, the way they stare at each other." One corner of his mouth came up as he described the scene, and she obediently took in the married couple. "He dares to look upon her as though she is the only woman worth so much as a glance. And she, my younger sister, appears to completely adore him. That is always how it is with them. Quite rude, really, to speak to each other with no more than a glance, leaving the rest of the world out of the conversation."

Indeed, Millie saw the warmth between them. Felt it. Briefly, she wondered what it would be like to experience such love and devotion. She tried to cover the tenderness of feeling with her jest. "Yes, quite rude. Married people ought not act like that.

They ought to be cold to one another. We should, in fact, question whether they like each other at all rather than the opposite."

Isaac chuckled and leaned closer, his shoulder nearly brushing hers. His breath warm against the nape of her neck. "I completely agree. Imagine, though, how difficult it is for me as a brother to one of them. Here I must sit, through every event and gathering, and pretend I do not see how my sister flirts with her own husband. I am terribly ashamed." But the glint in his eye said the opposite. He was happy for his sister, for all he jested over the situation.

"One would think they would be more circumspect, at least with you nearby," she said in a whisper. "What does the neighborhood think of their overly affectionate display, I wonder?"

"That is the worst of it." He sighed and his eyes crinkled at the corners. "Everyone knows they are in love."

Her heart squeezed at the last word, and his gaze arrested hers.

Love. It was a terrible word, really. The word her sister used as an excuse to turn her back on the family, banishing them from their place in the world. Love ruined everything. Her sister's actions kept her from wishing to understand, kept her from sighing over poetry and novels the way other women in her position might.

Yet when Millie saw this new evidence of love, as honest and true as what the earl and countess felt for one another, she could not think it all bad. And the way Isaac stared at her, a depth in his eyes that nearly invited her in, offering to make her a part of something different—

"What are you two whispering about?" the deep voice of the earl boomed through the room, startling Millie. Isaac jerked away from her, and she abruptly realized how close they had been, nearly touching as they spoke. Leaning in to one another.

"We were whispering about how torturous it is to sit here while you flirt with your wife," Isaac said without apology. He leaned back in his chair and waved a hand to indicate how the countess stood with her hand on her husband's shoulder. "You are nearly as disgusting a sight as Hope and her castaway."

That was a puzzling statement. But Millie did not get the chance to ask what it could mean.

"No one is as demonstrative as those two," the countess said as though she disapproved, though she immediately bent to press a brief kiss to her husband's cheek. "There. That is an end to our flirting. At least until we are all at the dinner table together. You know how I like to flirt during meals."

Isaac groaned dramatically while the earl laughed.

"Both of you ought to stop," the earl said, "before you frighten away Miss Wedgewood. She will return to the marquess's house with wild tales of how we conduct ourselves."

"She would never betray our confidence, I am certain," Lady Inglewood said, casting a glance full of mirth in Millie's direction.

Millie's heart sank. Though the countess spoke lightly, her words brought what Millie planned to the forefront of her mind.

These were good people. They ought not be brought low by anything of her doing.

How had she ever thought herself capable of such duplicity? She could not go through with it.

"You have my word, my lady," she promised, sealing her silent conviction with her word. She caught Sir Isaac's expression from the corner of her eye. His eyes narrowed, and he appeared momentarily confused. Perhaps he sensed there was more to what she had said than continuing in the merriment.

Millie would have to find another way to appease Lady Olivia. Or else disappoint her mother even more, returning home without having assisted in their family's recovery. If they were ever to rise from the ranks of the inconsequential again, it was up to Millie to find a different way to lift them.

At last they were informed that dinner waited for them, and Millie was escorted into the dining room on Lord Inglewood's arm. A member of Lords, a staunch supporter of agriculture, and the man often said to be made of marble, had offered her a sincere welcome into his home and engaged her in pleasant conversation. He was much younger than she thought he would be, too.

"I hope you enjoy your time in our county. The Marquess of Alderton's house parties are famous for their entertainments. You must be looking forward to the arrival of the other guests."

"I am afraid I know almost no one else on the guest list," she admitted, her hand barely touching his arm. What would this powerful peer do if he knew her original purpose in befriending his wife? Kind as he seemed at the moment, his reputation as a hard man had come from somewhere.

The countess and her brother entered the dining room ahead of Millie and the earl, but that did not stop Lady Inglewood from replying to Millie's statement. "I hope that means you will have many new friends, Miss Wedgewood."

Millie accepted her seat at the small, formal table. The room was not meant for entertaining large parties. There must be another table in the house, in grander surroundings, for the sorts of fine dinners someone of the earl's standing must occasionally host.

First Mr. and Mrs. Barnes and now Lord and Lady Inglewood had invited her into their homes on an intimate level. Though she wondered at her inclusion, she did not mention her curiosity. Perhaps they simply preferred smaller gatherings.

"Miss Wedgewood, after dinner we must show the gentlemen your artwork," Lady Inglewood said after all had settled and began their meal. "I was never all that accomplished at the intricacies of ink on wood. It is not a forgiving medium."

"Is that all you ladies have done this afternoon?" Sir Isaac asked with a crooked sort of smile. "Paint?"

"What Miss Wedgewood does is not quite painting." The countess pursed her lips in thought a moment. "It is drawing upon wood, and occasionally woodcarving is involved, too. I confess, though I have seen the products of such work before, I never quite understood the amount of patience and talent it takes to complete them."

"Too busy with your paints to pay attention to other forms?" Sir Isaac asked his sister, sounding terribly disappointed in her, though the sparkle in his eyes indicated that he meant to nettle her.

It struck Millie as quite a contrast, how relaxed Sir Isaac was at his sister's as compared to how he had been the night of the marchioness's dinner party. Perhaps his change in social behavior was due to his comfort in more familiar environs.

Whatever the case, Millie determined she felt more at ease among the people of Inglewood than she had in quite some time. Though she had been in company with them at the vicarage, and that had been a uniquely awful evening, Isaac's acceptance of her changed everything.

She rose to the countess's defense, her own tone playful. "Elder siblings are forever causing trouble. Come now, Sir Isaac. You must know your sister is an accomplished artist. Why, I have seen a rendering of *you* she created with charcoal, and she managed to almost make you appear handsome."

Lord Inglewood laughed. "That does mark my wife as a talented artist, if she can manage such a thing for you, Isaac."

The baronet lifted his cup to Millie, as though toasting her. "I will admit to my sister's superior skill with charcoal and brush, and thank Miss Wedgewood for the compliment paid to me. For if she can find me handsome when my visage is naught but a smudge of coal on paper, she must be positively dazzled by me in person."

Everyone laughed, including Millie. She had seen evidence enough of Sir Isaac's wit once she realized he was the impertinent grounds man, and his more lighthearted conversation of the evening proved further he was not so stern a man as she had thought him at first. He merely exercised caution around newcomers, protective of himself and the people for which he cared. Most endearing of him, actually.

"While we were enthralled by paints and ink," Millie said at last, "what were you gentlemen doing to entertain yourselves?"

Sir Isaac groaned and leaned back in his chair. "Do not ask,

Miss Wedgewood. You will force us all to sit through my brother-in-law's long-winded explanations of politics. As I have already been forced to listen to him all afternoon, I would prefer you change the subject. With haste."

The earl did not appear at all offended. "Miss Wedgewood might have a better head for politics than you do, Isaac, but as you seem to equate the subject with torture, I will leave it alone for the time being." He turned in his chair to better face Millie. "We mostly discussed politics, Miss Wedgewood, and of all the things I should like to propose next Season. We discussed agriculture for a time, too. Nothing of great entertainment."

"How terribly sad for you both." The countess brightened. "I have had an excellent idea. Day after tomorrow, you should both come and enjoy some true diversion." She turned to Millie. "Do you think you can get away again, Miss Wedgewood? Or will your hosts mind? I thought we could spend time enjoying the seaside. And the gardener informs me we have enough odds and ends for a bit of a bonfire. If you can come, I thought I would invite some of our neighborhood friends to make an evening of it."

A seaside bonfire? Nothing had ever sounded as exciting, as grand, as that simple enjoyment. Yet with her decision to not aid Lady Olivia, she may not be welcomed in that house for long. She had to consider the invitation carefully. "I should very much like to join you," she admitted readily. "I feel I must ascertain if Lady Olivia would mind my absence another evening."

"Invite her, too, if you must," Lord Inglewood said, not at all enthusiastic. "So long as that brother of hers stays away, I care not who else comes."

The countess pursed her lips, looking as though she might disagree, but Sir Isaac came into the conversation as though to head off an argument.

"The bonfires on Inglewood beach are always enjoyable. We can usually persuade a few friends to bring instruments so there is singing. Sometimes dancing."

"That does not sound at all civilized," Millie remarked, turning her attention to her plate. "Dancing around a fire, on a beach. One must necessarily think such things are rather wild."

"With Grace Barnes in attendance?" the countess asked, a laugh in her words. "Never. I can assure you, Miss Wedgewood, we are all very well-mannered and respectable. The vicar and his wife will come, I am certain. Though Grace is not likely to take part in all the merriment, given her delicate state."

As delightful as the evening sounded, Millie still did not commit to attending. "I will certainly let you know, as soon as possible, if I can be present."

They took enough pity on her to turn the conversation to other things. Millie attempted to enjoy the simplicity of the evening, all the while ignoring the storm of worry brewing in her mind.

⌇⋯⌇

ISAAC PREPARED TO TAKE HIS LEAVE SHORTLY AFTER Miss Wedgewood and her maid left in the Inglewood coach. He had said good night to his sister and stood in the entryway, his hat in hand, when Silas appeared from upstairs.

"Isaac," he called down, voice low enough not to carry far. "Do wait a moment."

"Of course. Is something wrong?" Isaac tucked his hat beneath his left arm. He knew it looked odd; to place things there emphasized more of what he lacked than what still remained, but Silas would not care, so Isaac did not either.

Silas came down the steps quickly, though not with great urgency. "I wanted to speak with you about Miss Wedgewood."

With nothing to say to that pronouncement, Isaac cocked an eyebrow at his friend and waited for more. They had spent nearly all afternoon in each other's company and Silas never once brought up Essie's new friend. To do so at the end of a long day was odd.

When Silas stood only a few paces away from Isaac, his expression easily read as perplexed. "I did not want to say anything before. I know Esther likes the woman, and she does tend to be a good judge of character. But Esther also gives people around her more forgiveness and compassion than most. I have tried to remember where I heard the name, Wedgewood, before. You moved about in Society before the war. Do you know her people? Anything about her?"

"Not really. Nothing more than what she has shared. Her family fell out of favor a few years previous, and her parents think that Miss Wedgewood's time with the marquess's family might repair those circumstances." Isaac offered a doubtful shrug. "Society is fickle, so something as simple as Lady Olivia inviting Miss Wedgewood to spend the summer with her could restore whatever position they enjoyed before."

After a moment of consideration, Silas conceded that point. "I suppose I understand that logic, though it seems impractical. But still. It strikes me as odd how little Miss Wedgewood actually speaks of her family. Yet earlier this evening, when you were all speaking of painting, she spoke of 'troublesome elder siblings.' As if she had one of her own."

Thinking back on that moment in the conversation, which had seemed innocent enough at the time, Isaac gave a slow nod. "It may have been a flippant statement. But yes. The phrasing was odd."

"I should like to know why her family fell from Society's grace." Silas's eyebrows drew together, a hard line appeared along his jaw. "If she intends to mix with my wife, I do not want to discover something particularly nefarious. Esther has only just found her footing in Society, after all."

"It cannot be all that dreadful if the Marchioness of Alderton has allowed Miss Wedgewood into her home," Isaac argued, though why he felt the need to come to Miss Wedgewood's defense he did not know. It probably had something to do with the sweet picture she had made that afternoon, playing in the gardens with his nephew. She had appeared so innocent and happy, and then a moment later, quite sad and lonely.

"The marquess openly lives with his mistress in London," Silas reminded Isaac, somewhat icily. "The eldest son in the family gambles as though money falls from the sky. The rumors I have heard about the second son are even worse than that. And we cannot forget what Lord Neil attempted with my wife, or Lady Olivia with you. That family has few morals. If they were not protected by Prinny's friendship—"

Isaac clamped a hand on Silas's shoulder to stop his friend's litany before it turned into a tirade. As a man of principle and honor, Silas deplored lack of the same in others. The elite of England were well divided between those that lived however they pleased and those who held themselves to a moral standard where-upon virtue was more highly prized than vice.

"I agree," Isaac said quietly, firmly, "that Miss Wedgewood's association with that family is a mark against her, at least from our perspective. But in all of my interactions with her, even when I was behaving uncivilly, she has conducted herself well and given me no reason to think ill of her."

That much was true. Even her brief attempt at flirtation, while irritating, hadn't approached inappropriate behavior.

"I know. I agree; she seems kind and amiable." Silas rubbed at his forehead and looked over his shoulder to the stairs. "But I do not want to see Esther hurt by a false friend. That is all I am worrying over, like a nursemaid."

"Essie would not appreciate that comparison." Isaac chuckled. "Or the fact that you are considering ousting Miss Wedgewood from our company. Do not fret, Silas. Miss Wedgewood has been astonishingly open, forthright even, when we have been in conver-sation. If you like, I will see what more she will tell me in regard to her family. I will let you know if anything strikes me as suspect."

"Thank you, Isaac." Silas relaxed at last, the hardness fading from his expression. "I would appreciate whatever help you can offer. Your sister's happiness is everything to me."

"Thank goodness for that. If I ever suspected otherwise, I would have to challenge you to a duel." Isaac grinned at his oldest friend, then finally took up his hat and set it firmly atop his head.

"Do not worry so, old man. If I can face down a squad of French soldiers, I can certainly face down a woman such as Miss Wedgewood."

"But the French took your arm," Silas pointed out, his grin appearing. "That hardly gives one faith in your abilities."

"So they did. But I cannot imagine Miss Wedgewood taking more from me than that." He grinned slyly at his brother-in-law before bowing his way out the door to his waiting horse. He did not think upon what he had promised, or why, until he had nearly arrived at his own doorstep.

True, he had held some suspicion regarding Miss Wedgewood's place among them at first. But as he had told Silas, after several interactions, he thought her harmless. He even found her company pleasant. Her laughter contagious. Her gentle smiles...stirring.

Millie Wedgewood made him curious. Silas had just given Isaac the perfect excuse to feed that curiosity. Not that Isaac particularly needed or wanted to do so. Not at all. But—

"Anything to take my mind off of myself," he muttered aloud in the semi-darkness. His horse twitched an ear back at him, but otherwise there was no indication given he had spoken aloud.

Perhaps all he needed *was* a distraction of some sort. Something to think on other than his estate. Another layer of thought to cover the memories of war. Yes. That was why the idea of coming to know Millie better intrigued him. The fact that he would put Silas's mind at ease at the same time would only make the endeavor more worthwhile.

When Isaac retired that night, lying in bed, he tucked his hand behind his head. Staring up at the ceiling in his room, he conjured the image of the auburn-haired woman, delicately built, with warm brown eyes. Lovely woman. Still, the same niggling thought plagued him; however had someone such as she fallen into company with Lady Olivia?

Chapter Ten

Millie went in search of Lady Olivia shortly after she rose, only to be informed Lady Olivia had left for the day to make visits among her friends. Although Millie hardly expected her hostess to pay her much attention, the information that Lady Olivia had left the house for the day without a word stung her pride. They were not friends. They were temporary allies.

The difference in Lady Olivia's treatment of Millie, an insignificant person by nearly all measure, and Lady Inglewood's, firmed up Millie's resolve to end her agreement with the marquess's daughter.

Wandering about the house, Millie tried to find a diversion other than the art room. As much as she enjoyed her artistic pursuits, she could not abide the small room, and had spent all the previous day with the countess at that work. She needed something else to distract her. *Anything* else to distract her.

Somehow, she found her way out of doors, gloves in hand and a straw bonnet upon her head. She went to the stables, without any intention of riding, and stopped before a stall to greet the same horse she'd ridden her first day at the house. When she had met Sir Isaac for the first time.

He had played the part of an impudent servant with such easy charm, even if his accent was rubbish.

"What are you smiling about, Miss Wedgewood?" a voice asked, startling her from her thoughts. She turned away from the horse, withdrawing the hand upon its warm nose, and saw Lord Neil standing a few paces away. A groom led a horse into a stable; Lord Neil had returned from a ride.

"Nothing that would interest you, my lord," she answered, turning away from his narrow-eyed gaze.

"You really are terrible at falsehoods, Miss Wedgewood." Lord Neil came to stand beside her, laying his hand against the horse's neck and giving it a firm pat. "Which is why I cannot surmise why you and my sister are acquainted. You are not Olivia's usual sort of pet." He withdrew and kept walking down the wide lane between the two rows of stalls.

With nothing better to do, Millie followed along after him. "I cannot tell if you mean to slight your sister or me, Lord Neil."

"Both, I should think." He shot a cocky grin over his shoulder at her. "Olivia for being foolish enough to bring you here, and you for coming. Nothing the two of you do together could possibly be counted a success. I believe your goals must necessarily be at odds. Whatever it is you are planning."

"And here I thought you were all laconic boredom and indolence." She affected an innocent mien.

He cast her a look filled with supreme arrogance. "I am everything a man of my station ought to be."

Millie hastened her walk to draw up alongside the man as they stepped out of the other side of the stables, into the open air. He made his way to the kennels.

"Lord Neil," she said, daring to place her hand on his arm to pull him to a stop. "I actually believe that. You are what a man of privilege and high birth should be. Your kindness to me, though you certainly try to mask that part of your character, will never be forgotten. Thank you."

For a moment, his eyes widened as though she had surprised him. "There are few enough who would accuse me of kindness, Miss Wedgewood."

"There is more to you than I think you let on, Lord Neil." Millie released his arm and offered up a smile. He appeared confused, then his jaw tightened. Rather than continue on the subject of his character, Millie changed the subject with haste. "As to what Lady Olivia and I have planned, I believe you are right. I wanted to speak to your sister this morning, in fact. To tell her our agreement must come to an end."

His expression returned to one of smugness. "Ah, it is unfortunate I am not a gambling man. I seem to have a knack for predicting the future." Lord Neil swung the half door open to enter the kennels, where several dogs barked and bayed the moment he came into view.

Millie eyed the animals distrustfully, but as all were behind sound doors with slats in them, she kept pace with Lord Neil.

He stopped before a door that led into another room of the kennels and turned to face her. "What will Olivia do when she learns of this end?"

"I imagine she will send me packing." Millie forced the lack of concern into her voice, though she knew her mother would certainly punish her for the failure. "As that will likely be the case, that is why I wished to thank you."

His expression turned to one of amusement. "Completely unnecessary, Miss Wedgewood."

She lifted one shoulder in a shrug. "You are the only member of the family who has bothered yourself with me at all. The art room. Your conversation. Even the warning you offered. So. Thank you." She dropped into a curtsy and then turned on her heel, eager to leave the loud barking behind her.

"Miss Wedgewood," Lord Neil's voice called, louder than the dogs. She paused and turned around, curious. He came toward her at a quick, determined pace, his eyebrows drawn down and his mouth in a hard line. When he drew even with her, he spoke earnestly. "When you speak with my sister, send me word. Livvy will not be pleased with you going back on any agreement she contrived. If I am there, perhaps I can keep the situation from becoming disagreeable."

Millie considered the offer, and the complete seriousness with which he made it, before giving a nod of agreement. He bowed and went back about his business, leaving her to make her way out of the kennels alone. As all the barking receded, her thoughts cleared. If Lord Neil offered her protection from his own sister, what sort of unpleasantness awaited her?

She kept walking, taking herself out to the road. With nothing else to do, retracing the steps that had brought her into Sir Isaac's path would amuse her for a time. If she should come upon him during her walk, perhaps he would not mind her company.

She certainly would not mind his; now that her mind was fully made up she could more easily enjoy his wit.

But to her disappointment, no baronet appeared to enjoy the fine sun or the lovely summer breeze. After a quarter of an hour, she turned back, resigned to another day alone.

"Of course I am being silly." She spoke softly, but hearing the words aloud helped firm them up in her mind. "And why should I wish to meet him again? We are only friends. Hardly that."

She was partway up the drive to the marquess's estate, still nursing her unreasonable disappointment, when she saw a gentleman coming away from the house, on horseback.

Sir Isaac.

It was easy enough to recognize him, with his soldier's posture. What was he doing here? Now? Millie's heart lightened, the day somehow growing brighter around her. She waved at him.

He hadn't seemed to see her right away, his head lowered. The movement alerted his horse, and when the animal nickered, Sir Isaac looked up.

His somewhat stern expression changed into a smile of greeting, and he rode closer before swinging down from his horse. He accomplished the trick without pause, despite having only the one arm. Her eyes flicked to where the missing appendage ought to be, then up to his welcoming expression.

"Miss Wedgewood, I was told you were not at the house," he said. Did she imagine the warmth in his eyes? He could not possibly be as pleased to see her as she was to see him.

"I was out walking," she said, though the explanation was unnecessary. She stepped closer to rub the nose of his mount, attempting to distract herself from the delight of seeing him. Withdrawing from Lady Olivia's demands might make her situation more complicated, but it did allow her to relax the tight grip she had kept upon her admiration for the former soldier.

"I am come to press the invitation upon you to join our friends tomorrow evening. My sister has instructed me to be absolutely charming so that you will not be able to resist saying yes." He chuckled and tipped his hat further back on his head. "Though why she thinks my charm will have any draw, I do not know."

Millie slanted a look at him from beneath her bonnet. "I cannot understand Lady Inglewood either. But you had better make the attempt at charm, I suppose."

He grinned and then comically pursed his lips, lowering his eyebrows. "Miss Wedgewood, would you please consider attending the bonfire night with our friends? My sister and I would consider it a great honor."

She laughed. "That is what you believe your sister meant by charm? I am afraid I cannot qualify your brooding scowl as something that would entice me to accept an otherwise appealing invitation."

He folded his arm over his chest as he had the day before, cocking his chin upward. "No? Whatever else could my sister have meant by charm? Or by sending me as messenger instead of another? I am naturally charming."

"Perhaps she thought I would pity you." Millie narrowed her eyes at him. "Pity Sir Isaac, who cannot abide to even be flirted with and so does not know how best to use his charm. You must not have very many female friends."

His expression as she spoke went from shocked surprise to something else, something that made him turn pale and drop his gaze. "I have a few," he muttered quietly, almost too softly for her to hear. What had happened? In a handful of words she had managed to send him into a cast down state, as though she had proclaimed a death sentence rather than attempted a jest.

Millie stepped closer to him, put a hand upon that arm barring his chest, and looked directly up into his eyes. "Sir Isaac, I can see I have wounded you. I do not know how, but I am sorry for it. Please, forgive me."

He stared down at her, his eyes distant still, his jaw clenched over words or an emotion before he spoke, his body as rigid as ever.

"Was it the remark about friends? Or flirting?" she asked, aware she stood too close. But he had to see, especially after how difficult it had been to gain his trust before, that she did not mean to hurt him. "I am sorry—"

"You needn't be." His words were gentle. His posture relaxed again, and he dropped his arm, but caught her hand in his before it could fall back to her side. "Miss Wedgewood." His nose wrinkled. "It is a horrible surname, you know."

She dared a smile, though she kept it small. "I know. Thankfully, as a woman, I might one day change it. But you, sir, are changing the subject. I was still apologizing."

"As I said. It is unnecessary." He gave her hand a gentle squeeze before releasing it. He started walking down the path, his horse following like an obedient dog. "You jested about pity. That word is not a favorite of mine. Indeed, I rather dread having it associated with me in any way."

"Oh." Her eyes lowered to the path. "Because of the war? Your arm?"

"In part, I suppose. Foolish of me, of course. Many a man lost an arm, and many more never even came home. But there is something to it, you know, when someone stares at where your arm should be. When someone pretends to ignore the way in which you lack the ability to function as a man ought to."

"Dear me. That does sound rather daunting." Millie's mind searched for what to say on the subject. She had no experience with such a loss as his. She had seen artwork in the Royal Gallery depicting battlefields in France, full of soldiers, lunging horses, death on both sides. It was quite grim. But she hadn't spoken to many who had actually fought in the war, or witnessed such horrors the way Isaac had.

"We all have our hardships to bear," he said with false levity. "I imagine you could tell a few tales of woe yourself." He offered a weak smile to her, which was not at all acceptable. He had been so cheerful before. So delighted to see her. Then he'd revealed a weakness, forced to it by her thoughtless words.

"Not quite the same as yours, but yes. I've had my share of difficulties." She tipped her nose up in the air, briefly wondering if she ought to return to jesting, if laughter would be enough to restore balance. But that was a coward's way out. A fool's. She was tired of being both of those things. "Can you keep a secret, Sir Isaac?"

"A secret?" Isaac turned to his horse to take its lead, as the beast had started to lag behind to nip at the soft grass on the side of the path. They were at the road. "I think I can. Providing it does no harm to anyone I know." He turned to her, curiosity in his eyes. "I cannot imagine you have too many secrets of a clandestine nature."

"Not too many," she agreed, tucking her hands behind her back. "But you ought to know this one. For a time, and among certain circles still, I am a person to be stared at, pitied, and ridiculed. You see, due to an unfortunate circumstance, I am actually quite ruined."

His head jerked back. "What?" Then he leaned forward, eyes narrowed. "I cannot—do not understand."

She forced a smile, projecting a nonchalance she most certainly did not feel. "It is true. Ask anyone in Society about my elder sister, Emmeline. She ran off the night before her wedding. With a man decidedly beneath her station, and her prospective husband's honor was damaged. He lashed out in every way he could, socially. Ruined my entire family. Father was turned out of clubs, had notes called in, lost several investments. Mother was given the cut direct. I was only fifteen at the time." Her bravado failed her at last and she ducked her head, hiding beneath her bonnet's brim.

Perhaps she had miscalculated. She hadn't spoken of her sister's wrong-doing to a stranger before. But Sir Isaac—she desperately wanted him to understand, to see why she could not see a lack in him as other's might.

She knew too well that what a person could see on the outside had nothing to do with their honor, their virtue, or their heart.

When Isaac spoke, it was quietly, almost to himself. "That circumstance explains so much." He appeared as though a great revelation had come to him.

"It does?" She tried to keep her surprise out of her voice. "What...what do you mean?"

"The Marchioness of Alderton would take no exception to a reputation such as that, and the family is quite above any censure. The Crown Prince himself would have to deliver a harsh blow to lower their importance and esteem. I understand your presence here now." Sir Isaac turned away from her, his expression darkening. "From what you have said of your reputation, they really are one of the few families capable of restoring that sort of damage."

Millie's heart sunk. Damaged.

Yes. She was that.

There was no use giving him the rest of the story. He need not know exactly how close she had come to losing everything. She withdrew a step from him, moving back to the house.

"Miss Wedgewood." His voice stopped her from moving again. "Are you safe in that house?" He jerked his chin in the direction of the manor. Why would he ask? He could not possibly care. He was all cold formality again.

Millie looked up the drive to the stately house, all shining white stone and tall pillars. "Yes. I believe so. Although I do not think I will be a guest there much longer. Lady Olivia and I do not suit one another. I believe she will ask me to leave. Possibly this evening, or tomorrow." Not that he would care. Why did she bother telling him as much?

"Oh." Sir Isaac tucked his horse's lead beneath his arm and finally fixed his hat, adjusting it to the proper angle. "Esther will be terribly disappointed." His sister. Not him. Of course not. How silly she had been, to imagine—it did not matter.

"As will I. Your sister is one of the kindest people I have ever met." Millie did not bother to offer another smile that would surely falter and fall into a frown. "I had better return. My maid and I should start our packing."

Millie started away, but Sir Isaac dropped his horse's lead to put his hand upon her arm. She kept her eyes averted from his, no desire to speak to him more, not after his reaction to what she had revealed. She ought to have known better. No one accepted her once they knew of her sister's choice, of Lord Carning's anger. The might of his family's importance brought to bear against the Wedgewoods' insignificance cowed many who may have thought to continue a friendship.

"Then this is goodbye?" the baronet asked, voice lowered. Why did he pretend it mattered?

"I suppose it must be. And good day." She tugged away from him and kept walking, refusing to look back at him. Disagreeable, horrid man. Damaged. What if her family was out of favor? It did not make them useless. It did not make *her* worthless.

Her brisk walk away from him became a firm march, her head tilted up, and she kept her back stiff and straight. If she withdrew with dignity, she would be well enough. At least until she had to face her mother and explain what she had done. Why she had made an enemy of Lady Olivia.

But the marquess's daughter had lied. Sir Isaac could not be capable of anything dishonorable. He did not deserve whatever problems her prying would cause. Lady Olivia had something against him, which reflected more poorly on her than it did her intended victim.

It no longer mattered. Millie would get well and truly out of the whole mess, go home to the strictures of her mother, the wounded silences of her father, and continue as she had for the past six years.

Seven years of weight, of worry, of being *less* than every young lady of her standing. All because Emmeline married for love rather than position and chose an honorable solicitor rather than a brutish lord. Emmeline might have escaped her unpleasant future, but she had left behind enough misery to make up for it.

Worse, she'd never once tried to explain herself to her sister, no matter that Millie had always looked up to Emmeline. Millie had always been there for her, as a friend as well as a sister. Well. Millie was used to facing life's difficulties alone. She would manage. She had no other choice.

ALTHOUGH ISAAC HAD PROMISED SILAS TO DISCOVER Millie Wedgewood's secrets, it was to Esther that he went immediately after parting from the mournful Miss Wedgewood. Esther possibly would have insight into solving the problem her new friend faced. Isaac could assuage Silas's concerns over the matter another time.

But how to make certain Esther understood the situation? He could tell neither his sister nor his friend of Millie's past. He had as good as promised to keep what she said to him in the lane a secret.

But he hadn't promised to leave the situation entirely alone. How could he? Knowing her story, and the sort of people who lived in that house, he could save her from being put out in a humiliating and public manner. Perhaps even prevent her from returning home a failure. If Esther thought of a way to help.

The Earl and Countess of Inglewood might not have the same amount of clout as the Marquess of Alderton, but they both had friends in Society. Silas had a strong reputation as a man of honor. The couple's championing of Miss Wedgewood's cause, among a different set, might prove more valuable than the marquess's influence.

If Esther gave her assistance to Millie.

Isaac entered the house with his usual casual air, and then wasted a quarter of an hour in search of his sister. Finally, he came upon Esther in the library. She sat at a writing desk near the window, busily scratching a letter upon paper. He entered the room at the same moment he called out his greeting.

"Essie, here you are. Do you know, I have been in half a dozen rooms in this house before finding you here?"

She looked up from her letter writing, one eyebrow arched at him. The expression reminded him of Silas, somehow. "If you would have asked any one of the servants they could have told you where I was. Why you insist on wandering about my house rather than ask for direction, I cannot understand."

He grinned at her and came all the way into the room. "I suppose that would have been a quicker way to go about things."

"And the way most people would have gone about it. Did Bailey not let you inside?"

The old Inglewood butler had. "Yes."

"A single question to him—"

Isaac waved a hand to interrupt his sister's lecture. "I know, I know. I was not thinking." He winced the moment he said it as a triumphant gleam appeared in his sister's eyes. She had often accused him of that very thing. Of the two of them, Isaac had struggled to put thought before action. It had nearly cost him his life and had certainly led to a great deal of heartache. "I did not return here to talk about my failings, Essie."

His sister gestured to the chair nearest her desk. "Please, sit. It sounds as though you have a specific topic in mind. Though, when we saw each other half an hour ago, you seemed quite done with talking." She rose from the desk and came to a chair beside his, the two of them facing one another over a little table with a stack of books upon it. "In fact, you were put out that I asked you to speak to Miss Wedgewood."

"I was. But then I went and delivered your invitation for tomorrow evening as you requested."

Esther's eyes widened and one corner of her mouth tilted upward. "Oh?" A great deal of suggestion underscored that single syllable. Her eyes gleamed. "What did she say?"

Isaac's posture stiffened at his sister's expression, which went from delighted surprise to something far more calculating.

"Miss Wedgewood is a friend to you, is she not?" he asked, somewhat hesitantly. He did not like Esther's response to his words at all. That canny gleam put him off.

"I would count her so, yes, or else I would not have extended so many invitations to her." Esther folded her hands daintily in her lap as she spoke, not quite losing that scheming smirk. "Why do you ask? I know you were not overly impressed with her at first, but I thought at dinner last evening you had warmed to her somewhat. Even so, I worried you might not deliver the invitation."

"Perhaps I was too quick to judge before." Isaac shifted in his chair and tapped his fingers upon the arm of the furniture. "While I was speaking to her to extend your invitation, it became apparent that she is having a difficult time of things. In fact, Miss Wedgewood believes that she is soon to be dismissed as a guest. I am uncertain why, but she was quite out of sorts when I left her."

"Oh dear. Out of sorts how?" Essie leaned forward, her eyebrows tilting downward with the weight of her concern.

"Sad. Quite sad." Isaac well remembered the way Millie's eyes had changed from bright and shining when she greeted him to dull and withdrawn by the time she took her leave. Just as she had that night at the Barnes' home, when he had caused her harm with his words. He had made that moment right by apologizing. He would make this right, too. "I thought you might help her. Perhaps invite her here, as a guest in your home."

Esther considered his suggestion quietly for several long seconds, to the point he was ready to ask it again in case she had gone temporarily deaf.

"I cannot think that a wise idea, Isaac. We barely know one another. Her family knows ours not at all. It would not be appropriate. I will write to her mother, of course, and extend the invitation. But I can do nothing without the consent of her guardians. She is only one and twenty."

"What has that to do with anything?" He scoffed. As though age had any bearing—

"She cannot legally make decisions for herself. If we transferred her to our home, and her family made objection, it would not go well for Miss Wedgewood or any of us." She sighed deeply and leaned toward him. "Perhaps it would be best for her to return home. I might extend her an invitation to visit us next Season, at our house in Town."

Isaac stared at his sister and attempted to make sense of all she said. "You will not help her."

Her shoulders slumped and the look in her eyes came very near to pity. "I cannot. We must think these things through, Isaac. If I were to put on my bonnet and descend upon the Alderton manor, demanding that their guest be turned over to my care, that would not do the already strained relations between our families any service. The marquess and Silas are at odds over Silas's refusal to step foot upon their property and his banishment of Lord Neil from ours. The only reason the two have not come to more public arguments over things is because they are part of the same party."

Though she might have a point, Isaac refused to concede the matter. "What has Silas's grudge to do with Miss Wedgewood's present need?"

"You cannot save everyone, Isaac," Esther said, her tone growing softer. "And nothing truly dire has happened. Miss Wedgewood only suspects she will be sent away. We do not yet know if that is the case. The absolute worst thing that can happen is that she will be put into a mail coach with her maid and sent home."

"But the gossip will not help her situation." Surely, if Esther understood anything, she would understand that the wrong sort of gossip would hurt Miss Wedgewood further.

But she was already shaking her head. "Miss Wedgewood made it clear to me that her family occupies a low rung of Society. So long as she is not compromised, being sent away as a guest will not harm them."

Isaac jolted to his feet and paced away, his agitation too much to bear sitting still.

"Why does Miss Wedgewood's fate matter to you, Isaac?" The directness of the question halted him in his steps. He looked over his shoulder, then slowly turned about. "You hardly know her, and you did not at all like her only a few days ago."

True enough. But that hardly seemed the point. "What is right is right, no matter whether or not I like a person." Isaac did not suffer injustices done upon anyone within his sight. He would as resolutely stand for a vagabond as a prince, should he have the ability to prevent a wrong. "Miss Wedgewood has explained why she is present, what is at stake for her and her family. We know the marquess and his family are not entirely honorable."

"Isaac." His sister stood with grace and elegance, as befitting her station. "I'll say it again. You cannot save everyone."

Her words struck him like a blow to the chest. His arm fell uselessly to his side. "Just as I did not save you."

Color flooded his sister's cheeks. Esther lowered her eyes to the carpet between them. "That is not the issue here, Isaac. Though I can see this discussion has upset you. I am sorry for that, and sorry that I cannot help Miss Wedgewood at this time. I do like her. If I think of another way to be of aid, without making matters more difficult, I will do what I can."

He recognized his sister's dismissal, even though she would never voice it as such. Esther had finished the conversation. As he could not pretend satisfaction with its ending, he had no choice but to leave. Isaac bowed. "Good afternoon, Essie. I will see you tomorrow."

He left the instant he saw her dip her head in acknowledgement. There was nothing more to do. As a bachelor, and no more than an acquaintance to the young woman in trouble, Isaac could offer no direct assistance. Esther's refusal to help was less understandable.

Once Isaac had his hat and glove, he made his way back out the door to his waiting horse. Mounting one-handed had become a matter of some pride to Isaac. Yes, a block made things easier, but he hadn't used a block to mount since childhood.

Strangely enough, it had been Hope's husband who had helped Isaac gain more independence in his riding.

"Vaqueros ride one-handed; they mount in all circumstances and in all weathers. I will show you."

Had the man done no more than love Hope, the Silver Birch Society would have embraced him well enough. But when he gave Isaac back the ability to mount and ride unassisted, the entire group had claimed him as one of their own.

He hooked the toe of his left foot in the stirrup which had been adjusted to specifications given by Alejandro. Then he leaned his left shoulder into the horse, using what remained of that arm to steady himself. With two quick hops of his right foot, his right arm came up and took the saddle by its lip. With the momentum of his jump, leverage against the saddle with his toe in the stirrup, Isaac propelled himself up onto his mount's back.

"You are a good fellow, Prophet." He picked up the reins in one hand. They had tried several of Isaac's horses, from those trained as hunters to the carriage horses, until Prophet proved he had the patience and intelligence to work with Isaac's unique mounting style. Not to mention the horse's ability to follow verbal commands and whistles.

The horse nickered softly and flicked his tail. He was not so tall a horse as Isaac had once favored, but the animal was worth his weight in gold, so far as his rider was concerned.

Isaac turned them toward home, still mulling over his disappointment in regard to Miss Wedgewood's situation.

Why could he not shake the feeling that it was wrong to leave her to fend for herself? Esther thought his desire to help was uncalled for, unnecessary. But she had a point. Knowing he hadn't helped his own sister when she needed him most had left his pride wounded. Not that helping Miss Wedgewood would heal that old hurt, but it might do something to lessen the sting.

Especially given all that she had told him. Her elder sister's betrayal hurt her, leaving her to feel abandoned. As Esther had felt when Isaac left her alone.

He arrived home at Woodsbridge, affectionately named Fox Hall by his friends. He dismounted at the stables. After giving instructions to the groom, Isaac took himself off to the house. The wide, empty rooms made him shudder. They were too large, too empty, for anyone to be truly comfortable inside them.

Isaac entered his study and sat without thought on posture or concern for the furniture, rather heavily. The whole evening stretched before him still. Alone, with his thoughts, there was nothing with which he could occupy himself. Not with any success.

His hand twitched. He curled it into a fist. Even after more than a year without his left arm, his natural reactions to certain things had continued. Like the desire to scratch an itch on his left hand that no longer existed. Or the thought that he might reach for something with both hands only to have one appear ready to obey him.

In his dreams, he had both hands still. Sometimes he fought with them. Sometimes he wandered endless battle fields alone, with only the refuse of war scattered about him. Very rarely, he had pleasant dreams. After his day spent with Silas, Esther, and Miss Wedgewood, his dreams had been calmer.

Isaac shoved his hand through his hair, then loosened his cravat with a few tugs at the white fabric. It hardly mattered what he looked like. No one would see him but the servants, and if he took a meal in his room or study, only one servant need see him at all. His valet.

Despite the fine day before, Isaac had still awoken before dawn that morning, in a cold sweat. Still, he'd pushed away the laudanum his valet had suggested as a helpful method of sleeping. Too many of Isaac's friends now depended upon laudanum. Or strong draughts of bourbon.

But Isaac, as much as he longed to forget his pains and memories, preferred to keep his mind sharp. To do that, he needed problems to solve. Needed things to turn his attention toward. He had found papers detailing some of his father's old investments. Those ought to help him repair the decline of the estate. Silas had assisted with the dam project that would start in a few days' time, when the laborers were free from other business.

That left Isaac to pursue what he wished in his evening hours.

Yet there was little to distract him. Little that interested him.

Millie had been a pleasant distraction. First, trying to determine what her game was, why she had expressed her curiosity about him. When she had grown more open, more honest about herself, that had intrigued him still further.

Now, she would leave, and that would be one less thing for him to think upon. One less person to befriend. And he was powerless to aid her.

Powerless. Unable to do a thing to ease her way, to spare her grief when she deserved none.

Isaac groaned and dropped his forehead into his hand, then rubbed at his eyes. Helpless.

Chapter Eleven

Waiting for Lady Olivia to return made the hours pass slowly. The marchioness had gone for most of the day and returned in time to nap before the evening meal. Millie took up her usual chair in the art room, Sarah at the table with her this time. The maid had apparently taken pity on Millie's lonely state.

Pity. What a powerful, horrible word that was. As Millie etched another line of ink onto the wood box, turning a sweep of her hand into the tail of a fox, she reflected on her conversation with Sir Isaac that morning. He had hated the very idea of pity, of it directed at him. How could he think himself the object of such a thing? She hadn't seen him as any less of a man for the loss of one arm.

Half of one arm, really.

"Sarah," she said aloud, filling her brush again with the ebony ink. "What hardship do you think a gentleman faces without the use of both arms?"

Sarah peeked up from her work, tatting lace. Not all women of her position had such a skill, which made Sarah take extra care and pride in her work. She created beautiful lace collars for Millie's gowns, as well as pretty bits and pieces to add to Christening gowns and handkerchiefs. "You mean Sir Isaac, miss?"

"He simply made me think on the question. I am not thinking of him specifically." Millie lowered her eyes to her work. Of course she did not mean to think only of him. As a woman, had she lost an arm, a great many of the skills most prized by the gentry would be out of her reach. Sewing, playing an instrument, even many of her artistic skills would no longer be achievable. And she would not cut the right figure in gowns, which always made a lady less than desirable.

"I imagine it's just about everything, miss," her maid said lightly, turning her attention back to her tatting needle. It was made of fine bone, a gift from Millie's mother to encourage the maid to practice her skills. "Except maybe writing. Gentlemen are expected to hunt. How does he fire a rifle? They're expected to be sportsmen. How does he play cricket, or row a boat? Riding would be difficult."

"He rides quite well, from what little I've seen," Millie murmured, keeping her eye on yet another stroke of her brush meant to make the curve of the fox's shoulder.

Sarah sounded far too amused when she said, "I thought we weren't talking about Sir Isaac, miss."

Millie bit the insides of her cheeks and put her brush down. "Sarah. We both know the reason I am here is to help Lady Olivia revenge herself upon Sir Isaac. I cannot be his friend." She leaned back against her chair and rubbed at her forehead, the beginnings of an ache forming just behind her eyes. "But I cannot do what Lady Olivia wants, either."

Sarah dropped her hands into her lap, her work forgotten, as a bright smile appeared upon her face. "That's a mercy. I could tell you like the lady countess, and you seemed to enjoy your time spent with the whole family yesterday. I never did like the idea of doing what Lady Olivia asked. Not once."

Her maid's vehemence drew a laugh from Millie, though it was not so much mirthful as rueful. "I know, Sarah. I could feel your disapproval at every moment. But this puts us in a difficult position. Most likely, Lady Olivia will send us home. And you know how my mother will take this latest failure on my part."

To Sarah's credit, she never said a word against either of Millie's parents. Her loyalty ran too deep for that. But she did allow herself a deep sigh and sage nod over the pronouncement. "It will not go well for you, miss."

A knock at the door made both of them raise their eyebrows. Millie rose, as did Sarah.

"Come in."

Lord Neil stuck his head inside but did not enter. "My sister is at home. She arrived only a moment ago. I know you had something rather pressing you wished to tell her."

"I do. Yes." Millie looked down at her brushes and hesitated.

"I'll take care of everything, miss. I know how particular you are." Sarah immediately began to gather things up. Bless her. Millie had depended upon Sarah many times since they had come together as mistress and servant, and Sarah had never let her down.

"I am coming, my lord." Millie went to the door, which Lord Neil opened wider to allow her through. Together they walked down the hall toward his sister's rooms. "It is good of you to offer your support, Lord Neil," she said.

The tall, fair-haired man shrugged his broad shoulders. He was a sportsman, through and through. Nearly every day she had been present, he had been out riding, training with the dogs, and hardly seemed to spend a moment indoors. That he gave her any attention at all, given at least a decade of years between them and her insignificance in the world, was a mystery to her.

Yet she sensed a kindness to him, lurking beneath the surface. There was a depth to him he did not show.

"Here. This is Livvy's sitting room." He knocked on the door, and his sister instantly invited whoever was without to enter. "Here we are. I promise only to keep her from drawing blood." He made the jest lightly as he swung the door open and gestured for Millie to enter first.

Millie walked inside, reminding herself that she had to appear confident, or Lady Olivia very well might draw blood. The woman had something of a cruel streak. "Lady Olivia." Millie offered the requisite curtsy. "I must beg a moment of your time."

On an elegant couch with a curved back and plump cushions, Lady Olivia was lounging in a day dress and robe. She barely stirred when she saw Millie, but her eyebrow arched when she spotted her brother entering the room as well. "Can it not wait? I have been gone all day. I am fatigued." She closed her eyes and leaned back upon the couch.

Lady Olivia was several years Millie's senior, though younger than her brother. She no longer had the freshness of youthful beauty but had taken pains to cultivate a more sophisticated appearance. But women of her wealth and standing need not marry for their security or place in the world.

"I think you ought to listen to your guest, Olivia." Lord Neil came through the room with an arrogant laziness, and he took a chair near his sister's head. "You will find what she has to say fascinating, I am certain."

"Oh? Very well, then." Olivia sat up and wrapped her robe more tightly about herself. "What is it, Miss Wedgewood?"

Millie took in a breath; she did not look to Lord Neil. She had no wish to betray that he was actually on her side of the matter. "I have considered our arrangement, Lady Olivia, and I am afraid I cannot go through on my end. I wanted to tell you directly, so that we might end things before your mother's house party guests arrive. I should not wish to cause a scene of any kind. I will pack my things and take my leave right away."

Beneath her honey-colored curls, Lady Olivia's expression barely changed. She appeared as bored as she had when Millie entered the room, and hardly more awake. "Is that all? What happened? Were you found out?"

"Not at all." Millie kept her hands at her side, though bringing them together to twist her ring about her finger usually calmed her. Showing weakness of any kind in front of Lady Olivia could leave Millie in greater trouble. "But the arrangement is no longer prudent. I cannot, in good conscious, do as you asked regarding Sir Isaac."

"Really." Lady Olivia stood slowly, languidly, and came toward Millie. Lady Olivia was much taller than Millie's petite form. She moved with all the grace of a swan, too. Everything about her spoke of privilege. "Perhaps you will rethink this when I tell you what I have learned about *you*, my dear."

Every hair on Millie's arms stood on end, while each muscle in her body grew taut. "There is nothing especially interesting in my past," Millie said, barely keeping her words even. "Everyone knows about my sister."

"But not everyone knows where she is now. I do." Lady Olivia did not hide her feline grin when Millie's jaw dropped. "Did you not know where she is, Miss Wedgewood? And that is but one thing I have learned." She waved her hand dismissively. "I have sent a note requesting that Stephan Maritain and his wife attend our house party. They have agreed."

Millie's knees went weak, and she watched Lady Olivia come closer the way a mouse watched a cat prepare to pounce. She swallowed. "The Viscount, Lord Carning." Her words came out hoarse.

"What does that have to do with anything?" Lord Neil asked, sounding bored and far away.

Millie had forgotten he was there, listening. She went cold all over but directed her eyes to his. "He is the man my sister was to marry."

"Not just any man. The grandson of a duke, poised to one day inherit the title." Lady Olivia walked behind Millie, circling her. Toying with her. "He has given me his word to help you, my dear, and your family. It has been, what, six years since your sister disappeared with her Welshman?"

Millie's stomach turned. "Yes."

"Lord Carning has graciously agreed to forget the past and put your family back in his good graces. If you insist upon going back upon our agreement, perhaps I could persuade him to remind people of the past. Of the insult you offered to his family. And leaving my home, quitting my offered friendship, would also be a rather black mark upon you." She stopped when she had come all the way around Millie and stood closer. Her green eyes were cold as stone. "How would your dear mama take that bit of news, Miss Wedgewood? More debts might be called in. What few cards and invitations trickle into your mother's grasp would cease. Are you prepared to be a complete outcast?"

Lord Neil cleared his throat, loudly, before his sister had quite finished the question. "Olivia. Are you threatening Miss Wedgewood? I believe she said she would like to go home. Torturing her hardly becomes you."

"Really? I find it most suitable." Lady Olivia smirked and turned to look at her brother over one slim shoulder. "You know nothing of my plans, brother. I suggest we keep it that way. Miss Wedgewood and I entered into an agreement. It would be quite unacceptable for her to go back upon it now. Dishonorable, in fact." She turned back to Millie and tilted her head so that it nearly rested upon her shoulder. The effect of her chilled smile at that angle disconcerted Millie. "Do you still wish to go home, Miss Wedgewood? Or would you rather stay here, and enjoy our house party?"

Millie's stomach rolled, but she lowered her chin and shuddered as she answered, "I will stay."

"What of Sir Isaac?" The nobleman's daughter stepped closer, whispering her words. "What of our agreement?"

"Livvy—"

The woman turned a glare on her brother, hissing like a cat. "I have asked you not to call me that anymore, Neil."

Millie's heart grew cold, gripped in icy dread. What choice did she have now? "I will do as you ask, Lady Olivia." She caught a glimpse of Lord Neil coming to his feet, wearing a concerned frown. But he said nothing. She did not blame him. Things had turned quickly. She drew in a breath and dropped her curtsy again. "I am sorry I disturbed you." Then she turned and left the room, forcing her steps to remain slow until she closed the door behind her.

She ran. Down the halls, her slippers making hardly a sound on the plush carpets upon the shining wood floors. She ran to her room, flew through the door, and directly to Sarah. There was no one else who would understand. But Sarah, arms full of clothing as though she had begun to pack, took one look at Millie and dropped everything in order to embrace her mistress.

"What happened?" the maid asked, dread in her words.

Millie cried and told the whole story through her tears.

The man who had destroyed her family was coming. She spoke his name and Sarah immediately sat down upon the bed, shocked.

"Not him," the maid whispered. "He's terrible."

They both knew it was an understatement. Terrible did not begin to describe Lord Carning. Sarah had seen the sort of man he was, and her presence alone had saved Millie from far worse than social ruin the night Millie had told him about her sister running away.

"You can't be in the same house with him, miss," the maid whispered, her whole face pale beneath her cap, nearly the same shade of white. "Under the same roof."

"What choice do we have?" Millie asked. She climbed onto the bed, her tears spent, and covered her eyes with one hand. The ache she had felt before had grown into a harsh pounding in her head.

"Write to your mother. Tell her what's happened. Then we catch the post coach when everyone else is sleeping." Sarah shook her head even as she spoke, doubting the plan as it formed.

"Mother will not suffer more damage to her reputation." Millie turned on her side and drew a pillow close, wrapping her arms about it in a vain search for comfort. "I have to do what Lady Olivia asked. I have to find a way to break Sir Isaac's heart." She closed her eyes against those words, finding tears stinging anew. "I thought he had started to like me, too." The admission was weak and meaningless now.

Because no matter how much the man did or did not care for her company, she had to hurt him. Or allow her family to sink too low for anyone to pull them out again.

Chapter Twelve

JULY 21, 1815

Millie penned her acceptance of Lady Inglewood's invitation when she woke the next morning. Dread pulled at her limbs, making each of her movements slow and ponderous. Every stroke of the pen was a lash upon her conscience. Sarah took the folded note with her lips pressed tightly together, her face pale.

"I am sorry, Sarah," Millie said quietly, her pen falling from her limp fingers to the desk. A drop of ink fell onto the wood. "This is a mess of my own making. There is no other way to look at it."

Sarah lowered her eyes to the paper in her hand. "But what if— what if you don't have to do this? What if we find another way?"

Millie dabbed at the ink upon the finely polished wood, staining her thumb. "What other way?"

"You're supposed to hurt Sir Isaac. Humiliate him, somehow. Isn't that right, miss?"

"Yes." Millie rubbed her thumb and forefinger together, then took out her handkerchief to rub off the ink. She had dozens of handkerchiefs stained with ink, from her work creating the delicate black designs on pale wood. She kept them all for use in her art. One more would hurt nothing.

"What do you think he did to Lady Olivia, that she harbors such a desire to cause him pain?"

"I would think it's obvious, miss." Sarah's nose wrinkled and her lips pulled back in an expression of distaste. "She tried to win him for herself, and he spurned her. I can't say that I blame him at all, miss."

That did seem a likely cause for Lady Olivia's bitterness. "No. I would not blame him either. Though she certainly appears harmless enough, at first acquaintance."

"Until her claws come out." Sarah shuddered and tucked the note in her apron pocket. "I'll see that this goes to her ladyship at once, miss. But might I offer up a suggestion?"

"Hm?" Millie's mind had drifted into imagining the rather satisfying scene of Sir Isaac rejecting a woman as beautiful and well-connected as Lady Olivia. "What suggestion, Sarah?"

"I think you ought to tell Sir Isaac what's happening. He could maybe find a way out of all the mess." Sarah offered a hesitant smile, followed closely by her curtsy. "I'll be back in a trice, miss."

The maid left Millie alone in her room, nothing to distract her from her thoughts. Millie rose from the little table by the window and went to look outside. Her room was placed as to give her a view of the stables, placed a distance from the house, and nothing else particularly lovely. She opened her window to let in some air, then leaned against the sill.

Telling Sir Isaac would only create a bigger problem. He had already been suspicious of her when she first arrived. What would he think once he learned her entire reason for being in Suffolk was to humiliate and hurt him? It would hardly garner his trust. He would see everything she had done as her attempt to win her aim.

With her head leaning against the windowpane, Millie considered her options anew. She had sent a letter to her mother that very morning, sparing no detail in what Lady Olivia had threatened. Any advice her mother might have would be welcome. Given that Mother only wanted to return to a position of prominence,

however, made it unlikely she would do more than encourage
Millie in her task of hurting Isaac.

As the hours passed, Millie's thoughts lingered upon the man
she had tried to only think of as her quarry. His crooked grin. His
sweetness toward his nephew, and his sister. He carried himself
with such confidence and had the bearing of a soldier. He was
handsome, too. There was no reason to pretend otherwise. He had
a lightness in his eyes, and she suddenly wished she had seen more
of it in his actions. But life had dealt difficulty to him, and that
weighed upon his shoulders.

An abhorrent task lay before her. Humiliate him. Hurt him. Satisfy Lady Olivia's desire to see him suffer.

When the hour for the bonfire came, Sarah helped Millie to
dress for it. There were no silks for beaches and bonfires, but a
comfortable blue muslin gown. No jewels in her hair, but a
matching ribbon to assist in holding the plaits and twists of her
copper-colored tresses in place against the beach's wind. Then a
shawl, soft and gray, to keep her warm.

Millie looked herself over in the mirror, then turned to offer a
smile to her maid. "Thank you."

The maid curtsied. "Good luck tonight, miss."

Millie needed more than luck. She needed cunning. She needed
cleverness. And a heart of stone.

But maybe not yet.

The house party began tomorrow. She would have no choice
but to take up her assignment from Lady Olivia in full. For one last
evening, Millie gave herself permission to simply be herself.

ISAAC WALKED THROUGH THE GARDENS OF INGLEWOOD
Keep, each terrace leading him closer to the beach path. He kicked
at a rock that dared leave its place beneath the shrubbery. He wore
the same clothes he had on the day he met Miss Wedgewood
spying upon his property. Comfortable. Old. Not at all befitting his

status, but perfect for an evening upon the beach enjoying the surf and a bonfire.

On the lowest terrace, Esther would have lanterns and a meal spread upon tables. Many of their friends and neighbors would be present. Esther and Silas, Jacob and Grace, Isaac, the Ashfords, Jacob's unwed sisters, his married brother, and possibly Miss Parr, whom Grace and Esther both were attempting to befriend and guide before she went to London next Season.

People he had known nearly the whole of his life. Friends, most of them. Ready to share laughter and memories, to sing while they sat around the bonfire and forget about all their responsibilities until the morning.

Yet for all the pleasure such an evening promised, Isaac's thoughts lingered on Millie's plight. Had Lady Olivia sent her away, as Millie thought she might? What cause would the marquess's family have to give their assistance to someone of such low rank in the first place?

None of it made sense to him, but then, Isaac had never been overly concerned with what Society thought of him. After coming back from the war, Society held even less of a draw for him. The whole of Society's machinations and rules had lost its appeal to him. It was meaningless, vying for popular opinion to turn in his favor.

Seeing all the helpless of London, all the men broken by the war, the women left widows and children orphans, had cured him of ever wishing to step foot into that town again. The nobility and other elite refused to see the pain and suffering all around them. Isaac could not wish to be part of that.

Yet others needed that approval. The Wedgewood family believed they needed it. He could not judge Millie for that, though it grated upon him that the path Millie's family had chosen involved any member of the Marquess of Alderton's family.

Laughter pulled him from his thoughts, and Isaac stopped just shy of entering the lowest terrace. Tall hedges on either side of the step, and an archway of twisting ivy, marked this part of the garden as separate, as a doorway marked a room. He drew in a deep breath and put a smile upon his face, then stepped through.

Esther had outdone herself. Though not yet dark, the garden was lined with torches. A small fountain merrily sang and reflected the firelight. Tables laden with covered dishes were surrounded by people filling their plates. A little over a dozen people conversed, laughed, and drank from elegantly curved cups.

Isaac took in a deep breath, though his shoulders already ached with how tightly he held everything within himself. If the group was any larger, he might find himself ill. Indoors, he often sought the edges of the room near the windows.

You are not trapped, he told himself, as firmly as he would a subordinate. *You are in the open air. These are your friends. All is well. The war...* Before Napoleon's escape from Elba, his familiar litany included a reminder that the war had ended. Now, however, the Corsican was upon the Continent again, stirring up trouble.

Isaac shuddered, despite the warmth of the evening air.

A small hand touched his arm, fingers curling about his wrist. "Sir Isaac?" a familiar feminine voice whispered. "Are you well?"

His gaze fell to his side, to a familiar pair of warm brown eyes and hair that glistened a fiery red in the fading light of evening.

"Millie." Her Christian name escaped him so naturally that it took him a moment to understand why her eyebrows rose nearly to her hairline, and her cheeks colored. He felt his cheeks warm, too. He cleared his throat. "I apologize. Miss Wedgewood. You are still here."

She must not have appreciated his tone. Her eyebrows fell as she narrowed her eyes at him, and removed her hand from his arm, which made him immediately regret the stumble in his words. "Yes, I am afraid so."

Isaac reached for the withdrawing hand, catching it before she could tuck it out of sight. "No, you misunderstand. I meant to say that I am glad you are not gone. That you were not sent home." He let out a shaky, awkward chuckle. "I did not think to see you again, after our meeting yesterday."

She lowered her head, allowing him to glimpse the ribbons sliding through her hair like rivulets of water. "I know. I did not expect to be here either." A line appeared between her eyebrows, though she smiled. "There was only a small misunderstanding between myself and Lady Olivia. I spoke to her. It seems I will be a guest until the end of her mother's house party after all."

"I am glad to hear it." The moment Isaac spoke the words, he recognized the truth in them. She intrigued him. Amused him, even. Her conversation was unusual, but comfortable. Honest. And that smile of hers—

One corner of her mouth crept upward and revealed her dimple. "Do you know what I thought after our conversation yesterday?"

"No. Tell me." His lips twitched, tempted to match her smile with one of his own.

"That you would rather not associate with one of my tainted reputation." She looked down, pointedly, at their joined hands. "It seems I was mistaken."

Isaac released her and stepped back, tucking his hand behind his back. "I apologize if I gave that impression. Your standing in Society has no bearing on our acquaintance. Your personal conduct and character are more important than whatever your popularity might be."

She lowered her head, her expression changing to one of contemplation. "There are few enough who say such things, and fewer still that mean them."

Isaac bent to catch her gaze. "You have my word, Miss Wedgewood. I mean every word I say." Then he offered his arm, and she took it hesitantly. "Have you eaten?" He nodded to the laden tables. "Met everyone?"

That brought a truer smile to her face than he had seen thus far that evening. "Yes, I have. Unlike you, I arrived on time."

He hung his head as though shamed. "I suppose I am rather late. I apologize."

"To me?" She gave him an amused nudge with her shoulder.

"For shame. I am not the hostess. Your sister was not sure you would come at all." She fell into step with him easily, notwithstanding the disparity in their heights and stride.

"Essie will forgive me." He straightened his posture, unrepentant.

He did not direct her to the tables, knowing she had already visited them, but to the archway leading to the sea path. While he had tamped down the urge to escape, he yet preferred the open stretch of beach to the gardens.

Beyond the small hill covered in long grasses, the sand stretched north and south, and the waves lapped at the shore. "The moon will rise soon," Isaac said, as though that were the reason he directed them away from the small crowd to the sand. "Directly ahead of us, as though from the sea."

"A full moon," she added softly, her words a breath on the night air. "I watched it, last evening, come into view of my window. Just before dinner." She looked up at him, her eyes bright. "My family stays in London most of the year, and the skies are never so clear there as here. I have wanted to take a walk in the evening many times since my arrival in the country." She raised her chin upward, her eyes turning to the heavens above. Her smile fell away, yet a softness came into her expression. She had such a gentle soul, a kindness about her he hadn't encountered often outside of his circle of friends.

"I watched many a moon creep across the sky during my time on the Continent," he murmured, then clamped his mouth shut tightly. He had no wish to speak of the war. Ever. Yet when she turned her attention back to him, a question in her eyes, he found himself answering. "There were nights I could not sleep. I had a tent, of course. Officers were given the best of the worst accommodations." He forced a chuckle but turned his gaze away from hers to the ground as they walked upon the sand. "But it was easier to be in the open air, before it filled with smoke from battle. To lay beneath the stars and find my favorite constellations from boyhood. From a time before I knew the truth of what it meant to be a soldier."

When she spoke, her words were slower, as though each came with the weight of her thoughts. "I think we all look for peace where we can find it. At war, in the noise of London. Even in the midst of a ballroom, with music, swirls of silk, and heavy perfumes. There are quiet corners. Windows for peering out to remember there is a wider world than where we find ourselves."

That she echoed his thoughts, that she could understand what he had never attempted to explain to anyone, made his heart take up speed. She *knew*. "Yes. I—I often feel that way. That I need to look beyond a crowd, a room, and remember there is more."

His reasons were different from hers. He knew that without asking. She likely had no wish to escape, for fear of revealing a weakness, for fear of breaking apart. But she understood, and that alone brought him comfort.

Millie nudged his shoulder with hers, then stayed near, her arm upon his. "Are you telling me we have something in common, Sir Isaac?"

He let his shoulders droop and lowered his head dramatically. "This truly is the end of all things, if we find ourselves at such an accord."

"You are a terrible man." Her laugh was soft and warm as the breeze. "But I suppose that makes me terrible, too." She turned her face away from him, to where the Inglewood groundskeeper and his crew of six men worked to arrange scraggly branches and drift-wood into a mound that would burn well. "That will be a large fire. Will it burn all night?"

"Most likely several hours, should we keep feeding the flames." He nodded to the shoreline. "Would you care to walk until it is lit?"

"Thank you, I would." She adjusted her skirts, taking them up a touch with her free hand to keep the hem from sand.

They kept to their walk, southward. The sun had faded away beyond Inglewood Keep in the west, and a soft glow above the sea indicated the moon was ready to take the sun's place. He did not take her far. They were within full view of anyone upon the beach, though details might not be so clear in the moments between the sunset and the moonrise.

"Sir Isaac," she said, her voice hesitant and faint against the sound of the surf. "I have a most impertinent question to ask."

"I am not the least surprised, given our conversations of the past." He turned her about, ready to walk again to the fire. A soft orange glow low upon the sand indicated the bonfire had at last been lit. "Ask. I will not take offense."

They took a few more steps before she stopped them, tugging gently upon his arm. Isaac looked down at her, and the moon broke the surface of the North Sea, turning her copper hair silver. His breath caught. For the barest moment, he wondered what her reaction might be were he to lean down and kiss her.

"What is it that makes Lady Olivia dislike you so?" she asked. The question removed temptation more soundly than a slap. Though she asked it gently, there was a pleading in her tone as though something important depended upon the answer. As though she depended upon it.

He released his breath, turning away from her. The moment of enchantment had left him confused, but not so befuddled as to answer that question honestly. Not entirely.

"As a gentleman, I cannot answer that. No matter how I feel toward Lady Olivia, it is not something I ought to tell."

"I understand." Yet she did not, given the disappointment in her eyes.

He sighed heavily, the weight of his concerns over Millie returning. Her place among the marquess's family could only cause trouble, but whether for her or someone else, he could not decide.

If only she had come to the country as the guest of some other person. If he had met her at a gathering such as this, with moonlight and the surf to lend a touch of magic to her first glimpse of him. Instead, his perception and hers were colored by the likes of

Lady Olivia. But on their own, on a night such as that, perhaps they might have—

Isaac caught himself before completing that thought. It did not matter who had brought her to Suffolk, to Aldersy, or to the very door of Inglewood. Miss Millicent Wedgewood was nothing to him but the friend of his sister. Perhaps his friend, too. But she had no more desire to entertain notions of more toward him than anyone else had. A baronet. A damaged man, in body and soul. A burden to all those who actually did care for him with his ill-disposed humor.

He took her back to the fire, and she asked him nothing further. They said not another word. The rest of the party began to come down from the gardens, and servants were putting benches about the fire.

Millie's hand started to slip from his arm, and he let it this time. "Thank you for the walk, Sir Isaac." She curtsied, as though they were in a drawing room for her to take her leave, rather than upon a beach.

"Miss Wedgewood, wait." He did not touch her, though he had to remind himself to keep his hand to himself. "Will you sit with me, near the fire?"

Her eyes flashed up at him, surprise in their depths. "You are a strange one, sir." She angled her head to one side, narrowing her eyes at him. "One moment, I am certain we are friends. The next, I think you wish me away in your silence. Then we are friends again. Which is it?"

What was he to say to that? He could not answer. He was not certain of himself. Not in the least. But when the moon caught upon her, as it did just then, he rather felt like leaning down and kissing her.

He must not give in to such a foolish whim. It would not be gentlemanly. She certainly would not welcome that action.

"Sir Isaac." She said his name the way one might speak an endearment, bringing him out of his befuddled thoughts. "Are we friends or foes, sir?" Though her lips pressed together, she smiled at him.

Perhaps she would welcome a kiss, given the dancing mischief in her eyes.

A burst of song, loud and wobbly, led out by Mr. Matthew Barnes, Jacob's eldest brother, put an end to all thoughts of a stolen kiss.

A laugh escaped those all too kissable lips. "Come. You can tell me how much you detest me another time."

With a gentle tug of his arm, she led them to the benches set about the fire, where many of his friends sat and sang a ridiculous song. Once seated next to each other, Millie joined in the singing.

Her sweet soprano gave him yet another reason to enjoy having her near.

Chapter Thirteen

The house thundered with the clamor of servants, the doors in the corridors opening and closing, all the day long. The guests had arrived for the house party, fully a dozen of them along with twice as many servants, and their voices filtered through the cracks around Millie's door. She remained in her room, in a chair she had dragged to the window. Sarah stayed with her, sitting within arm's reach of Millie. The maid's presence was the only comfort Millie could rely upon.

Millie's gut twisted whenever she thought of Lord Carning. He could have been the first guest to enter the house, or perhaps hadn't even arrived yet, but the knowledge that he resided under the same roof as she made her abominably ill.

In an attempt to distract herself, Millie thought of Mr. Weston. He was yet another of her targets, at the behest of Mrs. Cecilia Vanderby. Millie had absolutely no idea why the woman could not find happiness with her wealthy Dutchman and leave her former suitor to his own devices.

"Misery seeks its own, miss," Sarah had said when Millie voiced her confusion. "People can't accept that they're the only ones unhappy. They're jealous, and waste their time trying to make others feel the same, when really they ought to put their energy into fixing their own problems."

Millie could not agree more with her servant.

"I am only to find something for Mrs. Vanderby to use against Mr. Weston in Society. It need not even be the man's darkest secrets. Only something she might taunt him with before others." Millie massaged her temples. "How very juvenile."

"That's Society, miss." Sarah kept at her tatting, a nearly complete lace collar resting upon her apron. "Everyone wishes to prove themselves better than anyone else. No matter the cost."

Not for the first time, Millie wondered at her mother's desire to rejoin such a herd of unscrupulous men and women. Though, the reasons her whole family needed to regain their footing were easy enough to understand. Better opportunities for her father, for their income, and for her own advantageous marriage.

Sir Isaac's crooked grin flashed in her memory. Millie brushed it aside rather than dwell on the fact she must hurt him, too. What choice did she have? The previous evening, sitting next to him while the Earl of Inglewood told ghost stories that left everyone shuddering, she had wished Isaac would put his arm around her. Comfort her and protect her from the unseen ghosts. But she had sat on his left side. Even had he wanted to, and he most certainly did not, there was no arm there to wrap around her.

How ridiculous. How utterly foolish of her to entertain any notions of friendship, let alone greater affection, existing between them. She had tried to do the right thing, and Lady Olivia effectively destroyed that plan.

"What will you do if Lord Carning attempts to speak to you?" Sarah asked when the dinner hour drew near.

"Make certain I am never alone with him. That will require that anything he says to me remain appropriate for others to hear." Millie shuddered, remembering the one and only time she had been in a room alone with the man. "He never acted as anything other than a perfect gentleman until that night, Sarah."

Sarah said nothing, merely rose to prepare Millie's evening

dress. They said little except what was required for Sarah to prepare Millie for the evening. She chose a gown of blue with a glimmering silver overlay. The gown had always reminded her of a starlit sky. And thinking on such a scene now reminded her of standing beneath the stars with Isaac.

Perhaps the warmth of that memory would be enough to protect her from the cold gaze of Lord Carning.

After Sarah looped and twisted Millie's hair into an intricate swirl upon her head, she put her hand on Millie's arm. "There's one thing more I'm putting in your hair, miss." She pulled out a long pin with a bright blue stone on its end. She held it up in the mirror, showing Millie the point. "We'd normally use it with a fancy cap. But I can make it look like it belongs in your hair. Like this." The maid carefully put it through Millie's hair, concealing the six-inch metal most cleverly, running it from just above Millie's forehead through to the back of her auburn curls.

"A weapon?" Millie asked, her hands went cold inside her gloves. "You think it necessary—"

"I hope not. But it's there. My mum, she always told me to keep something at hand to defend myself. A rock in my coat pocket. A pin in my apron. A needle. Anything." Sarah met Millie's eyes in the mirror. "It's not a fair world for any of us, miss. I just want to look after you a bit."

Millie's eyes filled with tears at that kindness. She sniffed and found a handkerchief to quickly swipe at the moisture in her eyes. "Thank you, Sarah. What would I do without you?"

Sarah only offered a smile that did not quite make it to her eyes. "Well, miss, you'd not have nearly such well-made hair." She sniffed and tipped her chin up as though proud.

Millie laughed and rose, then wrapped her arms around her maid in a brief embrace. "You are a wonder, Sarah."

Then the two of them looked over her dress one more time and applied the smallest amount of scent behind her ears and at her throat. Sarah handed Millie a fan to hang at her wrist before opening the door to allow her mistress out into the rest of the house.

Once in the drawing room, where everyone had started gathering in preparation for dinner, Millie realized she needed every good wish Sarah had sent with her. Lady Alderton, Lord Neil, and Lady Olivia were at the center of everything, greeting their guests and making introductions.

Lord Neil saw her before his sister or mother, and the man gave her a commiserating sort of grimace before coming her direction. "Miss Wedgewood. I have not seen you today."

"I thought it best to rest," she said quietly. He offered his arm and she took it.

"If you need rescue," he said quietly, "signal me with that fan of yours." He did not leave her time to respond. Lord Neil raised his voice and brought her to a couch full of guests. He introduced her to two sisters and their parents, then to a handsome gentleman with black hair and a charming smile.

"Mr. Weston, this is Miss Wedgewood, a particular friend of my sister's. We have made the two of you dinner partners this evening." Lord Neil spoke with his usual slow, almost bored tone. The man certainly was a gifted actor. He hid his emotions quite well, yet Millie sensed his thoughtfulness, his good heart, every time they spoke.

"A pleasure, Miss Wedgewood," the object of her current hunt said, appearing not the least put out that he would be expected to escort a nobody to the table.

Lord Neil kept her there, making conversation with Mr. Weston and one of the other young ladies. Weston was something of a flirt, she realized in only a few minutes, bandying about compliments to both unmarried women and attempting to draw Lord Neil into the same. While that might make it easy to converse with him, flirts rarely shared personal information.

An all too familiar deep baritone voice interrupted her thoughts. "Miss Millicent Wedgewood. What an unexpected pleasure, to see you again."

The breath froze in Millie's lungs, and she turned woodenly to greet the owner of the voice by dropping a curtsy more worthy of his grandfather, a duke, than him. "Lord Carning. Good evening." She barely raised her eyes to the level of his cravat.

"Allow me to introduce my wife," he said, his voice dripping with haughtiness. "Lady Carning, Miss Wedgewood is an old acquaintance. I have known her since before she came out in Society. You have come out by now, I would assume, Miss Wedgewood? I cannot recall seeing you at any event in Town."

"Yes, I am quite out," she whispered, then swiftly turned her eyes to the woman on his arm as she curtsied. "Lady Carning. It is an honor to meet you."

The viscountess was much taller than Millie, with alabaster skin, golden hair, and blue eyes. She looked, except for her height, very much like Millie's sister. The woman held herself with the poise of a Greek statue.

"Miss Wedgewood. A pleasure," she said, her voice like a harp in its gentle musicality. Millie realized, quite suddenly, that the woman was likely younger than herself. The viscount was at least forty-five. His wife could be no more than twenty.

The poor woman.

Millie was saved from further exchange when the butler arrived to announce dinner, and doors opened to allow them into the opulent dining room and heavy-laden table. Mr. Weston took her arm, and Millie briefly put a hand to her head where the blue-gem pin rested in her curls. Though unlikely as she was to need it, its presence soothed her.

The house party's beginning made her long for its end. But no matter what happened, Millie had to come out the victor. Had to satisfy Lady Olivia. Or else disappoint her parents, thrust her family into obscurity, and forgo her own dreams of a titled husband and home of her own.

Chapter Fourteen

I saac sat at his breakfast, turning a thick sheet of ivory paper over and over in his hand.

The itinerary and invitations for the various events for the Alderton house party had arrived. The marchioness always sent out a complete schedule to the neighborhood, at least to those privileged few whom she wished to attend the daily activities. Isaac had turned down the invitations the previous year, except when escorting Esther.

Silas had tasked Isaac with the role of escort, as the earl refused to even step foot on Alderton land. His dislike of Lord Neil had grown to include the whole family when the marquess had made a veiled reference to the strange timing of Silas and Esther's marriage.

Esther would attend fewer of the events this year, given her more matronly status as a mother to a young child. But Isaac had another reason to appear at each event. The reason, of course, was a woman with copper hair and kind brown eyes.

Millie needed a friend. That much anyone might see. But few would act upon it, including his sister, though she had sent the letter to Millie's mother as promised.

He took the invitation to his study and tossed it upon his desk before he pulled drawers open in search of ink and paper for his formal response. Every event, every outing, every moment he had been invited to be present, he would be there. So long as Millie needed him.

That very afternoon, they were to go to the ruins of the old Orford Castle. The ancient tower had been neglected for decades. But the old piles of stone proved an interesting spot for picnics. It was scenic. Took two hours to get to in good weather. He would need the carriage, whether Esther agreed to join him or not.

Once he had the note written, he rang for a footman and gave instructions to rush it to the Alderton estate immediately. Then he started giving orders for his carriage's preparation, for his valet, for cook to prepare a basket full of foods for him to contribute to the picnic.

Each and every one of his servants stared at him with wide eyes, fairly gaping as he gave instructions. When Harper, his valet, outright grinned at Isaac's demands, the baronet grumbled.

"I cannot understand why everyone acts as though my attending a picnic is extraordinary."

Harper tried to hide his smile, poorly. "It is unusual is all, sir. We are happy for you."

Isaac frowned deeply, but Harper kept hold of his good cheer. Isaac stared at the mirror as Harper adjusted his cravat. He had been socially selective. Unless he escorted Esther, he limited his acceptances of dinners and parties, even balls, to those his friends sent. It was easier to stay home. To avoid crowds.

What the devil was he doing, seeking out the very sort of situation he had avoided for over a year, all for a woman he barely knew?

But her laughter tickled his memory, pulled him out of the gloom. He took in his reflection in the looking glass. What would a young woman think of his appearance? He checked the lines of his waistcoat and critically eyed the empty left sleeve of his shirt.

"Would you like the use of the wooden arm, Sir Isaac?" Harper asked.

Isaac jerked his eyes away from the mirror.

He hated that arm. Hated the process of attaching it to the stub of flesh he had been left with the year before. Shuddering, Isaac shook his head. "No. It is unwieldy, awkward, and unsightly. Even with a glove upon it."

Though he had paid well to have the arm carved into a mirror likeness of his remaining arm, it was disconcerting how stiff it was upon him. Putting a glove upon the oddly shaped fingers made it look worse, like he had stuffed sausages into the fingers of his best gloves. The whole thing had been a waste. It threw him off balance. Irritated him.

Admiral Nelson had appeared in all his portraits without a false arm. If it was good enough for one of Britain's greatest heroes to be without a false-arm or hook-handed, it was good enough for Isaac.

"As you wish, sir." Harper helped Isaac with his favorite dark green coat, a perfect choice for a visit to the ancient abbey. Isaac intended to take his carriage to the marquess's home, to offer up additional seats should anyone need them. Perhaps Millie would wish to ride with him.

That prospect brought him out of the somewhat sour mood the false arm had thrust Isaac into moments before.

Upon his arrival at the Alderton estate, Isaac's hackles came up at once. It was Lord Neil who greeted him in the main hall, after Isaac had been shown inside.

"Sir Isaac." The man sounded slippery as ever. He came into the entryway from another room, dressed for the outing with his hat upon his head. "I did not expect you to join us. Though Olivia insisted upon inviting you."

"Lord Neil." Isaac inclined his head the barest amount. "I find myself in want of a change of scenery. What better opportunity than an outing such as this?"

"I can think of none." Lord Neil adjusted his hat to sit at what he likely thought a rakish angle. While Silas made no effort to hide his dislike, Isaac put up with the marquess's son mostly because he knew the man had never been a real threat to Esther. A nuisance, of course. But that was all.

"Do you intend to join a carriage or lend yours to the venture?" Lord Neil asked, tucking an unnecessary walking stick beneath his arm. "I am in charge of putting people into the correct boxes for the ride, you see."

"I am lending my carriage. It can seat three more quite comfortably."

"Splendid." Lord Neil eyed Isaac carefully. "Will the countess join us?"

"Not today, I am afraid."

"That is disappointing. I know Miss Wedgewood quite depends upon her ladyship's friendship."

Isaac studied the other man's expression, noted his tone. Considering how thoroughly Silas had commanded Lord Neil to stay away from Esther, the marquess's son still showed too much interest in her.

With a shrug of one shoulder, Isaac responded with feigned disinterest. "My sister is a woman with much to occupy her time. I will do my best to alleviate Miss Wedgewood's disappointment with my company."

That made Lord Neil's somewhat bored expression flicker with momentary interest. "Is that your intention in coming today? I imagine she will be most grateful for your attention."

Before Isaac sorted out whether or not Lord Neil meant to imply something other than what he said, a door opened at the top of the stairs. Feminine laughter drifted through the foyer and corridors. Isaac's gaze took in several women coming down the steps but did not glimpse the copper curls for which he searched.

Lady Olivia and her mother appeared from the ground floor corridor, speaking with animation to each other and a servant who followed them.

The marchioness's tone was light and airy, though none could doubt she meant her words as commands. "Make certain the wagons do not leave more than a quarter of an hour after the first carriage departs. We will want refreshment after we arrive at Orford Castle. The Earl of Montecliff will meet us there with his set, and I will not be unprepared."

Lord Neil stepped away from Sir Isaac to bow to his mother. "I have all the assignments for the carriages, Mother."

"Good. Take everyone outside and see to it they are all properly placed. Olivia and I are riding with Lord and Lady Carning?"

"As requested." Lord Neil bowed again, then turned back to Sir Isaac. He made his way to the door, gesturing with the tilt of his head for Isaac to follow. Reluctantly, Isaac followed the other man back out into the late morning sun. "I will direct three guests to join you in your box, Sir Isaac, if you will take up your place beside it.

A row of carriages had joined Sir Isaac's before the house. He did not have a chance to respond to Lord Neil before the man had approached a group of ladies and gentlemen, gesturing for them to take certain vehicles. Two women, sometimes three, and two gentlemen each were put into the four carriages ahead of Sir Isaac.

Lord Carning and his wife came out the door after nearly everyone else had climbed into their wheeled boxes. Isaac bowed as Lord Carning passed. He had met the duke's grandson some years before, though their gap in age and rank meant theirs was no more than a nodding acquaintance. The couple went to the first carriage, and as soon as the door shut behind them the carriage pulled away, and the others followed.

Lord Neil walked back to Sir Isaac's carriage, which set to one side of the line. He had to raise his voice to be heard over the crunch of gravel beneath wheels and the clomp of horse's hooves. "My apologies, Sir Isaac. The ladies for your carriage are apparently not yet ready."

As he hadn't yet seen Millie emerge from the house, Isaac remained relaxed. "I am not pressed for time."

Lord Neil smirked and went back to the grand front door. He disappeared inside, likely to search out the missing guests.

Isaac shifted beside his vehicle, a groom standing nearby while the driver remained on top of the box. Anticipating Millie's pleasure at seeing him, Isaac checked his cravat and the tilt of his hat. Then he caught a look of amusement upon his groom's face. Isaac stopped fidgeting and adopted his most soldierly stance instead.

When the door to the house opened again, Isaac turned his full attention toward it, his heart inexplicably picking up speed. First Miss Ashford, a neighbor rather than a house party guest, emerged. She bounced down the steps cheerily, but Isaac's eyes immediately went back to the open door.

Millie emerged, closed parasol in one hand, a fetching bonnet decked in green feathers atop her copper curls, matching the green of her shawl. Despite his promise to act merely as a friend, to do no more than keep her company, Isaac took a step toward her. He could feel the smile upon his face growing.

She came down the steps at a quick pace, coming even with Miss Ashford at the instant the other young lady made her curtsy to Isaac.

"Good afternoon, Miss Ashford. Miss Wedgewood." He bowed to them in turn, then met Millie's gaze. She shared with him a much less radiant smile, her face somewhat pale.

His enthusiasm waned, replaced by immediate concern. Was something amiss?

The door shut and Lord Neil came to the carriage. "That is everyone. We had better be going."

Why Lord Neil arranged to ride in Isaac's coach, he did not know, but he handed both ladies in and allowed Lord Neil to go up before him, too.

Once all four were settled, the door shut and the carriage started forward. The men sat on the rear-facing seat; the ladies adjusted their skirts and tilted their bonnets to allow for more comfortable positions. They had nearly a two hours' ride to get to

Orford, time Isaac intended to spend getting to know Millie better. Even with Lord Neil in the same carriage.

❦

MILLIE HAD WAITED UNTIL THE ENTRY HAD CLEARED OF all the guests before descending to the ground floor. The more she avoided contact with Lord Carning, the happier she would be. Sarah had given Millie another long, sharp needle to conceal in her bonnet before disappearing to join the servants in the wagons going to Orford. Though the servants attending were mostly meant to be those charged with laying out a picnic, a few of the ladies maids were going to help mistresses with wardrobe or toilette needs.

Having an ally in the form of her maid alleviated a fraction of Millie's anxiety.

When she saw Sir Isaac waiting at his carriage, that nearly removed all her worry. Sir Isaac might be depended upon in an emergency. Lord Neil had proved pleasant company thus far, and Millie had met Miss Ashford on the night of the bonfire. At least the journey to Orford would prove pleasant.

The entirety of her plan included nothing more than wandering around old ruins and a quaint little town with Mr. Weston. She needed to get to know him if she wished to expose a weakness in his character.

As much as she looked forward to the carriage ride with Sir Isaac, having him about in Orford could make things difficult. Yet she doubted he would spend the afternoon in her company. As kindly as he treated her of late, she would never presume to take all his attention. He would know the titled guests and his local neighbors better. They would likely be his focus.

The carriage turned into the main road, and everyone exchanged pleasantries. Sir Isaac kept his eyes upon hers with the slightest upturn of his lips promising a smile to come, if she but said the right words.

"I am pleased you decided to come with the party today, Sir Isaac," she said. "I understand we have a lovely day ahead of us. The picnic at the ruins, and a trip to the lighthouse. I have never seen a lighthouse up close."

Sir Isaac relaxed into his seat. "I would not miss the opportunity to enjoy a day in Orford. It is a charming village. Are all the guests attending today?"

"Yes, everyone decided to attend. Except for His Lordship, the marquess." Millie's eyes darted to Lord Neil, who leaned an elbow against the windowpane.

His chin was in his palm and he had put on another elegant, bored expression. "Oh, Father never troubles himself with any of the excursions."

Miss Ashford nodded with sympathy. "My papa tends to avoid stirring out of doors this time of year. But his lordship has an additional reason, considering he only returned home from London this very morning. I cannot say I would be eager to ride in a carriage again after such a long journey."

Lord Neil shrugged and directed his gaze out the window.

"One does grow weary of the road from London," Millie said brightly. Lord Neil had no wish to discuss his father's reasons for remaining home, and she did not mind turning the conversation for his sake. She directed her next words to the other woman in the carriage. "Were you in London for the Season, Miss Ashford?"

The young woman brightened. "Only for a short time. We stayed with my uncle. He is in the House of Commons, you know." She raised her chin at that pronouncement, then launched into a list of all the things she had experienced during her stay in London. Millie listened, somewhat helplessly, as Miss Ashford delighted in activities and sights that were a part of Millie's regular day as a near-permanent resident of the city.

She caught Sir Isaac hiding his amusement behind his fist. His eyes sparkled when her gaze met his. Apparently, Miss Ashford's enthusiasm for conversation did not come as a surprise to him.

The young woman did not even appear to mind the fact that Lord Neil ignored the entire conversation.

When Miss Ashford finally paused for breath, Sir Isaac hastily spoke. "I believe I should like to visit London next winter. I am not usually fond of Town, but I understand there will be important votes coming in regard to aiding those who returned from war wounded."

Millie picked up on that topic before Miss Ashford's puzzled frown turned into more chatter. "You are uniquely placed to help influence the politics of such discussions."

Sir Isaac blinked at her. "I cannot see how. I am not in either house, myself, but I do hope to prove a support to my brother-in-law." He sounded as though he did not even consider the good he might do. Perhaps he meant to be modest.

"Do you not think you could meet with others who make those decisions? As a baronet, and with your connection to Lord Inglewood, you would certainly receive invitations aplenty into the homes of representatives from both Houses." She gestured to his left sleeve. "You are in a unique position as one who understands a man who has experienced a personal loss in defense of King and Country. Sharing your experiences may well influence many to ponder the subject a little longer."

To Millie's surprise, Sir Isaac turned quite pale, and his gloved hand curled into a fist upon his knee. "I do not hold any influence in political arenas, Miss Wedgewood." He pointedly turned his face to Miss Ashford. "But perhaps Miss Ashford might suggest places to visit while I am in Town."

The young woman happily began naming her favorite parks and theaters. Millie stared a moment at Isaac, wondering at the abrupt end of the topic he had brought up in the first place. She glanced at Lord Neil, who still stared out the window but had lifted his eyebrows slightly. Then she dropped her gaze to her lap.

For the remainder of the carriage ride, she confined herself to more appropriate subjects of conversation. Perhaps straying into the world of politics had been her mistake. Not all men enjoyed conversations of that depth with women. Her father had spoken to her of politics often, given that they had few people to debate in their semi-exile from the fashionable world. She supposed her father was rather unique, including her in such topics.

The remainder of the ride passed more pleasantly, once Millie relaxed into less weighty discussion. Lord Neil even joined in a time or two, when the topic strayed to the other activities of the house party.

Lord Neil and Sir Isaac never spoke directly to each other, she noticed, though both were perfectly polite and civil. How interesting.

When the carriage arrived in Orford, passing through the village, Millie turned all her attention inward. Mr. Weston was her quarry. She had to hunt him down. Spend every possible moment at his side, on his arm if possible, and let the outrageous flirt flatter her until she could gain his trust enough that he would drop his guard. She needed a scent to follow if there were to be any secrets uncovered.

Millie suffered a moment of regret. Spending time with Sir Isaac would be much more diverting. More pleasant. She sighed and checked her bonnet when the carriage rolled to a stop.

The groom opened the carriage door. Isaac stepped out first, then held his hand out to Millie. She took it with a smile and descended from the carriage, then immediately turned her attention to the crowd of people entering the rubble-strewn area around the castle. A castle that appeared more like a single tower of a larger fortress, if she were truthful. It was a strange, small piece of architecture, but it made for an interesting study.

Millie popped open her parasol and hurried her steps to catch the group, heedless of leaving the others from her carriage behind. They would not miss her. Not even Isaac. He would look after himself well enough, and she had an assignment to fulfill.

The more time she spent concentrating on Mr. Weston, the less she had to worry about fulfilling the part of her bargain that included harming Sir Isaac.

Chapter Fifteen

Before Isaac said a word, before he asked Millie if he might escort her as they explored the ruins, she rushed off. The woman did not even glance over her shoulder to see if he —or Lord Neil and Miss Ashford—followed. It was as though she could not wait to leave him behind.

Had he done something to upset her? Their time in the carriage had been amicable. Enjoyable, to him, even. Despite sharing a box with Lord Neil. Apparently, Millie hadn't felt the same given her haste to leave him behind.

Had he miscalculated?

Lord Neil offered his arm to Miss Ashford, leaving Isaac to follow behind them, making him feel more the fool. No one to take his arm, no one to even walk alongside, put him at the rear of the entire party. Not that he particularly wished for the company of others, but he had rather hoped—

It did not matter what he hoped. Though he had thought Millie regarded him at least as a friend, his company did not seem to suit her.

Isaac finally started moving in the same direction as the others, to the castle he had seen a dozen times in his life. The structure no longer impressed him, even though he remembered well the story of the Orford Wild Man. It was a story he had meant to tell Millie as they walked about the ruins, to see what she made of it, to amuse her.

Foolish of him, really. She had no wish to keep him company. He had misread all her friendliness of the bonfire night, all her jests from the dinner at his sister's home.

He walked through the crumbling stones that marked where the castle's outer wall had once stood, following a well-trod path. He turned his eyes up to the tower, to the crumbling stone. What a waste. The Marquess of Hertford held ownership of the castle but had done little to maintain it, despite the castle's usefulness as a location to signal ships at sea. From a purely military standpoint, the quiet port of Orford would provide a place for enemy ships to invade, and friendly ships to resupply in an emergency.

Isaac shook his head at the stones, as though it was their fault his mind still turned to military strategies. If he did not leave behind that way of thinking, he would never rid himself of his nightmares. Burying the memories and training of war deep within had proven nearly impossible, but it was the only hope he had.

Members of the party scattered throughout the ruins. Several ladies carried sketchbooks. Some walked about arm-in-arm. The servants had yet to arrive with the picnic. Isaac's eyes wandered until they landed upon the waving green feathers of Millie's bonnet. She was on the arm of a man he did not recognize.

I am ten times a fool. Isaac swallowed back his disappointment and turned his attention to the hill. He would go to the top, enjoy the air and the view, and leave directly after the picnic. If Lord Neil insisted on using Isaac's carriage rather than put additional people into the other vehicles, Isaac would ride back with the servants.

He had no intention of spending an entire day in company with people who had no interest in him and his lack of connections. Millie had no need of him. She had made enough friends among the members of the house party to amuse herself.

Perhaps Esther was right. Isaac did not need to save everyone. And not everyone needed saving.

The servants arrived and took their baskets, blankets, and all the pieces of a table made especially for such an event, into the ruins near the castle. What must the villagers of Orford think of the nobility descending upon the ruins only to set up a dining room? Isaac stood up and brushed the grass from his trousers before starting down the hill at an easy pace.

Footmen from the marquess's household put together the cleverly constructed table, sliding slots together in the wood until four legs held up long boards. Two maids came next, tablecloth in hand, and in a matter of minutes had spread out a feast of cold meats, pastries, fruits, and every food that might be easily transported. Wine bottles appeared, too, along with shining goblets.

More than a year before, Isaac had taken nearly all his meals out-of-doors, near a fire. Rations of dried bread, soups too thin with unidentifiable vegetables floating about, were often what the men ate. As an officer, Isaac's meals were slightly better. He never went hungry, but he had certainly grown used to humble meals.

"Sir Isaac?" a quiet voice asked near his elbow. Isaac looked down into the worried expression of a woman wearing an apron and cap that marked her position as a maid. Millie's maid.

"Yes." He nodded slightly, encouraging her to speak. Perhaps she searched for her mistress. Isaac had seen Millie and her chosen escort watching another lady sketch the castle.

"Forgive me, sir, but I have something I must tell you. In confidence." She glanced to where the other servants continued their work, far enough from where Isaac stood. "I am concerned for my mistress. There are members of this party, people who aren't—aren't good people." Her face went pale when Isaac frowned at her. "I mean no disrespect to my betters, sir. But I worry someone might do her harm. Miss Wedgewood—she says you're a good man."

Isaac's insides twisted. Millie had bothered mentioning him to her maid?

"What is it you expect me to do?" he asked the maid, keeping his voice soft. Her distress was real, and he had no intention of adding to it.

"Maybe—maybe keep a lookout for her, sir? Make sure she stays safe." The maid blushed terribly then and lowered her eyes. "I know I've no right to even speak to you—"

"Have no fear. What is your name?" he asked gently.

"Sarah Morton, sir."

"Sarah. Your concern for your mistress is a credit to you. I promise, I will do what I can to help, should Miss Wedgewood have need of it."

The maid's shoulders drooped as though a burden fell from them. "Thank you, Sir Isaac." She curtsied and hurried away without another word. Clearly, approaching him had taken a great deal of the maid's courage. She was a kind-hearted girl. And he would keep his promise.

Isaac took his watch from the pocket of his waistcoat, realizing he had hours to spend in the company he had wanted to leave minutes before.

If Esther had been present, she would raise one eyebrow at him imperiously and say, "You cannot resist protecting people."

It was true. Defending others had always come naturally to him. It was his role in the club his dearest friends had formed in childhood. Silas led. Jacob made peace. Hope stirred them to adventure. Grace plotted their course. And Isaac looked out for all of them, until they grew up, and no one, not even his sister, had need of him anymore.

Millie might need him, and that was enough to make him stay. He meant to spend the whole of the day in Orford, following her about.

⁂

IF ANOTHER MAN ENJOYED HEARING THE SOUND OF HIS own voice as much as Mr. Weston, Millie would be most surprised.

The man prattled on and on through the meal, sometimes around mouthfuls of food.

Once most of the group finished with the repast, Lady Alderton gave the party leave to explore the ruins or take themselves to the village for an hour, then they were to go to the beach and lighthouses.

Millie simpered up at Mr. Weston, in a way that would suggest she hadn't a single clever thought in her head. "Mr. Weston, I do hope you will take me about the village and show me the church. I am much inclined to hear what you think of the architecture."

"Of course, Miss Wedgewood. Have no fear. I will explain the whole of its construction to you." He was certainly the sort of gentleman who counted upon women being less clever than he, which made Mrs. Vanderby's desire to blackmail him almost understandable. His condescension grated upon Millie.

But if spending time in his company would allow her to win her mother's happiness and her father's pride, she could be a vapid miss more interested in a man's attention than her own pursuits.

They began their walk as soon as they left the table; during the five minutes it took to arrive on the grounds of Saint Bartholomew's, walking downhill from the castle, Mr. Weston told her a considerable amount about medieval churches. Or at least, all of his thoughts about them.

"Considerable waste of funds, if you ask me," he said when the old graveyard came into sight. "This whole building ought to be torn down. Put something more economical in place. A mill or a workhouse." He shook his head in some disgust and gestured to the ruins outside the building. "It is not even fit to hold services at present. Entire thing in disrepair."

The few others who had started to town, walking in groups of twos and threes, went elsewhere. To the bakery, to shops. No one else, it seemed, had any interest in the historic nature of the church.

Millie's eyes drank in the ruins of what once was an impressive sight. Arches had fallen, the roof of the building had seen better decades, and the whole church had an air of abandonment about it.

"I always find it rather sad when old places are left empty." Millie stared up at the broken panes of glass. "It is as though the soul has gone out of them."

Mr. Weston snorted. "Very like a woman, to ascribe things like souls to an inanimate pile of stone. It is not sad. It is impractical." Despite his disdain, he walked her about on a path along the side of the church, toward the rear of the building.

"Might we go inside?" Millie asked, looking over her shoulder where the entrance lay.

"The whole thing is unstable. Liable to collapse if someone sneezes upon it." Mr. Weston chuckled at his own wit, and Millie buried her disappointment. He looked down upon her, his fair eyebrows drawing together. "We might get closer to the walls, however. If you wish."

Somewhat surprised at this small consideration, Millie brightened. He took her to the corner of the church, to inspect the place where the west wall met the southern. She put her hand to the old stone and could not hold back a wistful sigh.

"Think of all these stones have born witness to, Mr. Weston. They have been here since the time of King Henry the Second."

His hand caught hers, and he drew her around the corner of the wall where they were hidden from the road. Mr. Weston had put on quite a different expression. An intense, knowing look in his eye and a smirk upon his lips startled her. Millie took a step back, bumping into the wall. His arms came up, one on either side of her.

"Now then, Miss Wedgewood. We come to the point."

Millie sucked in a breath and tightened her hands into fists. She had given her parasol into Sarah's care, planning to retrieve it before they went to the beach. Now she wished she had it at hand. Her hat pin was out of reach, with how closely Mr. Weston had her trapped.

"What point, sir?" She kept the tremble from her voice. "Your behavior is too forward, Mr. Weston." It was better to sound coy, to bat her lashes at him and smile.

His smirk grew until she saw the flash of his teeth. "Am I? You have made certain I am aware of your interest, Miss Wedgewood. Your attention has been mine since the moment we were introduced last evening. Every excuse to be near me has been made. I was rather surprised you did not manage to find a way into my coach."

He came closer, lowering his voice. "Perhaps you might find your way into my quarters tonight."

Millie's head went back, her bonnet crushed against the stone. "You are mistaken, sir. My interest in you was not at all inappropriate—"

"What else would it be?" he asked, his much larger body growing closer to hers. "I could never court you. Everyone knows about your family. But if you wish for my favor—"

Millie was much smaller than he was. She often detested her stature, but it occurred to her to drop when he bent with the intention of kissing her. She did not even lose her balance, hardly having to duck to get beneath the cage of his arms.

Mr. Weston stumbled in his surprise, his face hitting the stone wall. He snarled, and Millie turned to flee, but he caught her arm. "Little vixen, full of tricks. That is what you remind me of, with that hair of yours. Shall we play at fox hunt?" He drew her against his chest, and Millie sucked in a breath in preparation to scream.

Would anyone hear her?

Would anyone bother to come if they did?

"I enjoy a good fox hunt." The words, calmly spoken, came from behind Millie. But she recognized the voice. She knew it at once. That wry tone, the rich timbre. Sir Isaac Fox. "Of course, it is the wrong season for it."

Mr. Weston slowly released Millie and stepped back, his eyes fixed on a point over her shoulder where Sir Isaac stood. "Have you a reason to skulk about here, Fox?"

"I do." He paused, the silence heavy with unspoken words. Was he glaring at Mr. Weston as she imagined? Millie longed to turn, to rush directly into him, where she might tuck herself against his side and find safety. But she kept still. Like a true fox. No sudden movements.

Apparently, Mr. Weston took Isaac's measure and determined he had no wish to test the baronet's reasons for appearing so suddenly. His eyes flickered briefly to Millie's, the heat in them greatly diminished. "Perhaps we will discuss medieval churches another time, Miss Wedgewood."

Though she wished to slap his conceited face, to snarl at him, or to kick him as hard as possible upon his shins, Millie answered him with nothing more than a tight nod. He did not even bow before vanishing from her sight.

Millie shuddered and went to the wall again, leaning against it for support, and keeping her back to her rescuer. How humiliating, for him to find her in such a compromising position. For the second time in her life, Millie had faced the attack of a man and only escaped by someone else's arrival in time to save her. The first time, when Lord Carning had come at her in anger, insisting she give him what her sister denied him, it had been Sarah who had saved her.

"Foolish," she whispered, wiping the perspiration from her hairline with her glove.

"I agree," Isaac said from behind her. "Completely foolish. What were you thinking, going off alone with a man of Weston's reputation?"

Millie turned, her back against the stone. Isaac stood a handful of steps away and glared at her from beneath the brim of his hat, his jaw tight.

"I did not know his reputation," she admitted. "And I had my reasons."

"Did you? I am intensely curious as to what they could be." She noted his hand had curled into a fist at his side, as though he still readied for a fight.

"It is none of your affair, Sir Isaac," she said, trying to keep her voice steady. Then Millie tipped her chin upward, tired of her place as victim. "I had the situation quite under control. The man only meant to take a kiss. Many a lady gives her kisses away without thought."

"Are you such a lady?" he asked, one eyebrow arching upward.

"Have you ever stolen a kiss?"

A laugh escaped him, deep and short. "Never, Miss Wedgewood. Though I have accepted a few that were freely given. That did not appear to be the case here."

"Perhaps it was," she said airily, pushing herself from the wall. "Perhaps I meant to let him have the kiss, and I meant to make him think he must take it."

Rather than appear frustrated, or defeated, Sir Isaac's expression fell into something like sorrow. "Then you do not know the first thing about giving or receiving affection, Miss Wedgewood."

Her throat closed, and it took Millie several swallows before she trusted herself to speak. "I know enough. I certainly know how to kiss." She bit her tongue.

Sir Isaac's lips quirked and he leaned closer to her to whisper, "'The lady doth protest too much, methinks.'"

"You are a horrid man," she whispered back, glaring at him.

"I thought we were friends." He came closer, so the distance between them was less than what was acceptable in a ballroom. "But perhaps not. Perhaps, instead, I ought to join the fox hunt. Since you are so liberal with your kisses, Miss Wedgewood, might you give one to me?"

Millie's cheeks filled with heat. She stared up into his warm brown eyes, which had turned darker in his approach. They glowed like embers, causing a slow, simmering warmth to grow in her chest and creep upward to color her cheeks.

His gaze lowered, perhaps to her lips, then up to her eyes again. It was a challenge. He meant to call her bluff. That was all it could be. He did not think she knew the first thing about kisses.

And she did not. But Millie would not let him know that truth.

"Of course, Sir Isaac. Come and claim it." She could call his bluff as well as he called hers. The man was too honorable. He would never kiss her. And she positively would not think upon how much that thought disappointed her.

Millie pulled in a sharp breath the moment Sir Isaac's hand brushed her waist. But he did not settle his fingers just above her hip, as she might have expected. No, he meant to make a point of the farce, it would seem. His hand slid from the curve of her waist around to the small of her back, his palm flat against her gown. He drew her closer with no more than a gentle press, and the heat from his hand melted through her dress.

Her hands raised of their own accord and she placed them flat against his chest, her lungs constricting and her throat closing. She ought to push him away. Back out of the dare. But he already bent down, his head tilted just so. His thumb rubbed the back of her gown where her sash tied, and the emotions trapped inside of her swirled riotously.

She was not afraid. He moved slowly enough that she might withdraw. Might stop him.

Millie had no wish to end a moment she instinctively knew she would revisit in her dreams.

His lips brushed hers in the gentlest of caresses, and her eyes fluttered closed at the moment of connection. She returned the kiss, her lips pressing against his, and one of her hands slid up to the back of his neck. His arm tightened at her waist as his kiss deepened, causing every inch of her to feel as though she stood beside a roaring fire rather than pressed against a man of flesh and bone.

The kiss ended. He pulled back, and she followed him, standing on her toes to prolong the connection. It was like nothing she had ever experienced before, and she did not want it to stop. She wanted more. Needed more.

The man chuckled, and her eyes flew open, meeting his, seeing those lips that had kissed her so thoroughly turn upward in a smirk.

"There now, Miss Wedgewood." His voice was the low growl of a wolf, causing a shiver half fearful and half delightful to run down her spine.

She was nothing more than a helpless little fox. A foolish creature who thought herself clever and crafty.

His voice was low and rough. "We have both proven ourselves capable of exchanging a kiss which means absolutely nothing to either of us."

If only he were right.

The sob she had held at bay emerged, a quiet, pathetic sound. Millie walked away from him, along the western wall of the church, away from the path that would return her to the road and the sight of others. She wanted nothing more than to hide, to go to ground and escape.

She heard Isaac following behind her, his boots crunching along on the old gravely walk that might've once been a fine stone path around the whole of the church.

"Miss Wedgewood, come back. Please, stop." She heard his protests but ignored them. At least until he caught up to her, which was likely quite easily done considering how much longer his stride was than hers. "Millie, I am sorry." His hand brushed her arm, not taking hold, but it was enough of a touch to make her halt in her directionless flight.

"I apologize a thousand times over." Though he spoke earnestly, she did not look up at him. The tips of his boots came into sight as he stood before her. "Anyone who knows me will tell you that I often rush into things without thought. I do not measure my words before I speak them. This was a terrible example of both faults. Please, will you forgive me?"

Millie took the reticule from her wrist and pulled at the strings, attempting to free them enough to find her handkerchief. "There is nothing to forgive. You taught me a lesson."

She nearly jumped in surprise when he lowered himself to one knee before her, removing his hat as he did. The man looked as though he paid supplication to the Queen.

She sniffed and finally took hold of her handkerchief. She pressed the linen square to her face and glared at him over its edge. "What are you doing now?"

His grin appeared, crooked and contrite. "Begging you for forgiveness, Miss Wedgewood. Humbling myself before you. Please. Forgive my thoughtless words, my foolish actions. I was in a temper when I saw Weston with you. He is a cad. An unscrupulous womanizer. But I behaved as though he and I were cut from the same cloth. It is inexcusable." His shoulders fell, as did the smile from his face. Though he started his speech with dramatics, it ended with sincerity.

Her heart softened. "I goaded you, sir."

"I ought to have behaved better anyway, miss."

"I will forgive you." She let herself relax, ready to admit fault as well as defeat. "Thank you. You really did rescue me."

Sir Isaac had the grace not to gloat, nor even appear pleased at her admission. He stood again and replaced his hat, then brushed off the knee that had hit the dirt. "I am sorry it was necessary. Millie, please be more careful."

He spoke her Christian name with the gentle familiarity she needed.

It was such an exquisite kiss, to have it mean nothing—

How awful.

"I will do my best." She did not know what prompted her to add the next sentence. "But I am afraid I cannot avoid him."

"Why ever not? The man is a rake." Sir Isaac snorted, then he offered her his arm. She took it, as naturally as she ever had. "Stay in the corner opposite him the rest of the house party. I can inform him if he comes within six feet of you again—"

"Do not trouble yourself." Millie smiled despite the seriousness of her thoughts. "You would quite ruin my luck if you did that. You see, I have to spend time in his company. Not just because of the house party."

"Then why?" he asked, halting their progress at the corner of the building, where they were once again within sight of the road. "He is not worth a moment of your notice."

Millie wanted to tell him. But when Isaac learned of what she had agreed to do, he would think her too low a creature for even Mr. Weston's attentions.

Chapter Sixteen

When Millie did not answer him, Isaac's thoughts rehearsed every conversation they'd had since their first meeting. Reputation. That is what it came down to for Millie. Reputation and her family's place in Society. Somehow, Mr. Weston factored into her calculations to regain both of those things.

"Let us return to the castle and the carriages. I will tuck you into mine with your Sarah—" She started when he spoke the maid's name. "—and return both of you to the house. I will make your excuses—tell everyone you are ill."

Millie appeared tired. Whatever strength and fire he saw in her before had drained away. "Very well. Perhaps that is for the best."

She said nothing more on their walk, or as he put her into his carriage. Her silence, the paleness of her cheeks, would inform any who saw her that she wasn't in the pink of health.

It took hardly any time to find the maid, make the appropriate excuses to the correct people, and then join both Millie and her maid in the carriage. They began the journey back in silence.

Millie kept her eyes closed and her head tilted against the corner of the carriage. Sarah had taken the rear-facing seat, and rather than risk the maid's discomfort he sat next to Millie. They said nothing as they bumped along on the road leaving Orford. Nothing for a quarter of an hour.

Finally, the maid closed her eyes and leaned into her own corner, giving way to sleep.

Isaac had nearly decided to do the same when Millie turned toward him, her eyes open and full of a sadness no one should bear alone.

"Tell me," he whispered, barely hearing his own voice above the noise of the carriage.

Her expression did not change. But she spoke. So quietly he had to lean closer to hear. "I am not a good person, Isaac." She had dropped his title. Why did that make his heart leap? "I have an arrangement with Lady Olivia and two of her friends."

"Does someone like Lady Olivia even have friends?" he quipped, a tiny smile his only reward. "What do you mean? What arrangement?"

"My family is desperate," she said slowly, seriously. "My parents need to find their footing in Society again. For financial stability. For their future. For mine."

She lowered her gaze to the seat between them, and he looked too, seeing that their hands nearly touched. He lifted one gloved finger and placed it upon the back of her hand, tracing across her knuckles.

"I understand desperation, Millie." Did she mind when he used the short form of her given name? It was so much better than what her parents had put upon her. "But what does that have to do with Lady Olivia? With Weston?"

"Lady Olivia and her friends promised to reintroduce me, my whole family, into Society if I performed a task set by each of them. I completed the first task in London. The second task is to find something about Mr. Weston that is a vulnerability, a mark against him Society will not forgive, and share that information with Mrs. Vanderby. The third task..." She turned her hand over, inviting him to slide his fingers between hers. "The third task is you."

"Me?" He tightened his grip on her fingers and bent until he could see beneath the brim of her bonnet. He had to fold nearly in half, given how low her head hung. "What do I have to do with anything?"

"Lady Olivia wishes me to find a way to wound you. Not physically, of course. But she means for you to hurt." Though the pronouncement ought to have chilled him, Isaac found he wished to comfort the confessing woman.

"All of that, just to put in a good word for you?" he asked quietly.

Her head came up at last, her eyes blazing. "I told her I would not do it. The day I told you I feared I must leave, I told her the agreement must end. I promise. As I came to know you, I felt how wrong it was. But I cannot—she made certain I must do as she says, or my whole family will face worse than we already have." Her voice broke on the last word, and she tried to disentangle her fingers from his.

Isaac looked to where the maid sat, then decided he did not care what she thought. He released Millie's hand, only to put his arm about her shoulder and guide her into his embrace. She laid her cheek against his chest without protest.

The tearful explanation that followed was partly muffled. "The man once engaged to my sister, he is at the house party. The Viscount of Carning. He is here. He is a dreadful, awful, wicked, powerful villain. He has agreed to enforce Lady Olivia's agreement. If I do not do as she wishes, every tiny piece of respectability my family still holds will be gone. He can ruin us. Take away everything except the land my father inherited from his father. My mother will be heartbroken. And they even know where Emmeline is—though I have never heard from her since she left our home." Her shoulders trembled beneath the weight they held, the weight of an entire family's future.

His heart ached for her, for the trouble she faced. Brought upon herself, in a way. But he had seen many a desperate person in his time as a soldier. He had been desperate himself, since the war.

"When we see no way out, we do what we have to do to survive," he said quietly, noting that the maid had opened her eyes and appeared not the least bit as though she had slept. When she saw him looking at her, the young woman's expression turned pleading, as it had at the castle.

Sarah the maid thought he could save her mistress.

Essie would remind him it was not his responsibility to save everyone.

How could he turn his back on Millie? She had confessed everything to him. Had given him her trust. She needed an ally.

Isaac could not save everyone. But he could help Millie. "What can I do to assist you?"

"You cannot—"

"I can. And I will." He gently set her away from him, met her red-rimmed eyes with his gaze. "Tell me everything. Every word of the agreement you made. We will fulfill it, and the moment you are free, you will let my family introduce you back into Society. Into the part of it where you belong. Not Lady Olivia's circle of corruption."

In as few words as possible, Millie recounted her mother bringing her to Lady Olivia's notice, then went into greater detail as she told him the whole of the ordeal and the horrid bargain she'd felt forced to make.

Millie had put herself in a terrible position. But it was not an impossible one. "At least I know why I am Lady Olivia's target," he admitted, the weight of all she told him making his shoulders sag. He leaned back against the seat and removed his hat.

"You do?" she asked, somewhat shyly. He had never seen her shy since their meeting. It was rather endearingly sweet.

"Normally, I would never divulge such a thing to anyone." He shot a look of warning at the maid, who nodded mutely, her promise of silence in the gesture. "But Lady Olivia has dragged you into our past through her actions and threats. Shortly after I returned from war, she paid me a visit. She came to my home, alone. During a storm. My servants showed her inside my house, offered her shelter, and I came into the room where they put her to play the part of a good host." He released a frustrated sigh and rubbed at his eyes, as though he could erase the memory of that horrible evening. "When I arrived at the room, she was not appropriately attired."

Millie's soft gasp made his ears turn red. A gentleman would take that whole scene to the grave. But she needed to know where Lady Olivia's anger had come from, why the daughter of a marquess sought to avenge herself upon a lowly baronet.

"I was shocked, and she...made a request." That was the most polite term he could use for what the woman had said to him. "I left the room without a word. I locked myself in my study after telling the butler to have her removed. I might have handled the situation poorly. The servants saw things, heard her say things. I have no doubt she regards herself as humiliated and ill-used."

What must Millie think of the whole situation?

"I understand," she said. Not softly, but firmly. He saw a flash of anger in her eyes. "I understand entirely too well." She looked to her maid. "Sarah does, too."

"Yes, miss. Sir." The maid appeared ill.

Isaac wanted to leave the entire subject behind them. Never discussing it again. "So we understand now the motivations, and what you must do. We have to see it through, Millie. Free you from these troubles. If you will let me speak to Silas—"

She broke in at once. "No. Isaac, you can tell no one. What would he think of me? What would your sister think?" She shuddered. "You promised we spoke in confidence. Please. You cannot say a word of this to anyone else. This is my problem, my mess to clean up, not yours. Not the earl's."

"They could help, I am certain of it." Though he spoke with conviction, she kept shaking her head.

"No. Please, say nothing."

Isaac put his hat upon his head again. "Very well. I will say nothing unless you bid me to do so. But you cannot stop me from helping, Miss Millicent Wedgewood."

Her smile appeared, tentative at first. "I would not dream of it. You are my rescuer, as Sarah is, and I am grateful for that. Also, Isaac—" A little color came back into her cheeks. "Please, keep calling me Millie."

THAT EVENING, STILL FEIGNING ILLNESS IN HER ROOM, Millie sat in the window. Knees tucked beneath her chin, forehead against the cool glass, she stared out over the stables to the clouds creeping across the sky. Sarah took the gown for the next day out of the wardrobe and held the material out by the shoulders. "This one, miss?"

Barely adjusting the tilt of her head, Millie eyed the blue dress with interest. "If you think it best, Sarah."

"It does look quite lovely with your hair and complexion," Sarah assured her. "And tomorrow is the tour of the gardens, sewing, and then the evening card party."

"Yes. A long, wretched day. At least Lady Olivia cannot expect much from me, with the men out fishing on the marquess's yacht." Millie put her feet upon the ground and stretched her arms above her head. "Do you think I can avoid dinner this evening? It is only an hour away."

Sarah sighed and went about gathering Millie's underthings for the next day. "I wish you would, miss. Wish you'd avoid everything and go home. But it's like you said to Sir Isaac. We're caught in a trap."

"I wish Sir Isaac did not have to know." Though it was some-what of a relief to her. Millie started to pace the room, her slippers hardly making a sound on the carpet. "It complicates matters."

"*Sir* Isaac?" Sarah asked, turning away from Millie and busying herself with the dressing table. "I believe he gave you leave to use his Christian name after you said, 'call me Millie.'" Sarah peered over her shoulder at Millie, grinning boldly.

Millie felt heat at the back of her neck and in her cheeks. "He is a comrade-in-arms now, Sarah. That is all I wanted him to understand."

"Oh, is he?" Sarah adjusted the hairbrush. "Is that why you two looked all snug and safe in the carriage together?"

"Stop your teasing, Sarah Morton." Millie lifted a cushion from the chair beside the empty hearth and threw it at Sarah's backside. The maid giggled when it hit her and fetched it up again. "You know very well I cannot be more than friends with him. He is only a baronet. Mama would not approve." She dropped inelegantly into the chair. "He hasn't enough influence in Society to please her, or to help Papa."

Sarah brushed off the cushion and brought it back to the chair, setting it in Millie's lap. "So you don't think he's handsome?"

Millie hugged the pillow to her, fingers tangling in its fringed corner. "He is most handsome. I can think him handsome without being more than his friend." He had such an engaging smile. And how safe she had felt, leaning into his embrace in the carriage.

"And you don't think him especially noble or kind?" Sarah folded her arms and fixed Millie with a stare more appropriate to a nanny scolding a child than a servant barely a year older than her mistress.

"He is both of those things." Millie could not deny that at all. She twisted the fringe around her fingers, still thinking of their time together in the carriage. Their fingers interlaced had made her heart dance, then tucking herself against his shoulder had been the most protected she had felt since—since before Emmeline left. "He makes me feel as though I have found shelter in a storm."

Sarah nodded once. "I see, miss. So you're just friends with him, because that's how friends often feel about one another."

"I would not know. Aside from you, I have had no friends since my sister left." She smiled fondly at her maid, lest Sarah think any insult was meant. It was more than a little unusual for a woman to befriend her maid or trust her so well. "I have been thinking about Emmeline a great deal of late." Bringing up her sister would decidedly move the topic of conversation away from any affectionate feeling she had for Isaac.

"Quite natural, I'm sure." Sarah fetched her mending basket and took out the nearly finished lace collar. The intricate work required time and signaled that Sarah had no intention of helping Millie dress for dinner. Good. Millie could avoid the viscount and Mr. Weston, as well as Lady Olivia.

"I only wonder if Emmeline is well." Millie pulled the pillow tighter to her chest, staring at nothing as she remembered her sister. Emmeline had always shone like the sun, brightening every room she entered. She had the perfect golden curls, eyes so blue one felt that they had stolen their color from the sky. Emmeline hadn't been as short as Millie and had the more desired, willow-like figure of a sylph.

She had always treated Millie kindly, too. Like a friend as much as like a sister. They had told each other everything. Emmeline had been eighteen years old when the viscount proposed. Papa and Mama had been shocked, honored, and hastily agreed to the match.

Perhaps too hastily.

"For years I have been so angry with her," Millie whispered, more to herself than to Sarah. "But I cannot find it in me to be angry anymore. Especially after seeing the viscount again." She shuddered and tucked her feet onto the chair beneath her. "Imagine how horrid a life she would have had, married to him."

"It's wise to think on that." Sarah cocked an eyebrow upward but did not take her eyes from her delicate work. "My mam always told us that you can't change a person, no matter how you try. If she'd have married the viscount, he'd be as horrid to her as he was to you. I feel sorry for his poor wife."

"She does appear a rather downtrodden creature." Millie kept the pillow in place and took up a book from the small table beside her chair. It was nothing more than a collection of poetry, and not by a poet she recognized. It seemed anyone who wished could get a book published. "If Lady Olivia found my sister, I would like to know where Emmie is, and how she is getting on with her husband. I wonder if she has children. I might be an aunt and not even know it."

"More's the pity, miss." Sarah shook her head, true sympathy in her tone. "But it's good you're thinking on it at all. Maybe you should ask Lady Olivia where your sister is."

"She would never tell me."

"Then maybe you ought to see if you can find out in another way." Sarah said the words slowly, each dripping with hidden meaning. "Maybe that's how you can take care of that Mr. Weston. Perhaps some spying is in order, miss."

Millie went cold. "Do you mean violate their privacy? Search their things?"

Sarah put on a rather crooked smile. "Or find a servant what would do it for a price. There are more'n a few in this house not paid a fair wage. I imagine I could find someone to help."

"That is a dangerous suggestion." Millie turned the idea over in her mind. "But not without merit. I will put the idea to Isaac. I have bungled everything so far. I do not trust my own judgement."

Sarah's grin widened. "Ah. *Sir* Isaac would be the perfect person to ask. It's the best excuse I ever heard for meeting with a handsome—"

Millie's pillow, tossed by the blushing woman at the maid, halted Sarah's sentence. But it did nothing to stop the way her stomach flipped and turned when she thought of Sir Isaac's incredible kiss. It was a shame he'd only meant to teach her a lesson by it.

As complicated as her situation was, Millie could not help but entertain the tiniest hope that perhaps there were other lessons he wished to teach her that ended in a kiss.

Chapter Seventeen

Drumming his fingers on the desk before him, Isaac glared down at the letters on the shiny, oak surface. The letters themselves were not particularly offensive. But Isaac's thoughts had wandered far from their words to those Millie had shared with him in the carriage the day before.

On a mission to elevate her family, saving them from the fall they had suffered after the viscount turned against them, Millie had made poor choices. He did not deny that. Nor did he condone it. But when she had come to the realization of her folly, had tried to correct it, she had been trapped into her agreement with Lady Olivia and her cronies.

A way to help her had to exist. If he could settle on the right course of action, he could free her from the agreement. Grace Barnes would know what to do. The woman was a natural strategist. But Isaac had made a promise which prohibited him from speaking to any of his friends of the trouble Millie faced.

He pushed away from the desk, taking a book from its surface with him. Isaac went to the bookshelves and returned the book to its place.

A knock at the door made him turn, almost with gratitude, to answer. "Come."

The butler entered the room and bowed. "Sir. A Miss Wedgewood to see you."

Isaac drew himself up. To call on a single gentleman, on her own—

"But she insisted upon waiting outside, sir," the butler added before Isaac's thoughts ventured down an uncomfortable path.

"Oh. Very good. I shall step out directly." The butler bowed and left. Isaac tugged at his waistcoat as he followed, then he paused before a mirror hanging in the corridor. His hair was mussed, his cravat in fair shape, and nothing else was amiss with his appearance. He attempted to smooth his hair back, but then noticed his butler standing a few feet further in the corridor, watching.

Isaac straightened from the mirror and lifted his chin in the air, as though unconcerned, and passed the butler at a quick clip to get to the door. He opened it himself and stepped into the light of the early afternoon sun.

Millie wore the raspberry dress he had seen before, when she called upon Esther, with a floral shawl upon her shoulders. She faced slightly away from the door, her eyes upon something at the side of the house.

"Millie." It was much easier to speak that familiar name than stumble through the whole of her formal address. It suited her better, too. Suited the smile she bestowed upon him when she turned around to greet him. "I am glad to see you."

"That is a relief to hear." She held her hand out in response to his approach. Without thought he took it in his ungloved hand. "I was forced from the house today by Lady Olivia. All the male guests are out upon the sea today, and the ladies are meant to sew and arrange flowers." She sighed deeply. "I am to be on task."

He brought her closer, drawing her to his side. "If Mr. Weston is not available, it makes perfect sense to dispatch you after the other man." He kept his tone light and the way her shoulders relaxed confirmed levity was the right path to take. "How are we to pass our afternoon? Will you try to discover all my deepest secrets?"

Her cheeks pinked. "Isaac Fox, are you flirting? I thought you detested flirting."

"I detest unwelcome flirting. Shallow flirting." He allowed her to move her hand from his so she might take his arm. They started to walk down the drive. "I have not flirted much myself, since the war. Perhaps I ought to take it up again."

"That would make you quite the hypocrite, unless you allow me the same privilege." She kept her head turned forward, so he heard more than saw her smile. "I thought we might walk for a time. Or perhaps we could pay a visit to your sister. As alternative ideas to sharing secrets."

He sighed dramatically and took her off the path, making for a large oak tree. "You need my secrets, Millie. How else will you escape Lady Olivia's clutches?" He nodded to an iron bench that his father had put around the tree to serve as a place of reflection. "Come. Sit for a time. Then I will have my gig brought round to take you to see Esther."

"Your concern for my reputation does you credit, sir." She took her seat upon the old bench, tucking her skirts carefully to the side so he might sit beside her. He did not hesitate to do so, laying his arm along the back of the bench above her shoulders.

"As does your concern for mine." He crossed his legs and leaned back against the bench. "Did you experience anything unpleasant after I left you yesterday?"

"Only the expression of Lady Olivia's impatience this morning, but as the result of that discussion brought me to your door, I cannot mind it." She tipped her face upward. "No one has tried to kiss me again, if that is what you were specifically wondering."

"Ah, I see. Is that the most unpleasant thing that might happen to you?" he asked, tempted to grin. He'd enjoyed their kiss. Though his intention had been to stun her, he had ended up surprised by how much he had liked it.

Her amusement faded into a tired sigh. "Unfortunately not.

There are many things for me to worry over, at present. Sarah locked my bedroom door last night and insisted she sleep in the same room. She already had her concerns over Lord Carning, and now she thinks Mr. Weston a threat."

Isaac winced at his own thoughtless inquiry. "You are fortunate to have such a loyal servant in your employment."

"I know it. Which brings to my mind a plan I had, but I wish to put it to you." She turned still more toward him, her left shoulder brushing against his arm. She explained an idea of shuffling through the personal rooms of not only Lady Olivia, but Mr. Weston. Isaac listened, his concern growing, as she first described taking action herself or, alternatively, bribing a servant to do the same.

"The more people you involve, the more likely you are to be found out." He sighed and his hand lifted a bonnet ribbon from her shoulder. He wistfully remembered when his nephew had played with the very same ribbon. Why had such a charming woman fallen into such an odd fate? More importantly, how was he to help her? "It was true in the army. Orders were never shared down the ranks until they absolutely had to be told. It kept secrets from slipping out, movements from being discovered."

"I had rather not send Sarah to do the job. If she is discovered, it would be terrible for her. But if I poke about Mr. Weston's quarters—"

"The consequences would be far worse." Isaac idly rubbed the satin ribbon between his thumb and forefinger, his thoughts turning about in his mind until he found a solution. "Tonight there is a card party at the house, is there not? I have my invitation. Esther planned to attend. What if I search Mr. Weston's rooms?"

Millie's eyebrows drew down and the lightest of creases appeared just above them on her smooth forehead. "How would you go about that?"

"Tell Sarah to wait for me, near the guest chambers. I will make an excuse to slip away a moment. Fresh air. A trip to the water closet. Something of the sort." He released the ribbon in favor of taking up the hand she had rested in her lap. Not that she needed his reassurance, but it felt right all the same. "She can tell me which room is Weston's and I can take a few minutes to see if there is anything of interest. Though I would think most men leave their secrets at home rather than take them to house parties in the country."

"I know." Her shoulders drooped along with the corners of her mouth. "I cannot think what else to do now. I have no wish to encourage him into behaving as he did before. I doubt the man will reveal anything of an intimate nature to me."

Isaac had already written letters of inquiry that morning, to a few fellow officers who held positions at home posts. Perhaps one of them would turn up something of use, but telling Millie of his efforts would be premature.

"Absolutely do not engage him that way again," Isaac said quietly, lifting her hand to his chest, holding it there to emphasize his sincere concern. "Millie, the man could overpower you. I would not have you hurt for anything."

Her cheeks reddened, and she lowered her eyes. "Do you always take such care of your friends, Isaac?"

It was the first time that day she had said his name, and it had the same effect as a hammer hitting upon his chest with a thud. He could not let Millie know what she did to him. That he had accepted his attraction to her, looked forward to knowing more of her.

He was captivated by this woman whose troubles would take work to solve, who inspired his desire to protect her, to save her.

"Millie." He thought of confessing, but his sister's admonishments of rushing headlong into impossible situations stopped up those words like a topper in a bottle.

She waited, then prompted with a shy smile. "Yes, Isaac?"

He shifted and looked down at her hand, still resting in his, her knuckles brushing his coat. "We can stave off Lady Olivia's impatience if I pretend to fall in love with you."

Millie's whole body pulled away from him, her face white with shock. "Forgive me. Did you really just suggest—Isaac. You cannot be serious. How would that help matters at all?"

"If I act the part of a lovelorn suitor, Lady Olivia will see it as evidence of your work upon the task. What better way to hurt a man than win his heart under false pretenses?" He tried to smile, to make the plan sound sensible even as she slipped her hand away. "You know her well enough by now to guess that she cares little for Mrs. Vanderby's plans regarding Mr. Weston. If Lady Olivia thinks you are succeeding with the part of the agreement that most concerns her, she will exert less pressure upon you."

A laugh escaped her, though it was short and surprised.

"Is the idea of loving me so laughable?" Isaac attempted to smile and tried very hard to make the words a jest, but his heart protested with one horrid stab of pain.

"Not at all." The mirth faded from her eyes and she sighed deeply, as though weary. "It is only that I suggested such a thing at the beginning. Lady Olivia scoffed at me. And here we have come back to my first suggestion."

He watched as Millie pulled in her bottom lip, worrying it between her teeth. Then she stood and walked to the very edge of the shadows cast by the oak. "It would be a relief to have her somewhat mollified. Lord Neil would attest to a claim of affection, given what he saw of our friendship in the carriage."

Isaac's curiosity grew. "Would he? I cannot think I have ever known Lord Neil to be particularly helpful."

"I think he is woefully underestimated." Millie turned enough for him to see a secretive smile upon her face. Because she thought of the shiftless son of the marquess? The two were not closely acquainted, surely. "Lord Neil has proven a help to me once or twice. He is the only person in that entire household that has shown himself to be something of a friend."

"Interesting thought." And unsettling. Millie and Lord Neil— friends? He stirred uneasily a moment, then stood. "Have we decided then? I will play the besotted suitor and you the clever huntress who ensnared me."

Millie hesitated, then gave a tight nod. "Yes. And the plan for the card party tonight—it is a good one. I will alert Sarah so she will play her part as guide. As lookout, too."

"Excellent. Allow me to get the carriage and we can pay our respects to Essie." Isaac bowed, making certain to show nothing but confidence in his smile, and he returned to the house with a quick step. His enthusiasm dissipated when he entered the house and called for a footman to go to the stables. He needed to fetch his hat and gloves, change footwear, and look the part of an eligible baronet. Not because he wished to impress Millie, of course. Not at all.

Whatever affection he felt for her, he must quell. She needed a friend and confidant. But playing the part of a smitten man, intent upon courtship, would prove quite easy. Perhaps, when it was all over, when Millie was safely away from Lady Olivia, he might visit her in London. Then he would see if there could be something real between them.

Chapter Eighteen

As bidden by a note scrawled in Lady Olivia's hand, Millie appeared in the lady's room before the card party. Dinner had ended an hour previous, and Millie hid herself away, rather than force herself to make conversation. Lady Olivia's note had waited for Millie atop her dressing table.

"You wished to see me, Lady Olivia?"

"Yes." Lady Olivia wore her dinner clothes and sat on the edge of her lounging couch, snapping her fan before her face. Her eyes flashed irritably. "You were gone the whole of the day. What happened with Sir Isaac? And why do you avoid Weston?"

This was the moment. Millie had to sound confident, and she had to press upon Lady Olivia that all went according to plan. "I do apologize for my absence, but I had good reason. I spent my time away from the house with Sir Isaac and his family. I felt it important to concentrate my efforts on one man at a time, as dividing my attention caused confusion during the Orford excursion."

Lady Olivia snapped her fan closed, her cold green eyes narrowing. "And? What happened?"

"I believe I have won Sir Isaac's trust." That much she could say without even batting an eye. It was the truth. He trusted her. "And I am on my way to winning his heart."

It shocked her how much she wished it were true. She should not want to win him. She should forget the very idea of Isaac feeling for her anything other than friendship. Millie had to fulfill her family's wishes—and her own. For as long as she could remember, she had been groomed to take a place of prominence in Society. It was up to her to fix everything Emmeline's decision had broken.

Even if Emmeline had made the right choice when she escaped her engagement to the viscount.

The silence stretched between them. Lady Olivia's cold glare did not abate. Millie did not flinch or quell beneath the ice.

Finally, Lady Olivia opened her fan with a slow, graceful movement. "His heart." She stood and walked languidly to Millie, towering over her with her greater height. Lady Olivia was the swan to Millie's peahen. Tall, elegant, wearing a gown that likely cost as much as Millie's entire wardrobe. "I attempted something similar, once. I presented him with everything he could want from a woman of standing, of nobility. All I received was his scorn." Her eyes narrowed and she bared her teeth as she snarled. "If you try to make a fool of me, Miss Millicent Wedgewood, your family will regret it for generations to come."

Millie kept her gaze straight ahead, looking at the wall across from where she stood lest she lose her bravado. "Yes, Lady Olivia."

A knock at the door prevented Lady Olivia from saying more. Instead she raised her voice, her tone changing to one of boredom. "Who is it?"

The door opened and Lord Neil leaned against its frame, wearing an exasperated expression. "Mother wants you downstairs to greet the neighborhood guests with her."

Lady Olivia huffed, then waved dismissively toward Millie. "Very well. We will speak later, Miss Wedgewood."

Millie curtsied, then preceded Lady Olivia out the door. Lord

Neil offered his arm to Millie, not his sister, and immediately started speaking of whist. His sister cut him an annoyed glance and sailed away, as graceful as ever. Lord Neil kept his steps shorter, slower, until his sister turned down the hall out of sight.

"I noticed you both missing," he said, voice lowered and no longer as languid. "Have you some secret enjoyment of being flayed by my sister's temper?"

"Not at all." She relaxed her hold upon him. "Do you know the whole of the agreement between us now?"

"I believe so. Though not why Olivia is so determined to cause ruin. She can be a vindictive creature, I suppose." He cut a fine figure in his dark blue coat and golden hair. He acted the part of a lay about, yet there was a strength to him that peeked out on occasion and gave Millie pause.

Though he had shown himself as an ally of sorts, Millie had no doubt his greater loyalty would always remain with his sister. "My only desire now is to leave your home unscathed by her wrath, my lord."

The man could be better. If he wished. Perhaps he had never had the chance to be good, trapped within his family as he was.

He cocked an eyebrow at her and smirked. "Look after yourself, Miss Wedgewood. It is the only advice I can give. Though I have reason to believe you are avoiding certain members of our party." His voice lowered. "There are rules here, Miss Wedgewood. No one may cross your threshold without your permission. Your maid need not sleep in your room."

Millie sucked in a surprised gasp, then set about coughing when her lungs protested. "How did you know?"

"This is my home. I know what goes on inside of it." Lord Neil lifted one shoulder in a lazy shrug. "To the card room?"

She nodded her acceptance. When they reached the corridor, they were not the only couple ready to step inside. Sir Isaac and his sister had arrived at the door nearly at the same moment. Both of them appeared surprised to see her. Or perhaps surprised by the company she kept.

Lord Neil paused outside the door and bowed, deeply, to the countess. He spoke not a word to her, though he nodded to Isaac. "Fox."

Isaac nodded but said nothing.

"This is where I leave you to make your own way, Miss Wedgewood." He offered her the barest of smiles, but she caught a cautionary look in his eyes. If she said the word, asked it of him, he would not abandon her.

"Thank you, Lord Neil. I look forward to the evening." She released his arm, then properly greeted her friends. "My lady. Sir Isaac. I am delighted to see you both here."

"It is always pleasant to be among others for an evening," Lady Inglewood said, her usual cheer subdued. She looked to Isaac, who still stood stiff and still as a statue. "Will you excuse me? I see Mrs. Ashford inside, and I must speak with her."

"Of course, my lady." Millie waited until the countess withdrew to step closer to Isaac. "Is something wrong? You appear...unsettled. Do you wish to abandon our plan?" What else could have him take on such a grim appearance?

Isaac offered her his arm. "I am surprised by Lord Neil's attention to you, I suppose." He cleared his throat and looked away, at the other guests in the room they had entered. There were tables scattered everywhere, footmen bearing trays of treats and goblets of wine. "You are quite lovely tonight, Miss Wedgewood."

Ah, yes. Their plan. Over the course of the evening, Isaac intended not only to make everyone believe him a besotted man, but he meant to engage in a clandestine search, too. The easier she made the whole of it for him, the less work he had to do.

"Thank you, Sir Isaac. You are most kind. Might I interest you in a game of Whist?"

His gaze came back to meet hers. "Perhaps. If you will consent to be my partner."

They were soon seated at a table with Miss Parr and Mr. Ashford. The four of them exchanged pleasantries during the first round of the game, and Miss Parr dealt the second round.

Millie did not particularly care for the game. When she played at home, with her parents or people from their small set of friends, she never exactly knew what her partner expected of her. Did they play a low card in hopes she would play a higher, winning the trick for them? Or did they anticipate that she would play low as well, forfeiting a point to the other team? Even with discussing strategy ahead of time with her father, when he consented to play, she inevitably made mistakes enough that her team lost the game.

When the third trick in a row went to their opponents, Millie raised her stare from the cards, a blush upon her cheeks. "I am sorry, Sir Isaac. This turn will be better."

A boyish smile appeared on his face, revealing that hidden sparkle in his eyes. "Do not worry your head over it. I have never enjoyed a game of Whist more than this one."

Her stomach twisted. This was part of his playacting. How could anyone enjoy losing?

Apparently, Miss Parr wondered the same. "If you two do not win this round, you forfeit the game to us. I can hardly see how losing is enjoyable."

"Can you not?" Mr. Ashford reordered his cards in his hand, contemplating which card to lay atop the first for the round. "I am certain it is the company Sir Isaac enjoys. Not the cards." The gentleman winked across at Miss Parr, who blushed prettily.

Sir Isaac said nothing, but his eyes glittered at Millie with pleasure. His ruse was working. Of course he was pleased. He had laid down the first card this time, a high card the other couple could not possibly beat without a trump. Millie put down the lower card in her possession, and Miss Parr did the same.

"You see? We won that one." Millie sat a little taller in her chair, though she knew she had no right to be pleased. He'd had the trick for them with his Queen of Spades.

"That we did." He flashed a smile she barely caught from around his cards. He held them up close in his hand, tapping his forefinger on the backs of them without any purpose to the movement. After they had sat, Millie wondered if he could manage the cards one-handed. Of course, he'd proven himself perfectly adept at gathering the cards and fanning them in his hand; he even played without having to put them down to select a single card.

Millie pursed her lips and put her left hand in her lap, taking up the cards only in her right. Simple.

When her turn came, she attempted to do as Isaac had, using only her thumb to push the card she wished to play up in the fan of the hand. Three cards came up. She frowned and tried to lower the two she did not wish to access, only to have a card at the edge of her hand drop to the table, face-up.

"Bother," she muttered, laying the whole hand down and playing the unfortunate card that had already been revealed to all.

"Not so easy as it looks, is it?" The corners of Isaac's eyes crinkled. "Still, valiant effort, Miss Wedgewood."

Millie blushed and very nearly stuck her tongue out at him.

Mr. Ashford dropped his left hand to the arm of his chair. "I bet I can manage it better."

Miss Parr, not to be left out, did the same. "How long did it take you to manage playing with one hand, Sir Isaac?"

"I have no idea." He thumbed his next card easily into the pile, without revealing the rest of his hand to them as Mr. Ashford did a moment later. "My friends were patient with me as I practiced. That is all I remember of it now."

Millie inadvertently dropped another card, but face-down. She frowned at it and played a different one before trying to return it to her hand. "I cannot fathom the amount of patience you must have exercised. I have seen you ride, manage all your utensils at meals, hold a baby, and now play cards."

"Hold a baby?" Mr. Ashford smirked. "I had no idea you were domestic, Sir Isaac."

Isaac shrugged one shoulder. "My nephew is a fine lad. I have no objection to entertaining him. I quite enjoy it."

"It is my opinion," Millie added, slanting a mocking glare at Mr. Ashford, "that a man is never so handsome as when he proves himself kind to women, children, and animals."

Miss Parr tipped her delicate nose in the air. "I quite agree."

"I shall have to make use of my own nieces and nephews then." Mr. Ashford sighed deeply, then dropped his entire hand of cards. He muttered a less than appropriate word, causing Miss Parr to blush and giggle.

Millie studied the card Mr. Ashford played, then looked to Sir Isaac. Did he wish for her to lay down a lower card? Had he a trump card? When all he did was raise his eyebrows at her, giving her no indication of what he wished, she glared at him and put down the highest card she had.

Miss Parr swiftly covered it with the smallest possible trump. "We win this one again, unless you have a higher trump card, Sir Isaac."

"Alas, I do not." He played a throwaway card of the wrong suit entirely. Millie's shoulder dropped.

"I am the worst of all Whist players. Do forgive my ineptitude, Sir Isaac."

"Only if you promise you will play chess with me after." He tipped his head in the direction of a chessboard near the window overlooking the dark gardens. "Or do you claim to be the worst of all chess players, too?"

Millie played her second to last card. "My father regularly outmaneuvers me in less than ten minutes."

"Chess is such a dull game," Miss Parr muttered.

"What games do you enjoy, Miss Wedgewood?" Sir Isaac asked, not even batting an eye when Mr. Ashford claimed the pile of cards for their partnership. "Which do you win?"

Millie put down her last card, already knowing they'd lost. "Badminton."

"We won." Miss Parr cheerfully counted out their tricks.

"Bad luck, Sir Isaac." Mr. Ashford grinned and jerked his head to the chessboard. "Are you two off to play at kings and queens?"

Isaac rose from his chair and came around to help Millie from hers. "Perhaps. I might ask about a possible game of badminton instead."

Millie took his arm and the two of them walked slowly to the window, though Isaac made no move to the table and chairs set aside for the chessboard. The room buzzed with conversation and activity, yet Millie sensed a few stares upon them. They both turned to the window, the better to speak without anyone knowing what they said.

"Are you well?" Isaac asked, his voice rich and warm.

"Well enough. Lady Olivia did not believe me when we spoke earlier, when I told her you had feelings for me. But perhaps when she comes into the room and sees us...."

"I intend to make certain she cannot doubt my feelings for you." Isaac's crooked grin made him positively dashing.

"You mean you are not already acting?" she asked, leaning a little toward him. "Dear me. We are in for a show."

He chuckled but did not say more on the subject. He released her arm and leaned his left shoulder against the windowpane. "What do you wish to do tomorrow? I intend to take you away from this house as often as possible. Perhaps you would care to ride with me?"

Millie's heart accepted the invitation before she could voice it, with the way it picked up in tempo. It wasn't good to give in. Isaac was playing a role. He was a good friend, nothing more. "I would enjoy that. Tomorrow evening there will be a musical performance. Will you come?"

"Are you performing?"

"No."

He narrowed his eyes at her. "Are you not a talented performer?"

"I sing well enough." She stepped a little closer, lowering her voice still more. "And I play the harp, but Lady Olivia will not suffer anyone to play upon her instrument."

"Is that so?" His eyes brightened, undoubtedly with mischief. "Esther has a harp. Perhaps I will convince her to bring it."

"You horrid man. You must do no such thing. What an insult to my hosts." Millie tried to hide her amusement, looking over her shoulder at the room to be certain no one heard, and she caught sight of the viscount standing in a corner at the opposite side of the room, speaking with the marquess and Lord Neil. "I have no wish to perform for these people."

Isaac's eyebrows furrowed, and he followed her gaze with his. "I cannot say that I blame you. This room is full of disagreeable sorts."

Millie shuddered and turned away before Lord Carning caught her stare. "Thank goodness you are here."

His eyes met hers, and she caught a flicker of emotion in them. Tenderness. Relief. Something of that nature which caused his shoulders to relax and a smile to return to his handsome face. "I am pleased to be of service to you, Miss Wedgewood."

The air in the room shifted, growing stifling before Millie could offer her gratitude to Sir Isaac yet again. She and he turned as one to the entrance, where Lady Olivia stood regally framed by the wide doorway.

"Are we supposed to applaud?" Millie asked, taking in the woman's haughty pose.

"Thankfully, I am excused from ever doing so on that woman's account." He raised his right hand and his eyebrows, rather comically drawing her attention to his inability to clap hands together.

A laugh escaped Millie, and she did not cover it quite soon enough for Lady Olivia to miss the sound. The daughter of the marquess descended upon them, fan already cutting through the air.

"Sir Isaac. Miss Wedgewood. You are not playing any games. Are our offerings not good enough for you?" she asked, eyelashes beating fiercely. "Not tempting enough?" Though she had addressed them both, the woman kept her gaze upon Sir Isaac. Measuring him. Perhaps reminding him of what she had offered in the past. What she may yet offer.

Millie resisted the urge to be sick, but only just.

"The diversions in your home are well known." The lack of

emotion in Sir Isaac's voice bordered on rude. "I have found Miss Wedgewood's company preferable to the other entertainments."

If Millie hadn't been made privy to the history between the two people before her, their veiled meanings would certainly make her curious. When Lady Olivia's face turned a dark red, and one of her eyes twitched involuntarily, Millie hastily constructed an innocent expression before the woman rounded upon her.

"And you, Miss Wedgewood. Do you enjoy the company more than the games?"

There was hidden meaning there, too.

"The games are most diverting, my lady." Though she pressed her lips together tightly, Millie gritted her teeth after speaking, hard enough they might crack.

Lady Olivia was called by another guest. She gave Sir Isaac one last dangerous glare before turning her back on them.

Millie still held her breath when she felt Isaac's hand at the small of her back. He touched her gently, where no one might see the reassurance he offered. "We will beat her at her game, Millie. I promise."

She nodded once. "Perhaps you ought to excuse yourself now. I will speak to your sister." She had spotted the countess in conversation with other matrons near a table of punch. "Mr. Weston has just joined a game of cards."

Isaac took her measure before he agreed. "Stay with Essie. I did not tell her your secrets, but I did say you might need a friend this evening." He bowed, then left the room by walking along its edges, stopping to speak occasionally to card players, drawing little attention to himself.

Millie did the same, in the opposite direction, winding her way to Lady Inglewood. Esther welcomed her into the conversation at once, which centered upon the thought of using one's artistic skills to improve the home.

It took a great deal of Millie's discipline to not check the doorway, or the timepiece on the mantel, while Isaac was away. If he were caught, things might go badly for them both. But it was easier, far easier, to stand in a room with the viscount knowing Isaac was nearby.

THOUGH NOT INTIMATELY FAMILIAR WITH THE Alderton house, Isaac knew enough to find the guest quarters. He had barely stepped into the corridor when a door opened, and Sarah stepped out. He greeted her with a smile and tip of the head, hoping to set her at ease.

She did not seem to need his reassurance. "All the way down the hall, sir. Last door on the left. I've been watching it all evening. Mr. Weston's man is downstairs, enjoying a drink." She wrinkled her nose in distaste.

Isaac gave her a nod of understanding before making his way to the indicated door. She followed, a few steps behind. Then she took out a little box of sewing needles. "You go on, sir. If I see anyone coming, I plan to drop the box and make a fuss over picking up the pieces inside. The servant's stair is there." She pointed to a nondescript door down a small turn in the corridor. "No one will think it strange for me to be here. If you need to hide, I'll be especially clumsy."

Isaac gave her an appraising glance. "You sound as though you have done this before."

"Not at all, sir. Merely thought it through." She pointed to the door. "You better get a move on."

Bossy little thing. He did as she said, impressed by the servant yet again.

The guest room had a lamp burning low, which he immediately turned up to chase away the shadows. He shuddered, hating the confined, unfamiliar place. He had almost rather return to the gathering of people, though crowded rooms bothered him. Somehow, it was not as terrible as usual.

Millie made it bearable.

He paused, staring into the open drawer of a table, that thought catching him by surprise.

Yes, he had found himself attracted to her. Yes, he wanted to help her. But had she, somehow, helped him instead?

Isaac turned his search elsewhere. What sort of man traveled with any secrets he might possess? He doubted there was a thing in Mr. Weston's room that would be useful to anyone wishing to threaten him. But perhaps, as an honest man, it was naive of him to believe such a thing.

After going through the room, even checking beneath the pillow, mattress, and bed itself, Isaac admitted defeat. He stepped out into the hall to find Sarah still waiting, box of needles in hand.

"Nothing?" she whispered.

"Not a thing." Isaac gave her a reassuring smile. "Never fear. We will think of something."

The servant nodded thoughtfully, then dipped a curtsy and started to walk away. She paused after a few steps and turned. "Would you be willing to play lookout for me, sir, while I check Lady Olivia's room?"

What a brazen suggestion. But not a bad idea. Isaac considered, then removed his watch to check the time.

"Not this night, but perhaps another. I cannot be gone any longer."

"Of course, sir." She curtsied again and went to the door where she had been waiting for him, slipping inside. Was that Millie's room? Most likely.

He found his way back to the main room, where people mingled, laughing. Most now had cups of wine in hand. Millie stood by Esther, as he had instructed. He approached with a broad grin and shook his head the tiniest bit when she questioned him with no more than the lift of her chin.

Her shoulders drooped, but otherwise her disappointment did not show.

Somehow, Isaac would extract her from the situation. And enjoy her company all the more after.

Chapter Nineteen

I saac arrived in an open carriage at eleven o'clock in the morning. He had every intention of whisking Millie away with him and not returning her until absolutely necessary. The more time she spent with him, the better. He needed to study her more. He wanted to determine what quality she possessed that so put him at ease.

Yet that was not entirely the case, he reflected, as he waited in the foyer for the servants to locate Miss Wedgewood. He was at ease with her, yet sometimes when he thought on her, when they had kissed, it was as though he had been through an explosion a second time.

Things were changing, all because he had met Millie.

"Sir Isaac?"

He turned on his heels and rocked back, tone dry. "Lord Neil."

The lordling smirked. "Always a pleasure to see you."

The two had decided, long before Lord Neil's advances upon Esther, to tactfully dislike each other. It was not a spoken agreement, merely understood. They had exchanged more words between them in the past week than in the previous ten years together.

Isaac barely inclined his head. "Kind of you to say."

"You are here for Miss Wedgewood. She told me of your plans to take a ride through the countryside." He pointed out the front door. "I think she meant to wait for you outside. Did you not see her?"

Isaac shook his head, puzzled despite himself. "I did not. The butler did not even suggest she might be without."

Lord Neil shrugged and went to the staircase. "Perhaps she walked along the side of the house to the gardens. She went out some time ago." He did not bother turning as he spoke, but Sir Isaac bowed to the man's back anyway. He would remember his manners, even if Lord Neil did not.

Outside again, Isaac walked along the house to where it turned a corner into gardens that still maintained the stricter, geometric style of generations past. Esther had begun to change Inglewood's gardens into the more wild sort that many of artistic sensibilities preferred.

Which did Millie prefer? Clean lines of clipped hedges, or wildly swaying grasses and jumbled ivy?

He wound his way through a few shrubs and rose bushes, tempted to call out but resisting. He would come upon her soon or go back to the house and wait for the servants to run her to ground.

Then he saw someone else already had.

Millie stood next to a gleaming marble fountain, as pale as the stone itself, facing down the viscount, Lord Carning. Her small fists were clenched, her chin tilted up, and she glared fiercely at the peer. The man himself smirked down upon her, standing far too close.

What was it about the woman that attracted rakes and scoundrels?

Isaac quickened his step, though he maintained an aloof expression. "Miss Wedgewood, here you are at last. I have combed the entirety of the gardens looking for you."

Lord Carning stepped back, and Millie jerked around to face

him with an expression upon her face that pained him. She appeared afraid. And she clutched something in her hand—a long, slender object. A pin?

What had Carning done to frighten her?

There was no use trying to figure it out with the man himself standing there, smirking.

"Lord Carning." Isaac bowed when he came close enough, and the viscount returned the gesture gracefully. Then Isaac extended his hand, rather than his arm, to Millie.

Let the viscount see that she had friends.

She took his hand at once, allowing him to draw her close. "Are you ready for our ride?" he asked, voice pitched lower, almost intimate. He ignored the viscount's expression of interest. The man could go to the blazes for the look of fear he had put upon Millie's beautiful face.

"I am. Thank you for collecting me." Her fingers twined through his.

"Good day, Lord Carning." Isaac barely tipped his head this time, then whisked Millie away the moment she made her curtsy. The viscount did not say a word, though he stared after them.

Millie's hand trembled in Isaac's grasp, and he quickly drew her closer, the inside of her forearm flush against his. "Are you well?"

"Well enough." She smiled at him, still pale, her eyes shining with pain. "Please, get me away from here."

They were at his carriage, and he handed her up with swiftness. The moment she sat, she jammed the long pin back into her hat fiercely, as though she rather wished she was shoving it into something else. Perhaps someone else.

She already wore a dress, hat, gloves, and appeared entirely ready for the diversion. The diversion turned escape. He walked around quickly and found his seat with all speed before lifting the reins.

"I will drive you to the sea." With a quick flick of his wrist, the horses jolted forward, and they were moving away from the house at a fast clip.

The further they drove, the more Millie relaxed, until she leaned upon his left shoulder.

It felt natural to have her there, nearly tucked against his side. His only regret was that he did not have the ability to put an arm around her. Not that it would have been appropriate. But it would have felt natural, right, to hold her closer.

She did not seem to mind, did not even seem to notice or care, that the arm she leaned against did not possess an elbow, a crook to tuck her arm through, or a hand to hold.

He looked down at the top of her bonnet, barely able to glimpse more than a few curls and the tip of her nose from beneath its brim. What was she thinking?

Millie sat up abruptly. "I am sorry. I do not mean to be so cloying. You must think me weaker than a kitten." She rubbed at her eyes with her gloved fingers. "I am exhausted, Isaac. I thought this would all be so easy."

He missed the weight of her head upon his shoulder. "I do not think you weak, though I certainly question your decisions prior to your confession." He kept the words gentle, not accusing. She was distressed enough, he need not belabor that point with her. "What did Carning want?"

"Carning was the man engaged to my sister. And the man who attacked me."

Isaac turned to her, startled by that pronouncement. "What?" He had not drawn that conclusion from her stories.

"Years ago," she said with a dismissive wave.

Isaac pulled the reins, halting the horse pulling the gig, and turned fully to her. He arrested her with his gaze, the depths of his feeling unconcealed. "I do not care if it was this morning or a dozen years ago. He ought to be called out. Drawn and quartered. Publicly flogged. Why did you not tell me that he was the man? You should not spend another moment in that house."

Millie folded her hands in her lap, most primly. "That is all very easily said, Isaac, but not practical. Where do I go? Lady Olivia would not allow me to leave without doing her bidding first. Lord

Carning is as capable of ruining my family as ever he was before. Lord Carning is a peer, the grandson of a duke. An heir. An accusation toward him would be no more productive than digging a tunnel with a teaspoon. The teaspoon will only bend and break."

"I am not a teaspoon," he muttered. "And he is just a man."

"You could not even strike him without being brought up on charges." The exhaustion she spoke of was evident in her tone. "And then my name would be bandied about all over again, a joke for men at their gambling tables, gossip over teacups. There is no justice for him, Isaac. Only trouble for me."

Isaac stared at her, unable to argue. Though he wished to tell her she was wrong. Instead, he started the horse forward again. Without looking at her, he asked, "What was he saying to distress you when I arrived?"

He heard the slow intake of her breath, saw the way she shuddered before she spoke. "He reminded me of the past. Nothing more."

Isaac did not press further. He sensed she would say no more, and he had no wish to upset her. "Then we will not speak of the past at all. Only of the present." They continued down the road toward Inglewood and the sea, a path as familiar to Isaac as his own shadow. "You were quite terrible at Whist last night."

Millie glared at him. "I did warn you. I almost never win."

"I admit, I did not mind. Watching your countenance as you attempted to read my intent upon my face—it was as amusing as watching a play. Frowning, smiling, narrowing your pretty eyes." He mimicked one of her expressions from the previous evening, furrowing his brow, pursing his lips, and narrowing his eyes.

Millie smiled at last, though with only the barest amusement. "I did not look like *that*."

Isaac shrugged. "You did."

"Sir, you are contradicting a lady. That is terribly rude."

"The lady ought not tell falsehoods if she wishes me to agree with her." He mimicked her expression again, this time drawing a laugh from her. "There. You know I am right. Though I will admit that you are a great deal prettier than I am, so the expression was not so terrible upon you as it is upon me."

"Now you are just hoping I will call you handsome and soothe your vanity." She scoffed and folded her arms. "I refuse to fall prey to your wishes, Isaac."

"Positively unfair of you." He guided the horse down the lane to Inglewood. It was the fastest way to the beach, to pass through Esther and Silas's lands, and of course they would not mind. "We have been invited to take refreshment with Esther this afternoon."

"We have?" Millie cocked her head to one side. "And what does she make of all the time you spend in my company?"

That sobered him. When he had returned his sister to her home the night before, after an evening of sitting as near to Millie as he could without crossing the lines of appropriate behavior, Essie had been gleeful. His sister talked of nothing else until they parted company. If no one else believed Isaac smitten with Millicent Wedgewood, his sister certainly did.

"Exactly what we hope everyone thinks." He gave her an encouraging smile. "That I am falling in love with you."

Apparently, that was not the thing to say to please Millie. She turned away abruptly, her bonnet obscuring her lovely face from view. "Will she be terribly angry when she learns the truth? When I leave and nothing more is said?"

They crested a hill before the carriage path dipped down the beach, and Isaac halted the horse at the top. The beach spread as far as they could see, in either direction, and the North Sea laid before them. Isaac took in the beautiful sight, the shining silver of the water and brightness of the sand.

"Millie." He had to get the words right. Had to indicate just enough interest without leaving himself open for pain. "I have wondered, when all of this is over, if we can satisfy Lady Olivia, if you might be willing to see me again."

"See you again?" He could barely hear her over the sound of the waves crashing upon the shore, or his heart thudding in his ears. "After everything?"

He nodded and forced more cheer in his voice than he felt. "Perhaps I could call upon you in London. Or you could come back, visit Esther. I know she wishes to spend more time in your company."

"Only because she thinks the two of us might enter into a courtship." Millie turned her gaze to the sea, closing her eyes as she took in a breath of the briny air. "My family will still have a great deal of recovering ahead of us. Even if I am invited to parties and events, even if my mother is welcomed back to the circles that closed to her, there will be a lot of work ahead of me."

Isaac had called himself a fool before, but even he could not misunderstand what Millie tried to tell him. Polite as her words may be, her rationale pragmatic and straightforward, she was really telling him, "no, I will not see you again."

Despite telling himself that he had known it was a ridiculous notion to entertain, Isaac's heart cracked. He practically heard the sound as one would a branch snapping in two, or a vase dropped upon a marble floor.

He hid the pain behind a smile and a laugh, as he had when he first returned from war. "That is a shame. I find I enjoy your company. Even if you are a terrible partner at Whist."

Millie took his words as permission to smile again. "Are we going to sit upon this hill forever, or will we drive along the beach as you promised?"

Isaac's good humor did not falter as he drove her down the beach, then back again to Esther's hospitality. He laughed with Millie over his nephew's antics. Ignored Esther's knowing glance. Escaped to Silas's study and put Millie out of his mind until the time came to take her back to the Alderton house.

Until he was safely in his own home, in his room with his back pressed to the closed door, Isaac did not examine his heart.

He had no chance at making her love him. Millie had made that clear when she told him of her whole plan, of her need to reenter Society. Of course she would wish for the most advantageous marriage possible. And what was he?

A crippled baronet, with holdings that barely provided enough to remain self-sustaining.

Isaac went to the mirror which hung over a chest of drawers, staring at himself. He unbuttoned his coat and tossed it upon the bed. Then pulled off his cravat and threw it to the floor.

He stood before the glass, the white sleeve of his shirt hanging loosely on the left.

It wasn't just the arm, though that was what people saw. There were scars lining that side of his body from the shrapnel, from the blast that took his arm and the lives of men standing near him. Scars along his torso, his hip, his legs. Then the invisible scars upon his mind and heart, slicing their way across his dreams.

He would never be whole again. What woman would want him? Not someone like Millie, forced into a corner and fighting her way back to the top of Society's battlements. Little fox she might be, but the woman had ambition. And he did not even like to stand in crowded ballrooms.

Broken. He was broken.

Isaac undressed to his waist and forced himself to look in the mirror, to look at where his left arm ought to attach to the rest of him. How had he deluded himself into thinking he had a chance at a proper romance with that physical reminder ever present?

Tears burned in his eyes, but he refused to let them free. Refused weakness.

A drink would help. But that was the coward's way out. Essie had made that clear to him years ago when their mother had died. He could not go that route.

Each of his friends had found and claimed a love match. Their happiness had taught him to yearn for the same. But it could not be.

A knock on the door interrupted his morbid, pitying thoughts.

"Come."

Harper, the valet, entered. "Sir Isaac, do you wish to dress for the evening?" Harper eyed his undressed state with polite confusion.

The musical performance. He had that to go to directly after his dinner.

Isaac ran a hand across his chin, feeling the stubble coming in. He needed to shave. Dress again. Compose himself. "Yes, of course. My dark blue coat tonight, I think. And the silver waistcoat."

His valet nodded and began his work, speaking all the while of mundane things. Asking about cravats, stick-pins, shoes. They worked through the motions together, and Isaac approved the product of his valet's work at the end.

Still, he did not quite meet his own eyes in the mirror. He could not allow himself another moment of weakness while Millie still needed his help.

Chapter Twenty

My Dearest Daughter,

Your letter has left me most distressed. Your father and I quite depend upon you to set things to rights. Surely you are safe under the protection of the Marquess. You must remain and see this thing through, as you agreed....

Millie folded the letter, running her fingers over the crease. She walked from one end of her guest bedroom to the other. The letter had been penned before her mother knew the worst of it. Millie had written to her parents after Mr. Weston's attack.

She could not return home.

The night before, during the musical performances, Isaac had played his part admirably. He sat on her left, his sister on Millie's right, during each exhibit of musical talent. Isaac bent to whisper in her ear his thoughts on each performer, some of them not entirely charitable remarks, but anyone who watched the two of them had no way of knowing how intimate or casual their conversation.

Despite the unremarkable evening, Millie had barely slept. Her nightmares were growing worse with her repeated exposure to Lord Carning. Mr. Weston's unexpected advances likely contributed to the overly distressing dreams, too. Most of the night she dreamed of being hunted, running through trees with hounds baying, with hands grabbing at her, as though she was the prey they chased.

Another day of the house party upon them, Millie did not have much time to accomplish the tasks set by Lady Olivia. Her mother's letter made everything worse. Her exhaustion had drained her emotionally. There was no escape.

"Miss?" Sarah stepped into the room, her eyes bright. "Sir Isaac is downstairs. To call on you." The maid bounced on her toes as she made the pronouncement. Then she hurried to the small wardrobe and snatched up Millie's favorite bonnet. "You must take him for a walk in the gardens, miss. You will have privacy there."

Millie looked down at the letter in her hands, turning it over again. "Sarah. You know there is nothing between Sir Isaac and myself except friendship."

Sarah approached with the bonnet and a pair of gloves. "Nonsense, miss. The way that man looks at you, there is something more." She put the bonnet upon Millie's head without waiting for leave to do so.

Catching her maid's hands in her own, Millie fixed her with a stare. "There cannot be anything more, Sarah. Sir Isaac plays a part in order to help me. I play a part to get out of this house with my honor still intact. My parents have expectations—"

"They must want you to be happy, miss," Sarah said, staring at Millie without comprehension. "Mr. Wedgewood always says how important it is to him that you and your mother are happy."

"Emmeline is happy." Millie winced when she heard the sharp edge to her tone. "My sister did what made her happy, and they have not said her name since. They have not spoken of her. They do not want my happiness if it means their ruin."

A rebellious gleam appeared in Sarah's eyes, as though she meant to argue her point, but she abruptly lowered her gaze. "As you say, miss."

Hurting Sarah's feelings hadn't been Millie's intention, but before she could make her apology for speaking too harshly, the maid curtsied and fled the room. Millie took a moment to spear her bonnet with a pin, keeping it in place, and went to find Isaac. She would have to ask Sarah for her pardon later.

Isaac waited in the main foyer, studying a suit of armor near the grand doors. He looked up when she reached the top of the staircase, smiling in greeting. Millie hurried down to him.

He bowed to her. "I thought we might take a walk this morning, Miss Wedgewood."

"I had the very same idea." She took his arm at once. That was when she realized she did not wear any gloves. Sarah must have kept them when she made her abrupt departure from the room. Though walking about with ungloved hands was not the worst of sins, she still winced the moment she realized it.

Once they were out in the sunlight, Isaac spoke to her quietly. "Are you well, Millie? There is something not quite right about you today." He tipped his head to meet her gaze. "You smile, but you feel far away."

"I am sorry. I do not mean to be a puzzle to you." She sighed, but the sigh led to a deep yawn. She covered her mouth with the back of her hand. "Oh, I *am* sorry. I have not slept well of late."

"You apologize too much." He examined her face closely, then his eyes swept the front of the house. "No one is watching. Here, come with me. I have just the thing."

"Just the thing for what?" she asked, lengthening her step to keep up with his pace. He almost seemed excited.

"A nap."

Millie laughed. "What? Outside?"

"Precisely. The perfect place for someone suffering from nightmares."

"I never said nightmares—"

"You did not need to." He adjusted his arm, taking her hand. "As one who suffers regularly from horrid dreams, it is easy enough to recognize the symptoms in another."

Of course. His nightmares of the war. But her bad dreams were nothing like that. Nothing truly horrible had happened to her. She ought to give him sympathy, not receive it from him. She opened her mouth again, to decline his well-meant kindness, but stopped when they entered a stand of trees not far from the house.

"Here we are. What do you think?" Isaac stopped them before a net hanging from two trees. "The marquess installed it here years ago, after he returned from a trip to India. I had one during one of my campaigns on the Continent. Best sleep I had during the whole of the war."

"A hammock." She had heard of them, of course. Sailors slept in canvas hammocks aboard ships. Poorer families installed them in houses, for children to sleep one on top of another. Had she ever heard of one like this before? At a country estate?

"I have been sorely tempted to replace my bed with one of these." He gave the netting a push. "They rock in the breeze, like a cradle."

"It looks rather like a net for catching fish. Or birds." And she had no particular wish to be caught. Millie ventured closer. "How does one even use it?"

Isaac opened the hammock, raising one side high in the air. Then he turned, still holding it up, and moved backward as though he meant to swing. Once his backside was in the net, he leaned into it and let the net take him. Though nothing about his maneuver appeared elegant, as he shifted and finally settled, she found herself intrigued.

"You slept in one of those?"

"I did. Comfortably," he reminded her, looking up from his place in the net. Once he was in it, the sides of the netting cradled him rather than closing upon him. "Once you master the trick of getting inside, it isn't so bad. Here. Try." He sat up, threw his legs out, and stood.

"I will be caught in it, all tangled like a fish." Millie hesitantly touched one side of the dangerous thing.

"Here. I will hold it on this side for you." He took a firm grasp of the other end. "Back into it, as I did."

Millie eyed the net dubiously. "Very well. If I fall, I will hold you responsible."

"Noted." Isaac gave her his crooked smile, that dimple appearing in his cheek.

She mimicked what Isaac had done, and he held his end of the net steady. Millie closed her eyes tightly, up until the moment she pulled her legs inside with her, reclining in the netting. She opened one eye, then the other, to see the canopy of trees above.

"There you are. Perfectly situated." Isaac stood over her, releasing the side of the net slowly. "Comfortable?"

She wiggled her shoulders and her eyebrows raised. "Yes. What a surprise. Except for this." Her bonnet folded oddly against the net. She pulled the pin out and took off the bonnet, holding it up.

Isaac took it from her, then walked to a tree a few feet away and sat beneath its shade. "Now you may nap, and I will guard your rest."

"You will sit there. On the ground."

"Yes."

She frowned. "While I sleep?"

"Yes."

Millie folded her hands over her stomach and watched as the leaves above her trembled in the breeze. "Why?" Her heart sped as she asked, though it had no reason for excitement. The question was simple. A good question, too.

"Because you face a hard thing." His voice was quiet, carrying through the stillness of nature quite well. "And one should not face battle when tired. It impairs judgement. Slows reactions."

"Were you tired when you went to battle?" she asked, eyes still open. The green above soothed her, the netting of the hammock holding her in a gentle embrace. One could sleep quite well under such circumstances.

"Most of the time." He sighed, a heavy sound, the weight of all he left unsaid settling in her heart. How often had he marched into the night on a general's orders? Or laid awake, anticipating battle the next morning? Had he feared for his life or thought himself immortal until he took injury? They were questions she had no right to ask. No man would answer such things, either.

"I am sorry for that," she said instead. "Did you have nightmares for a long time after?"

"They have never stopped."

She closed her eyes, aching for him. They said nothing for a time, and the birds in nearby trees began to sing and call to one another again. She did not sway much in the hanging bed, but the summer breeze caressed her arms and cheeks and brushed her hair away from her eyes.

When careful fingertips brushed against her forehead, moving her hair back, Millie blinked awake. Had she slept an hour or only a few minutes? She could not quite tell. The sun was no longer bright with the new morning's light. Isaac stood over her, his hand upon her cheek.

Millie smiled up at him, warmth from sleep and from his touch mingling into a contentment she had never felt before. "Isaac. What time is it?"

There was a look, a warmth in his deep brown eyes that intrigued her. "Time to wake." He withdrew his hand and held the net again. She saw her bonnet pinned between his left side and arm. "Be careful."

Millie struggled to sit up, putting one leg outside the net most indecorously. "Getting out is more difficult—"

She gasped as the net seemed to give way, flipping her out upon the one leg unprepared to take her full weight while the other foot tangled somehow. She staggered forward, one hand holding to the rope and the other grasping Isaac's arm.

Without quite understanding how it happened, Millie abruptly found herself upon the ground, one foot still caught in the air, and Isaac beneath her. Laughing. The man laughed, as though he had never laughed before.

She had certainly never heard him laugh like that. Deep, and long, and then gasping. His arm went around her waist, and she pulled her foot one last time. She freed herself from the net, but her knee came down with such force into Isaac's leg that he cut off his laugh with a groan.

"I am sorry," she said, pushing herself up with both hands. One of the hands was on the ground, the other on his chest, so she pushed the breath out of him as well. They were a tangle of skirts, arms, legs, and it was all the dratted hammock's fault.

Millie looked down at him, uncertain if she dare try to move again. Their gazes caught, a wry smile upon his handsome face. "Millie."

It was only her name. He had said it many times. She had heard it her whole life. But everything changed when he said it this time, with the way he said it, as though it were a precious word. A declaration.

Her lips parted, she meant to speak. To ask him something.

Then she bent and kissed him instead. Carefully. Tenderly. Asking him something after all, but without using words. He touched her face, accepted the press of her lips and returned each token she offered with one of his own.

Nothing else mattered. Nothing in the whole world. Just Isaac.

Then she withdrew, sitting upon the ground, looking down at him. Isaac kept his gaze directed upward when she moved away, staring up into the trees. He dropped his hand to his chest, just over his heart.

Did he feel it, too? That tugging, that longing, that made her want to curl into his side and stay forever.

"Please. Do not do that again." Desperation filled each word.

The sweet fog that had wrapped around her thoughts, shutting out everything but Isaac, disappeared at once, chased away by the harsh winds of reality.

He remained upon the ground still, as though he had been felled in battle. Indeed, he spoke as a doomed man. "Not unless you mean to give me hope."

Millie picked up her bonnet, where it had fallen and been crushed. Ruined completely. She twisted one of the ribbons around her fingers. "Hope for what, Isaac?"

He grunted as he sat up, facing her, still there upon the ground. "I have never met anyone like you, Millicent Wedgewood. Prospective villainess." He shoved his gloved hand through his hair, his hat somewhere on the ground behind them. "I could love you."

Her gaze shifted up to his, and she quite forgot to breathe for several long moments. "You could?" Her heart pounded anew in her chest, but its hopeful rhythm did not last long.

"Yes. Enough to marry you." There was pain, so much pain, in his crooked smile. "But I do not think you want that." He stood and turned his back on her, going after the missing hat. Millie lowered her eyes again to her bonnet, the ribbons crushed in her grasp.

"No. I suppose I do not. Or, rather, I suppose I cannot." Everything would end for her family. Lady Olivia would revenge herself upon Millie, with Lord Carning's help.

Was this why Emmeline had run away, hidden from Society, without regard for who she hurt? Because she had fallen in love?

Millie loved Isaac. She saw that at last. Sarah had been right, as she always was. Isaac could tuck Millie away in the country and love her forever and always, and she would be happy.

But Lady Olivia would surely make it difficult for them to ever enter Society again. Lord Carning would spread rumors, too, whispering in ears as he did before.

Just the same, Millie could not do what Lady Olivia wanted. She could not hurt Isaac. Never, in a thousand years; she did not know how to even pretend to hurt him.

"I need to go." The words slipped from her lips, and she stumbled to her feet to obey her own pronouncement. "Thank you. For everything." Her hands shook, but she forced a smile when she met his eyes again. "Good afternoon, Isaac."

Millie did not believe in dramatics, so she did not run. She walked. Slowly and deliberately walked away from him. The short nap had helped, though the kissing had muddled her thoughts again. What was she to do?

She passed servants in the house. They either did not notice the state of her hair and clothing or they were exceptionally well-trained not to react to such things. Or perhaps they did not care.

She stepped into her room, and Sarah stood there. The maid stretched out her hand, a slip of paper in her grasp. "I know where your sister is, miss."

Chapter Twenty-One

I saac paced the nursery, his nephew cradled close to his chest sleepily sucking on his two middle fingers. The baby's eyes were closed, and he cooed to himself sweetly as he fell into a doze. The warmth, the soft infant sounds, of baby Isaac soothed his uncle more than anyone's words possibly could.

What was it about children, the tiniest in particular, that made one view life differently?

"I heard you were skulking in my nursery again." Esther came up beside him as softly as she had spoken, her son's only reaction to smile sleepily upon hearing his mother's voice.

"I cannot help that my favorite person resides in your nursery." He settled into a gentle rocking motion, swaying like a tree in a breeze.

"You ought to get married, Isaac. You will make such a wonderful father. Attentive. Doting. All your children will be spoiled rather terribly." Esther kissed her baby's head to punctuate her remark.

Isaac did not even try to make light of his sister's teasing. His mind rested heavily upon matters too close to his heart. "My nephew will be the only child in my life for some time yet."

"You sound as though you do not enjoy that idea. I will make certain my son does not take your remark amiss." Esther settled in a chair near the nursery's small hearth. "What happened, Isaac? I have not seen you in a bleak mood like this in some time."

"Bleak?" He came to sit in the chair near hers, keeping his nephew cradled close to his chest. He lowered himself slowly enough that the baby did not wake from his gentle slumber. "I protest your use of that word, Essie."

"It fits. You certainly carry on as a hopeless man. What is it that has upset you?"

Isaac leaned his head back against the small chair, meant more for a woman the size of his sister or a nursery maid than someone of his stature. "Nightmares. That is all."

"I am sorry those still trouble you." Her brows drew together in sympathy with his words. "Would it help if you slept somewhere else? I do hate that you are in that old house all alone."

"There are a dozen servants nearby at all times," Isaac countered. "I am not alone."

"Servants are not the same as family." Esther tapped the arm of the chair, studying him nearly as intently as she had when she'd painted his portrait. "You dine alone, you spend your days alone, and you go to bed alone with your nightmares."

"Essie." Isaac glowered at her. "I am a bachelor. All of those things are quite normal for one in my position."

"You are not like other bachelors. You have no family to distract you, but you do not go away to parties and entertainments. You spend all your time shut up in your house. Never going out into the neighborhood unless I insist upon your escort. I worry for you."

"Because you are a kind sister. But you need not trouble yourself."

"What do you think of Miss Wedgewood?" Esther asked abruptly. "You seemed terribly concerned for her before."

"Your evaluation of the situation was correct. I cannot abide to see someone in distress if I might be capable of offering assistance." He kept his eyes upon the sleeping baby, watching as the child's chest rose and fell. "I wish to help her. She means nothing more to me." Little Isaac's fingers had fallen out of his mouth, but the baby occasionally made small sucking motions with his lips.

Esther said nothing for a time. The peaceful silence was deceptive, however. Isaac knew his sister well enough to sense the way her thoughts churned before she spoke again. "Isaac. I think you have grown to care for Miss Wedgewood. I have not seen you smile as you have in her company since before you left for the war, and I don't think I've ever seen you as distressed as you were when you feared for her well-being."

Isaac shifted in the chair, but not enough to disturb the child in his arm. "I have compassion for her."

"No. You are smitten with her."

Why waste his breath arguing? Esther was right, but he would not admit it to her. He had thought on their shared kisses and nothing else for the whole of the day. Kissing her behind the church had been as much to test his feelings as to fulfill her dare. Kissing her in the grass, after her tumble from the hammock, had been her decision. One he had enjoyed, up until the moment he realized his heart was already too broken to be of any use to her.

He was too broken.

"Miss Wedgewood is chasing Society's good opinion." Isaac could state that truth with a firmness no one would argue. "I am not at all a suitable match for her."

"You are a baronet with a powerful earl as your brother-in-law. That is good enough for most hostesses in London." Essie tried to tease with her words, but when he did not even glance at her, his sister sighed. "Does she know how you feel?"

"Yes." He had as good as told her everything. *Enough to marry you. But I do not think you want that.* Millie's confirmation of his assessment had wounded him. His feelings were outside of her agenda to raise her family from the dregs of Society back to an elevated and respected position. She wanted to be someone of importance. She did not desire the title of Lady Fox, though no woman he knew would fulfill the role so well as Millie.

Esther made a sound of annoyance. A snort, truthfully, worthy of his horse. Then she came to him, bending to collect her son in her arms. "Out in the hall. I have something to say to you." She walked away with the baby, doubtless to put her son in his bed.

Isaac shrugged to himself, though what Esther might say intrigued him. His sister hadn't experienced a romance the likes of which poets or musicians would pen. Yet she was excessively happy, and very much in love, with Silas.

When he stepped out into the hall, the nursery maid waited. She curtsied and then went inside the room to see to her charge. A moment later, Esther came out and immediately linked an arm through his. "Walk with me."

"As you wish, countess," Isaac agreed with a dip of his head.

She gave him a slanted glare. "Do not think you can get out of this conversation with levity. It is high time we had this talk. You may be my older brother, but that obviously does not make you the wiser of the two of us."

Isaac walked down the steps to the first floor, not saying anything until they were on the landing. "I have never claimed wisdom, Essie. But tread lightly. I do have some experience in the world."

"I think I am qualified to give you this much advice, and as a former soldier, you will see the truth in it. Anything good in this world, especially the things and people we love, are worth the fight. Do not let your lady go without telling her of the depth of your feelings for her."

They stopped near a window overlooking the gardens. He stared outside, at the blue stretch of sky. "Your argument is intriguing, considering that the last time I fought for something I came back less one arm."

Essie gave him a gentle tug, forcing his attention to her. He looked down into her eyes, a match for his and inherited from the father neither of them had known well. "There is a risk, Isaac.

There will always be risks. When you left for war, I do not think you ever stopped to consider all the damage that might be done by your decision. The loss of your arm, the nightmares living in your head, what it meant for me to navigate the world and Society without you, they are all consequences of your decision to fight for what you believed to be the right thing."

Isaac's throat grew tight, and his heart gave a painful thud as the last fall of a stick upon a drum. "Essie—"

"However," she interrupted him with a warning glare, "good came from that decision, too. You served honorable men, those above and beneath you in rank. Silas and I married and fell in love. Now you have a nephew. A greater understanding of the hardships and losses of others are yours, too, with your own experiences. You can take what you have learned and do good in the world, with your family beside you."

"Good in the world." He shuddered. "I cannot even leave my house without the war haunting my every step."

"Yet you have, again and again, to spend time with a certain miss." Esther crossed her arms over her middle and regarded him with searching, curious eyes. "You have always been somewhat thoughtless about the feelings of others, Isaac."

He swallowed guiltily and tucked his fist behind his back. "I hate that you are right."

"Hm. You always went charging into the fray, though, when you believed someone had been wronged. At first, I thought that was all that your desire to aid Miss Wedgewood was, but I now believe it goes much deeper than that. I think you are more than smitten. I think you are falling in love with her. And I do not think she knows it, either. You must tell her, Isaac. At least let her know what she gives up if she chooses another path."

Isaac sighed. Esther did not understand and could not understand. He leaned down to place a kiss on her forehead. "Things are more complicated than you know, Essie. But I thank you for the advice. I will think upon it."

He bid her a good afternoon, then left while Esther yet wore a concerned frown. There was nothing more for him to say. Though he had found momentary peace in his sister's home he returned to the quiet loneliness of his manor. There was nothing so forlorn as the echo of his boots upon the floor. Nothing as bleak as the empty evening stretching before him.

Chapter Twenty-Two

Millie sat in the little art room, carefully putting the final touches on the box she had worked on from her first meeting with the Countess of Inglewood. The fox had turned out well. The creeping vines and flowers framing the handsome creature were graceful. The entire work was one of her best, despite the amount of anxiety in her soul as she worked.

Though there was danger in venturing away from her room, where a lock and privacy kept her away from the other houseguests, she had needed an escape. Isaac hadn't yet come to keep her company.

After that moment at the hammock, when he allowed her the smallest glimpse of his heart, she honestly did not know if he would ever return.

She had a decision to make, with the information Sarah had discovered about Emmeline. Somehow, all alone, Sarah had invaded Lady Olivia's room and found the woman's personal correspondence. Lady Olivia had found Emmeline through an acquaintance married to a London barrister. The woman had an entire web of people willing to do her favors, it would seem.

Millie pulled a sheet of paper from the small pile she had cut, to use for sketching out designs before committing them to the box in ink. Sarah did not even look up from where she sat, mending a hem in one of her own aprons.

Dipping her pen in the ink meant for the box, Millie considered a moment before writing.

My Dearest Sir Isaac,

My thoughts are muddled, swirling like mud and water, refusing to settle. I am at once grateful for all you have done, for your friendship, and regretful that we ever had to meet. Especially under such horrid circumstances.

She hesitated over that line, her eyes aching with her attempt to hold back tears. The words themselves were not eloquent, but her feelings ran deep. The letter would never reach Sir Isaac. So she poured out her heart for several silent minutes.

A knock on the door interrupted her pointless writing. Millie crumpled the paper in her hand and turned toward the door, calling her permission to enter.

Lord Neil. Of course it would be his blond head and wicked grin that invaded her moment of peace. "There you are. Miss Wedgewood, would you care to take a walk with me in the garden?"

"Of course, Lord Neil." Her words were shaky, but she stood. "Sarah, will you please tidy these things up? And bring the box to my room. It can finish drying upon the window."

"Yes, miss." Sarah curtsied to them both.

Millie exited the room and took the arm Lord Neil offered her. He appeared entirely too pleased with himself that morning. It lifted her spirits, somewhat, to see him happy.

"What has you smiling today, my lord?" she asked, allowing him to lead her down the corridor to the stairs.

"One of my favorite dogs has whelped an entire litter of healthy pups."

She studied him incredulously. "I had no idea you liked dogs so much."

"I never said as much. But I do. And these are fine animals. It has put me in good spirits."

"I can tell. Congratulations on your good fortune, my lord."

He tipped his head in acknowledgement of her words, then rattled on about the sorts of dogs he preferred. His tongue loosened a great deal under his cheer, and the man seemed more genuine than she had ever known him to be. Everyone had something they cared about, something that made them happy, and for Lord Neil that something was apparently the animals in the kennels.

During the turn through the garden, Lord Neil changed the topic to discuss what he thought of all his mother's guests. Apparently, he liked none of them, and did a fair impression of several of the more pompous members of the party.

"Where is everyone today?" Millie asked after an unsuccessful attempt to smother her laughter. "I have not seen a soul."

"There was an outing, to the beach." Lord Neil's eyebrows furrowed. "Did you not know? I thought it strange you were not among those who left an hour ago, after all you have said about your enjoyment of the sea."

"I did not know. An oversight, I am certain." Millie's stomach momentarily sank at being left out, as she so often was in London. But then, she cheered a little. "It is of no matter. I am afraid I feel toward the guests as you do. I am not inclined to spend more time in their company."

Lord Neil stopped their progress near a rosebush. He bent down to examine Millie, his eyes shrewd. "Ah. I see. You do not like the shallow, arrogant lot upon whom my sister lavishes all her worries and attentions?"

Millie slowly shook her head, befuddled. "No. I do not. But you do not, either—"

"I was born into this set," he said, voice low. "You, Miss Wedgewood, have no obligation to them. No desire to be with them. Yet you allow my sister to trick you into her service, merely for an opportunity to impress these people you do not even like."

A hard gleam appeared in his eyes as he spoke. A triumphant smile curved his sly lips.

Millie stilled, then fell back a step. She put a hand to her head and walked away from him to the edge of a stone urn. She sat down upon it.

Lord Neil came closer, steps light, wolfish grin in place. "Had you not thought of it that way?"

"Not in such clear terms," she acknowledged. Then she groaned and placed her face in her hands. "What do I do?"

"I haven't the least idea." He sounded pleased with himself, the villain. "But if I were you, I would not continue on in a course doomed to make you spend the rest of your life entertaining people whose company you do not even enjoy and whose morals you cannot respect." He executed a low, taunting bow. "Good day to you, Miss Wedgewood."

Millie glared at him as he left, then sighed and rubbed at her temples again. "It is not so easy as that," she whispered to herself and a passing bumblebee. "There is too much to consider."

But if she gave up her mother's ambition, if she lost Lady Olivia's favor, that would free her. Free her to look at Isaac as more than a friend.

Would he still want her, if the powerful people of Society ruined her family completely? Millie could only think on one person who might be able to advise her.

Emmeline.

Chapter Twenty-Three

An evening of entertainment at the marquess's house had once filled Isaac with dread. Yet Millie would be present, and even if she did not return his love, being near her soothed his soul. She needed him. That would be enough. It had to be enough.

Silas rode in the carriage with Esther and Isaac, grumbling the entire time. But the marquess had extended a personal invitation, and that meant Silas had to come or risk insulting a powerful member of his political party. Due to his brother-in-law's ill humor, Isaac said almost nothing on the drive to the Alderton estate. Esther did all the talking, and all the soothing of her husband's mood.

When the carriage stopped, Isaac exhaled gratefully.

"Mind your manners," Esther said to her husband once more. "It will all be over soon. We can return home early."

"Not if Isaac has his way," Silas muttered as he exited the carriage, ready to hand his wife down. He glared pointedly at Isaac. "He will want to stay the whole of the evening to spend time with Miss Wedgewood."

Isaac hesitated before he stepped out. "Essie told you about that?"

"Of course I did," Esther said plainly. "There are no secrets between a married couple."

"I think you two are the exception, not the rule. Given what I have seen of Society." Isaac looked up at the large house, lights blazing from nearly every window. "I can find my own way home, if the two of you find yourselves fatigued before the end of the evening." He turned a crooked smile to Silas. "Bachelors tend to stay out later than old married men, I am told."

Silas tucked Esther's arm through his before he responded. "If Esther is right, and she usually is, I am inclined to believe you will not be a bachelor long. I look forward to the spectacle you will make this evening, lavishing your attentions on Miss Wedgewood."

Isaac shrugged, unbothered by the teasing. He meant to pay attention to no one else, as he had agreed with Millie. But he would not be playing a part so much as indulging his aching heart.

They entered the house, and Isaac prepared himself for a difficult evening.

⁜

MILLIE KNEW THE MOMENT ISAAC ENTERED THE ROOM, though she had her back to the door. Impossibly, she sensed him, and turned to meet his stare. At her side, Lady Olivia snorted.

"I did not think it possible. But he does appear enamored by you, Miss Wedgewood. However did you manage it?"

The woman made everything that passed between Millie and Isaac sound cheap and farcical. How wrong she was. How blind Lady Olivia was to the truth of the matter.

"I am myself with him," Millie admitted quietly, watching as Isaac paid his respects to the marchioness and marquess, his eyes continually finding hers as he spoke.

"How droll." Lady Olivia sniffed disdainfully. "I grow weary of waiting for you to do my bidding, Miss Wedgewood. And you have yet to satisfy Mrs. Vanderby's request in regard to Mr. Weston. Your abilities are proving to be of little use to us."

Millie's hands went cold from the chill in Lady Olivia's voice. "I may have overestimated my talents, my lady, but it was not done purposefully."

Isaac had started to wind his way through the crowded room to speak to her but another neighbor stopped him for a word.

"I wonder what Lord Carning will say to that," Lady Olivia hissed. She bent closer, whispering in Millie's ear. "He has told me such a fascinating tale of the night you came to him in London, wearing barely more than your shift and a robe. How you pled with him to help you. To save your sister from her grievous mistake."

Millie's heart lurched, and she felt her stomach roll unpleasantly. "Did he tell you how he drunkenly attacked me?" Her tone matched Lady Olivia's. Cold. Quiet.

Lady Olivia's smirk was plainly visible from the corner of Millie's eye. "Is that what happened? That is not the story he tells. Not at all." Lady Olivia placed a finger beneath Millie's chin and forced Millie to turn her head to face her. "Mr. Weston says you are a vixen, tempting him only to push him away again. What is the truth of your character, Miss Wedgewood?"

Millie's eyes burned with angry tears. "You know the answer to that, Lady Olivia."

"Yes. You are a conniving little social climber. Like your mother." Lady Olivia's smile reminded Millie of icicles, cold and brittle, but dangerously sharp. "And you will do as I say, or the world will see you the way I tell it to." In a twirl of silk, Lady Olivia departed.

"Millie." Isaac had come at last. She looked up at him, and his whole countenance changed from one of welcome to deep concern. "What happened?" he whispered.

She shook her head and took his arm. "Isaac," she whispered, then a tear fell. "Get me away from here for a moment. Please."

He did not hesitate even long enough to draw breath. Isaac acted, quietly and decisively.

Isaac took hold of Millie's forearm and unceremoniously pulled her through a side door into a less crowded room, then led her into the corridor. A turn, a few steps, and he opened another door, into a darkened room.

He shut it behind them, and he turned to Millie as she wiped at her cheeks. She leaned back against the wall beside the door and closed her eyes against the firelight in the hearth.

"Millie," he whispered, and she felt him place his hand upon one wet cheek. "My heart, what happened?"

She laughed shakily, and leaned into his hand. "Isaac." That one word had enough heartbreak in it, a sound of pain she knew he could not miss.

"Look at me, Millie," he commanded gently. "Please."

She shook her head and kept her eyes shut tight. "I cannot. I— You need to leave. I have ruined everything, Isaac. She wants to hurt you. Lady Olivia, she wants to humiliate you, to break you. And she will use me to do it. We cannot outwit her."

Millie's heart broke as she spoke, but when she opened her eyes, she saw fire in the man before her.

Chapter Twenty-Four

"Leave? While you are in pain? Never." Though Isaac heard her words, they made little enough sense. His beloved was broken hearted. Nothing had happened to him. Nothing would happen. But Lady Olivia had somehow crushed Millie.

"If Napoleon's troops could not manage to put an end to me, what makes Lady Olivia think she has a chance at doing such a thing?" he asked quietly. Why would she not look at him?

"It does not matter how," Millie whispered. "Though she wishes me to do it, I cannot. I will not let her use me like that, no matter the consequences." She whimpered and her eyes filled with enough sorrow and dread that he could not doubt her word. But the fear unnerved him.

Isaac did not remove his hand, nor did he step back. He watched the woman he loved, the woman he had sworn to protect, even if he could not make her his own, as the hope left her eyes.

"What could that ridiculous woman do to me? To you?" he asked again, keeping his voice level, pleading with her to speak to him.

Pain flashed in her eyes. "She will turn the world against us."

He shook his head. "Impossible. You give her and her family too much credit. They do not have the power you think—"

She gulped in a breath. "Leave, Isaac. Please. She wants to humiliate you, all because you turned down her advances. She wants to mock you." Millie's hands came up, grasping his wrist. "You are a kind and honorable man, and you ought to stay far, far away from Lady Olivia and people like me."

"No." He forced a smile, tried to soften her words with his own whispered denial. He had to tell her. She had to understand. "I love you."

Millie made a sound part sob and part laugh. She pushed herself away from him and put her hand on the door. "Do not say that. Please." She opened the door and slipped away without another word.

The woman he loved, the woman who had filled the gaps in his soul and made him forget all that had been taken from him, left.

It was completely unacceptable. He had lost too much. Isaac would not lose her, too.

Isaac was out the door, his long strides catching up to Millie before she could reach the stairs. Before, he had taken her arm. This time, when she turned to see who came up behind her, he tucked his right shoulder down, caught her up with her arm, and carried the protesting young woman over his shoulder to the top of the stairs. "Stop your twisting, or we will fall," he warned.

She froze and caught hold of his waist with her arms. "Isaac, you imbecile, what are you doing?" she demanded in a hiss. "If anyone sees you—"

"We will explain you turned your ankle and I am helping you home," he said, looking about until he saw another abandoned room to duck inside.

"What are you doing?" she asked again, in the quiet room. "Have you gone mad?"

Isaac lowered her to the ground. This room had been well lit with gas lamps, a withdrawing room for the ladies of the party, still empty that early in the evening.

"Come away with me, Millie." He kept her hand, though she stepped away from him. "Marry me."

MILLIE'S HEAD AND HEART WARRED WITH ONE ANOTHER. Her mind immediately drew upon a list of reasons it could never be, but her heart thrummed painfully in her chest. Isaac hadn't really asked her—hadn't actually said those words to her. "You barely know me," she whispered. "You cannot mean it."

"I mean it." He drew her hand up to his lips, holding it so close his lips brushed her knuckles as he spoke. "You are witty and wise, kind, forgiving, and you see past my weaknesses while making me wish to be stronger, better. Marry me. I will spend the rest of my life protecting you and working for your happiness."

She stared up at him, wishing to say yes, longing to accept his hand and give him her heart. But then the reality of her situation broke upon her. "I cannot," she whispered. "Isaac. Say no more. Please. Go—go away." Millie withdrew her hand and stumbled back, grasping the handle of the door.

The pain in his eyes was sharp and drove a dagger into her heart.

"Why?" The single word was not plaintive but demanding. "Do you have no feelings for me? Could you never come to care—?"

"Isaac." She stopped him, closing her eyes and leaning back against the door. What could she say? It would ruin him, ruin her, break her mother's heart, devastate her father, disappoint his family. "I care for you. But I cannot marry you."

Silence hung between them, with him standing stubbornly before her, fist clenched and eyes storming. Millie's eyes stung with tears. "I wish I could say yes. But it is not possible. Not now. Lord Carning would tear my family apart. Lady Olivia would find another way to hurt us both."

"You think I care what that group of fools thinks?" he asked, jerking his chin to the door. "Millie, I have stood before the armies of our nation's enemies and led men into battle. I have been shot at, stabbed, and blown apart." He shuddered and closed his eyes, the memories too much for him, perhaps. "I nearly died in a canvas tent, feet away from a massive grave of my fellow soldiers. And Lady Olivia and the silk-swathed *ton* are supposed to frighten me?"

"They frighten me," she shouted back at him, then covered her mouth. She continued in a whisper. "Losing what is left of my family frightens me. The contempt of Society hanging over my head for the rest of my life stifles my very breath. And what of you? You say you do not care, but will you, when gentlemen turn their backs upon you? What about our children, when they cannot find friends, or support, to move forward in their chosen paths because of a choice I made?"

"We would manage. There are many who give no heed to what the likes of Carning and Alderton have to say."

Millie shook her head again. She had lived under the frowns of Society, she had been given the cut direct the first time she attended a Social event and had heard her mother weeping over the betrayal of old friends. Six years had been a long time for her family to stand at the edge of the world they had once belonged to, and Millie would not do that to Isaac.

There was no way to make Isaac see as she did. She drew herself up, she narrowed her eyes at him. "You think you are in love with me?"

"I know I am." His conviction would make what she said next hurt all the more.

Forcing her voice to remain even, to keep her tone cool as ice, Millie protected him the only way she could think of; she wounded him. "Then I have fulfilled my obligation to Lady Olivia, for I can think of nothing as humiliating as declaring your love to one who will not have you." She tipped her nose in the air. "Now there is only Mr. Weston to deal with. Good bye, Sir Isaac."

He stared at her with such shock that she knew she could escape at last, if she moved quickly enough. So she did. She slipped out the door and fled, not caring if anyone saw, all the way to her room.

A sob broke free of her throat, and Millie searched her room frantically for her trunk. Once she found it, she started shoving her clothing inside. Sarah did not find her until the room had been torn apart, and Millie sat on the ground beside her bed, sobbing into her hands.

Sarah gathered Millie up and rocked her back and forth, not saying a word.

"We leave in the morning," Millie said at last between shuddering breaths.

"Yes, miss."

"I want my things left for Lord Neil to see to. He will send them home for me."

Sarah released Millie and sat back on her heels, raising her eyebrows. "Where do you intend to go, miss, if not home with your trunk?"

Millie shuddered and wiped at her eyes with the back of her hand. "You and I will travel by post to see Emmeline." She forced a smile, though it likely appeared rather grim. "I need to speak to my sister. Will you keep packing? I have letters to write."

Chapter Twenty-Five

After calling himself every type of fool he could think of, Isaac walked home in the darkness. He knew the lands about his estate well enough that it was easily accomplished. But no matter how he growled and snapped at the bushes in his path like an angry dog, his heart continued to crumble. When he walked through his front door, startling the footman tasked with waiting for him to arrive home, the whole of his emotions finally fell to pieces.

Isaac went directly for his study where he knew he had a bottle of brandy. He had never hurt so terribly in his life, excepting when his arm had been removed from his body. And he meant to drown the pain in the burning alcohol. Forgetting everything. Forgetting Millie.

She loved him. He knew she must. She lied when she said it had all been for nothing, all to appease Lady Olivia's twisted sense of revenge. Every moment the two of them shared, excepting that first dinner when she had attempted to flirt with him, had been real.

He took up the bottle of brandy and a glass from a cupboard and went to sit behind his desk. He put both items down on the table, then froze when he realized he had no way of opening the bottle without help, or risking breaking it. He glared at the alcohol as it promised hours of relief, of forgetting.

Then he opened and closed his hand, the useless, single hand.

Yet it had saved him. Had he started drinking, Isaac knew he might never have stopped. Not until every drop of liquor in the house had gone, as it had after his mother died.

Esther had found him, inebriated, collapsed on the floor of the library. He had promised her to never dull his pain in that way again.

What was he to do? The raw ache in his heart pulled him apart from the inside. There was no place to go.

Isaac stormed out of his study again and back into the night. He went to the stables, and a groom saddled Prophet for him. It did not matter that he still wore his evening finery. He did not care if it smelled of horse, or if riding pulled every seam out of place.

He went to Jacob.

With Grace's time drawing near, Jacob did not leave her alone most nights. He hadn't appeared at Alderton. He had to be home. And a man might confess to his priest without breaking any vows.

The moon waned, nearly gone, but the horse and Isaac knew the way. When he arrived at the house, Isaac knocked loudly. Only one light could be seen, and when Jacob himself answered the door, Isaac met his friend's startled gaze.

Jacob hadn't been the vicar long, but the nighttime visit must have been one of dozens he had welcomed. He took one look at Isaac and opened the door wider. They went into the study, and when Isaac sat in a chair beside his friend, he cried at last.

It was not the desperate sobs of a broken man. But the slow, steady tears of a creature too long in pain. Millie's rejection, her claim of betrayal, had undone him. Where he thought he had grown stronger, for her sake, he realized he had only created a hole in the wall around his heart and given everything he kept inside a way out at last.

Jacob listened. He listened as Isaac told him of the war, of firing into a line of men to watch them fall. Wondering if his had been the shot to take a life amidst the chaos of smoke and blood. He made no comment when Isaac spoke of watching his men die from wounds inflicted in battle. Isaac spoke of grown men weeping like boys, of cowards failing to act and costing lives, of generals who moved them about like pieces on a board rather than men with beating hearts.

Then Jacob asked questions. Gentle questions, probing Isaac to reveal still more of what he had kept hidden. His failure as a friend and brother in regard to Esther. His reluctance to return to Society.

His brokenness, that was so much more than the lack of an arm.

The hour grew later, and Isaac gulped in air. "I am like a man caught at the bottom of a well," he said at last, into the quiet room and Jacob's attentive ears. "I must tread water or drown. But I cannot climb out and save myself. So I struggle to keep my head above water, hoping rescue will come, but it never does."

When Jacob answered him, Isaac saw tears in his friend's eyes. "I have worried for you. Prayed for you. I knew you were not as healed and whole as you pretended, but I did not know you needed me. I am sorry I let you do this alone for so long, Isaac."

Though his friend's words touched him, Isaac shrugged. "I did not want your help. Or anyone's. But I cannot do this anymore."

"No one can face what you have and remain whole," Jacob said quietly. "You are not the first soldier I have spoken to, you will likely not be the last. Isaac, you are not alone. Healing will come with time, with faith, and with love."

"Love." Isaac groaned and folded himself in half where he sat. "That is what brought me here at last. But not God's love, as I suspect you meant."

Jacob's lips twitched, though his eyes remained heavy. "Of course I mean God's love. And your family's, and your friends'. But who is it that drove you here? Miss Wedgewood?"

"You heard about the time we spent in each other's company?"

"No." Jacob's smile turned sympathetic. "Seeing you both together that night at dinner, when you were oblivious to her, and then again the night of the bonfire when you could not keep your eyes from her—it was such a contrast. For a woman to gain your interest with such speed, I knew she must be unique. Special to you."

"Yet I am nothing to her. What I say to you tonight, it is in confidence?"

Jacob nodded once, a solemnity about him that soothed what remained of Isaac's concerns.

Isaac kept talking, explaining everything to Jacob. Everything. Even kissing her. His friend did not offer censure, nor jest, but listened with his full attention. When Isaac came to the end of the disaster, to Millie's parting words, his voice faded away to nothing.

The clock on the mantel marked the passage of time. It was two o'clock in the morning. Isaac was nearly hoarse with talking, his eyes dry and burning. He rubbed at his eyes, yet the ache remained both there and in his chest. He met Jacob's gaze and waited, hoping for wisdom, for guidance.

Jacob's smile returned, the shadow of one he had often worn in their youth. Goading. "What will you do now?"

Isaac's thoughts halted. "What?"

Jacob repeated himself, slowly. "What will you do now, Isaac?"

"Are you not supposed to tell me?" Isaac asked, sitting back and gripping the arm of the chair.

His friend relaxed, his shoulders dropping and his smile growing. "I am a vicar, not a prophet. I have listened to all you have said. I offer you my support, my prayers, and a listening ear. Your struggles are real, and they are all in your heart. I cannot tell you what to do, but I can encourage you in your next steps. That is why I ask you, my friend, what will you do?"

Isaac opened and closed his mouth multiple times, then stood and paced away from the chair, hearth, Jacob, and to the window.

He stared out into the darkness, the light behind him only reflecting the shadowed room to him in the glass.

"What will I do." He pulled in a deep breath, then let it out in a laugh. "Take each day as I have, I suppose. One moment at a time."

"And?" Jacob prompted quietly.

Isaac turned, slowly, and saw the hopeful expression upon his friend's face. "And come to you when I struggle."

"I imagine Esther would be of help, too. And Silas. All of us you count as friends. You are as a brother to all of us." Jacob rose from his chair. "Will you do that, Isaac?"

Hours of talk had loosened the hold Isaac's fear, his guilt, had upon him. He was not yet entirely free. But his soul felt lighter than it had since his return from war. "I will. But you may have to remind me, from time to time." The admission humbled him, and he had to swallow back another display of emotion.

"What of Miss Wedgewood?" Jacob raised his eyebrows and folded his arms over his chest.

"I don't know." Isaac shoved a hand through his hair, examining his heart. "I love her. Esther would have me believe—she would say to fight for what I love."

"I suggest, instead of barreling straight into the thick of it as you did, you give the matter some thought." Jacob's smile turned amused. "Those of us who know you best know that you are prone to charge into a fray rather than consider a better strategy."

A laugh coming from his own throat surprised Isaac, but it dispelled the fog around his heart. "You are right, of course."

"Of course. I am a vicar." Jacob grinned. "And your friend. Never forget that."

"Never," Isaac promised.

He left without all the answers he sought, but at least felt himself prepared to find them. Prepared to form a plan and to wait, if necessary, until he knew how to approach Millie again.

Because he would go to her again. He would declare his love. New as it was, Isaac was too stubborn to give up on his heart and on her.

Chapter Twenty-Six

The early morning light did little to settle Isaac's mind on the matter of Millie. Despite finding a measure of peace in speaking to Jacob the night before, Isaac's heart still ached. He stayed in bed later than usual, merely thinking.

His heart belonged to her. It did not matter, how little time they had spent together. Nor did it matter that she had trespassed upon his land that first time in order to spy upon him. He knew her and recognized the beauty of her soul, the fiery spirit she possessed, the kind heart she kept guarded.

Jacob had advised him to strategize. Strategize, then, Isaac would.

After he had dressed and eaten enough of a breakfast to stave off hunger pains, Isaac went to his study and started writing out lists. The only practical purpose his work served was to help focus his thoughts. First, a list of things he knew about Millie. Her family, where they lived, how old she had been when her sister eloped, all her little comments about people she knew or wished to know in Society.

Then he made a list of all the reasons he had given his heart to her, and another of all the ways he might help her and her family from their predicament.

Silas would have to be involved, but Isaac would give up his solitary life for her, too.

He stopped. What did that mean, to give up solitude?

Isaac started another list of everything he might do in Society, everything he wished to do, and it was dismally short. He hated crowded ballrooms and parties. Theater boxes would not be so bad, he thought, though the noise of the audience might prove difficult.

His hand started shaking as he imagined it, pictured himself in a box above a hoard of men and women laughing, whispering behind fans. The scents of perfumes, powders, and bodies all stuffed together in one room.

He closed his eyes and leaned back in his chair, rubbing at his eyes.

"What a joke." He spoke to the empty room, to himself. "I cannot even pretend to be in that place without falling to pieces." Sweat had broken out along his brow.

The familiar building pressure in his chest warned him of an attack. Not an attack of French soldiers, but of the enemy within. His own fear. Esther had described her own dark moods as melancholia. But this was not the same. His sister fell into bouts of sorrow, from time to time. But Isaac was not sorrowful.

He was not fearful, either. Merely aware of every little detail in his life that could send him spiraling out of control, into headaches, into a panic.

What the deuce was wrong with him? He need never face war again. Britain would rout Napoleon.

He looked down at his lists. Meaningless drivel, most of it, except what he had written down about Millie. He could not take her into Society. Not as he was.

Isaac went to the largest window in his study and threw it open, hoping the fresh air would take away the smothering thoughts in his head.

Were other soldiers returned from war as plagued as he? Was anyone helping them?

Isaac grew still as the questions settled in his heart.

Esther accused him of attempting to save everyone. Play the part of the rescuer. But what if he felt that way, acted that way, for a reason? What if he was meant to be a rescuer? He had the ear of the Earl of Inglewood, and others of Silas's circle of political allies. He had the time, too, to do something for his brothers in arms who returned from war and felt as lost as he had.

A knock interrupted the productive line of thinking.

At Isaac's command, the butler strode inside and bowed. "Sir Isaac, Lord Neil Duncan is here to see you. I have shown him into the front parlor, sir."

"Lord Neil?" Isaac did not bother to hide the skepticism in his tone. "Thank you. I will go to him directly."

They avoided each other, except when it was absolutely necessary to converse. Showing up at Isaac's house was strange. Isaac did not waste time thinking the oddity over, however, and went to see what the man wanted.

Lord Neil stood in the middle of the parlor, admiring a painting hanging over the mantel. It was one of Esther's, of course, of Woodsbridge itself, bathed in cheerful sunlight. The lordling looked over his shoulder when Isaac entered the room, his sideways smile appearing.

"Your sister has a great talent. This is one of hers, is it not?"

"My sister will never be a topic of conversation between us, Lord Neil." Isaac did not bother to bow since the other man had already ignored common politeness. "What are you doing here?"

Lord Neil turned to fully face Isaac, and that was when Isaac saw the box in his neighbor's hands. A box he had glimpsed before, a time or two, while Millie worked upon it.

"I have come to deliver this to you, though why I am made errand boy I cannot imagine." He came forward and put the box upon a table near Isaac. Thoughtful of him, considering it would be difficult for Isaac to manage the wide rectangular object with a single hand.

"You should not have troubled yourself," Isaac said, unable to take his eyes from the artfully rendered fox upon the box's hinged lid. It was all in black and ivory, quite beautiful. The inked fox looked almost alive, peering up at him with its long tail lowered to wrap around a leg. Vines and grasses covered the rest of the lid and twined down to the box's sides.

It really was a work of art.

Lord Neil shrugged, his eyelids falling somewhat, as though he were bored. "I wanted to see your reaction to it, to be honest. I find that Miss Wedgewood stirs the strangest of emotions in people. The letter she instructed me to give to my sister, for instance, left Olivia shrieking and spitting rather like an angry cat. Most diverting."

"Why would you have to deliver a letter to your sister?" Isaac asked, approaching the table. "Surely the two women could pass their own notes to each other." He ran his hand across the edge of the box, feeling light etches in the wood made to keep the ink in place and providing greater depth to the image. It was not a painting, such as Esther's, but it was unique and quite fine.

Why had Millie sent it to him? He would not keep away from her. So if it was meant as a goodbye—

"Oh, you did not know?" Lord Neil's tone was sly and smooth as ever. "I suppose you could not. Miss Wedgewood disappeared from our house this morning. All her things were left with a letter instructing me how to dispatch them."

Isaac jerked his head up, unable to keep his shock inside. "She *what?*"

"Disappeared." Lord Neil waved his hand through the air. "Her note said she wished her things sent to her parents' country home, then there was a letter addressed to me. I had a note to send to her parents, a note for Olivia, and the instruction to bring you this box." He nodded to the box upon the table.

Isaac stared down again, swallowing back a string of oaths. She left without a goodbye. If she thought that would keep him from following her—

"There are notes inside."

His poor humor made him snap. "Have you read them?"

Without shame, the man grinned. "I have. As I said, the woman makes me curious."

This time, Isaac did swear, but Lord Neil only chuckled. Isaac flipped open the lid. Two papers were inside. One folded, neatly, and the other appearing to have been crumpled and smoothed out again.

He took the undamaged paper first and saw it bore the name of a street, town, and county in cramped, uneven handwriting. He narrowed his eyes, uncertain, before dropping it in favor of the crumpled paper. It was an unfinished letter. As he read, he wondered if Millie had meant to send it to him at all.

Dear Isaac,

My Dearest Sir Isaac,

My thoughts are muddled, swirling like mud and water, refusing to settle. I am at once grateful for all you have done, for your friendship, and regretful that we ever had to meet. Especially under such horrid circumstances.

From the first moment I saw you, pretending you were a groundskeeper, I have thought you handsome, witty, and most infuriating. Yet now that I know you better, I see so much more. You are kind, protective, honorable. You are a man without equal.

I wish I was worthy of you.

You said you could love me. I wish it were so. With my whole heart.

It was written before he'd confessed his love for her in full. Sometime between her nap in the hammock and their last words to each other. Why send him the letter, unfinished? It didn't make sense.

Isaac examined the paper again, then the direction. He raised his gaze from the scrawled words to Lord Neil, who appeared as perplexed as he. "You had nothing to do with these notes finding their way into the box?"

"Nothing at all." Lord Neil shrugged. "I confess to enjoying the mystery about them."

"And are you to report to your sister on my reaction?" Isaac asked, allowing his anger to taint the words.

To his surprise, the lord laughed at that. "Not at all."

"So you do not care that Miss Wedgewood fulfilled her part of the agreement?" he asked carefully.

Lord Neil's smile was slow and full of whatever knowledge the man thought he had. "My sister apparently bays for your blood, Sir Isaac. I do not know why, nor do I wish to, but she has been thwarted. Given her reaction to her own note from Miss Wedgewood, that is. How strange you would think the young woman accomplished the task set for her."

"I have never liked you, Lord Neil." Isaac watched the man as he spoke, saw the momentary flicker of emotion in his eye. Anger, perhaps. "But you inspired confidence in Miss Wedgewood. Enough for her to trust you with her things and her words. She seemed to have a certain fondness for you."

Nothing had prepared the man for that comment, apparently, given the way his smirk melted away. He cleared his throat. "Miss Wedgewood is a unique woman. She claims to have seen something in me. Something good. Decent, even. I could not let her down this time. I am unlikely to have cause to do her a favor again."

"That being said," Isaac went on, "thank you for delivering this. Perhaps you might find a way to keep your sister from adding Miss Wedgewood to her list of people to revenge herself upon."

"Perhaps." Lord Neil dusted off the sleeves of his coat. "Perhaps you and that brother-in-law of yours ought to come to the house today. My father is still at home. He might find what you two have to say about my sister's activities...interesting." He abruptly bowed. "For now, good day, Sir Isaac."

"Lord Neil." Isaac bowed as the man swept past him to the door, puzzling over his words no more than an instant before the painful news returned to the forefront of his mind.

Millie had left. All he had of her was a box, a letter, and a location. Then there was Lord Neil's suggestion. Intriguing as it was, Isaac sent word to the stables to ready his horse.

In little time, he was in Silas's study, explaining the situation as best he could. He had little evidence to support all that Millie had told him. Would his word be enough to involve the marquess?

"All we can do is try." Silas huffed and bestowed a dark scowl upon Isaac. "Why did you not involve me before?"

"I made a promise to a young woman." Isaac tried to smile. "But as she has fled the area I thought it best to confide in you. You know the Marquess. Will he listen to us?"

Silas rose from his desk with purpose. Apparently, there would be no delay in dealing with Lady Olivia. "It will take cleverness. Let me do the talking."

Isaac snorted. "Thank you for that."

The earl realized what he had said and chuckled. "Sorry for that. I did not mean to imply you lacked cleverness. But we all know you are apt to speak without thinking."

That trait had cost him a great deal over the years. If it had removed Millie from the possibility of loving him, he would ache for her the rest of his days. Then Lady Olivia would win.

"It irritates me how accurate that statement is, but I do intend to remedy that." He gestured to the door. "Shall we?"

A hard smile appeared upon Silas's face. The sort of smile his political opponents would be terrified to see if he ever showed them more than his stony mask. "We shall."

Given the serious nature of their visit to the marquess, Silas insisted on taking the carriage bearing his family's coat of arms. Though he wished to tap his foot with impatience, Isaac forced himself to maintain composure. Charging in to the marquess's home with accusations and little evidence would not achieve his purpose.

He distracted himself by thinking of Millie on the afternoon she slept in the hammock, beneath the trees. The world had been at peace around them for a precious hour, and then her kiss...

The carriage came to the door at last, and Isaac breathed easier. He kept Millie's image in his mind and heart, making her the center of his thoughts.

They arrived at the Alderton estate and were shown to the library to await the marquess. Given Silas's avoidance of the house for more than a year, his presence alone would indicate the seriousness of the matter to the other nobleman.

The Marquess of Alderton, Reginald Duncan, entered his library. He was an older man, nearing seventy, but still carried himself with confidence. His black hair was shot through with gray streaks, his eyes were the color of iron. Lord Neil, who entered after his father and closed the doors behind them, looked nothing like his father.

"Inglewood." The marquess offered an abbreviated bow. "To what do I owe this unexpected pleasure?" His eyes flicked briefly to Isaac, then back to Silas.

Lord Neil came into the room and took a seat, without waiting for either of the lords who outranked him to do so. His father briefly scowled at him, but Lord Neil ignored everyone. For the first time, Isaac wondered how much of Lord Neil's arrogant boredom was an act. He had as good as told Isaac to confront his father, yet acted as though nothing of consequence was to take place.

"It has come to my attention that a member of your household is abusing their power," Silas said, all lordly and stiff. "I have come to ask, as a personal favor, that you put an end to it."

Isaac's attention focused again on the marquess.

The old man appeared to consider Silas's words, raising his eyebrows. "Is that so? Abuse, hm? Have you evidence to support this claim?"

"Perhaps." Silas cut a look to Isaac. "I have the word of my brother-in-law, and the testimony of a young woman. I thought it best I bring the matter to you, Alderton. I would certainly wish to know if a member of my family promised favors and retribution upon members of Society in order to settle petty differences."

"Indeed." The marquess turned his attention to Isaac, all of them still standing still. Silas and Isaac were nearly shoulder-to-shoulder and the marquess had not come far into the room. "Tell me, Sir Isaac. I should like to hear—"

The door burst open. Isaac turned, as did the others, to see Lady Olivia standing within the doorway. She scowled, but not at Isaac or Silas. At her brother. Strange. Did she know he had orchestrated this confrontation? She stormed into the room and slammed the door behind her.

She snarled like a wild animal. "I do not care what they have said, Papa, you mustn't believe it."

"Olivia." Her father spoke her name sharply. "What is the meaning of this intrusion?"

"Neil is a traitor," she bit out, hands curled into fists.

The marquess's features hardened as he took in the state of his only daughter, and Isaac did not blame him for his shock. Lady Olivia's cheeks were red, her eyes snapping dangerously, and she appeared wild.

"Miss Wedgewood came up with the whole plan herself. I had nothing to do with it. She betrayed me, and our family's hospitality, using us for her own gain."

Lord Neil chuckled from his place on the long sofa, which only appeared to infuriate his sister more.

"Would you make sense of this for me, Sir Isaac?" The marquess regarded his daughter coolly, not looking away from her as he asked his question. "My daughter protests her innocence for a wrongdoing I have not yet heard, accuses her brother, and one of our guests, of crimes against our family. I should like to hear a more level-headed explanation."

Isaac exchanged a look with Silas. They had agreed to let the earl do the talking, but the balance had shifted. Silas gave a small nod, and Isaac took up the stance of a soldier.

"My lord, one of your guests has fled your house this morning, but not before she gave her reasons. Your daughter has threatened Miss Wedgewood with utter ruin if the other young lady did not do as Lady Olivia instructed. Lady Olivia meant to use Miss Wedgewood in an attempt to revenge herself upon me for a perceived slight. She has wielded Miss Wedgewood, an innocent young woman of gentle birth, as a weapon through her threats and promises—"

Isaac was cut off by a shriek. "Liar." Lady Olivia stormed forward, stopping a pace closer than her father stood to Isaac. "Why would I ever bother with the likes of a baronet? You are beneath my notice, beneath even my contempt."

He studied her, the cold fury in her eyes, the way her lip curled. And then, to his surprise and everyone else's, Isaac laughed. Not long, or loud, but enough that Lady Olivia paled and stepped back, confusion upon her face.

When Isaac spoke, it was still with a touch of mirth. "Come now, Lady Olivia. We both know exactly what lengths you have gone to in order to capture my attention." There was nothing suggestive, nor lurid in his tone. Yet she paled and darted a frightened look toward her father.

Apparently, the marquess needed nothing more said. "Go to my study, Olivia. Wait for me there."

She squeaked. "Yes, Papa." As she fled the room without a backward glance, Isaac almost felt sorry for her. The conniving woman had learned her viscous, hurtful behavior from someone. Most likely, given the sudden chill in his tone, it was from the marquess.

The marquess cast a suspicious glance toward his son, then turned his attention to Silas and Isaac. "It seems we are to trade favors today, Inglewood. If you will encourage your brother-in-law to forget whatever my daughter has done, I will ensure she does no harm to your Miss Wedgewood."

Isaac looked to Silas, his heart racing. Had they won so easily? If the marquess was aware of his daughter's intrigues, of her nature, he knew enough.

"We are willing to forget the whole of it, Alderton." Silas tucked his hands behind his back and nodded to Isaac. "Sir Isaac?"

"If you give me your word, Lord Alderton." Isaac kept his gaze steady on the older nobleman. "I want no repercussions, no harm to Miss Wedgewood or her family, and your guarantee that your daughter will leave my family alone."

The marquess, a man of great power even though he had few morals, nodded once. "You have my word. Reputation is everything, Sir Isaac." He looked to where Lord Neil quietly lounged upon the sofa. "I know all too well how damaging certain *rumors* can be. My daughter will not act in this manner again." There were layers to his pronouncement, but at least one message was clear. If Isaac never again spoke of Lady Olivia's attempted seduction, the marquess would see to it his daughter left Isaac and those he loved alone.

"Thank you." Silas and Isaac bowed, taking their leave. Just before Isaac took the last step out the door, he glanced over his shoulder to Lord Neil. He caught the man's eye, curious as to what part he had played in the confrontation.

Lord Neil had the audacity to smirk, but nodded once, as though in salute.

When they stepped into the open air again, Silas shuddered. "It's rather like escaping a den of snakes."

Isaac chuckled and put his hat upon his head, noticing for the first time what a glorious sky hung above them. The sky was blue, with dots of white clouds drifting by, and a sun so bright and glorious that it lifted his heart to stand beneath it.

"What will you do now?" Silas asked, still walking to the carriage.

"You need to ask?" Isaac grinned at his oldest friend, climbing into the vehicle. "I have a fox to catch."

Chapter Twenty-Seven

The mail coach stopped at last in Warwickshire. Millie stepped down, with the assistance of an elderly gentleman who had sat across from her, knees knocking against hers for the last several hours. She pulled her small trunk close to her chest, looking about with some uncertainty. Sarah came down next, clutching the bag of her essential items. They had only brought what they needed for the two-day trip, and a change of clothes for their final destination.

"That was an adventure, miss." Sarah sidled up next to Millie on the path.

Millie shuddered. "One I am not eager to repeat." They hadn't met with anyone truly unpleasant, but the crowded coach, full of people from various social stations, had been a rather cramped and smelly affair.

"Then we will hope your sister lets us stay a bit." Sarah offered her mistress a hopeful smile. "Now then. Where do we go?"

Millie had memorized the paper in her bag where she had written the instructions for finding her sister. She did not need to check them. She went to the innkeeper, who happily pointed them in the right direction.

Once upon the correct street, which was clean and tidy with two rows of neat houses and shops, Millie asked after the solicitor.

"Pardon me," she said to a woman who watered a flower box full of pansies. "I am looking for Mr. and Mrs. Cadoc Powell. Do they live on this street?"

"Yes, miss. Three houses over, with the dark green door." The woman smiled broadly, and without hesitation she asked, "Are you visiting the family, miss?"

Millie's eyes were already searching out the door, her heart beating rapidly. It was Sarah that answered. "Yes, missus. Thank you kindly."

"I have never said her married name before," Millie whispered as they walked down the wide footpath. "What if she does not wish to see me?"

"Have courage. Your sister used to dote on you."

"Up until the moment she met Mr. Powell."

They stood in front of the door, and Millie suddenly remembered that night when she woke to find her sister escaping out the window.

"Do not fret, Millie. And do not say a word. I cannot marry Lord Carning. I am in love with Cadoc."

She had kissed Millie on the cheek and resumed her escape. Millie had gone looking for the duke's grandson, hoping he would stop her sister from making a foolish mistake.

"Are you going to knock, or should I?" Sarah asked.

Millie shivered. "I will." She held her fist above her in the air, took in a deep breath, and rapped smartly against the door. Then they both waited. Though only the smallest increments of time passed before the door opened, it felt as though they waited years.

A young girl in an apron and cap answered. "Good afternoon. May I help you?"

A servant. Of course a servant would answer. What had Millie expected? Emmeline to rush out the door and embrace her?

She forced a smile. "Hello. I am here to call upon Mrs. Powell.

Would you please tell her that Miss Wedgewood is here to see her?"

The maid did not even blink. She likely did not know her mistress's maiden name. Why would she? But she stepped back enough to let them into the little corridor. She showed them into a room that faced the road. Sarah took a place near the wall and put her bag down beside her feet.

Millie drank in every detail of the cozy sitting room, her heart still racing. The room was decorated in soft hues, and the furniture appeared new and comfortable. Everything was clean, and the windows let in a great deal of light.

The door opened.

Millie turned, bracing herself, though she knew not for what. Emmeline, the sister she remembered, would immediately wrap her in an embrace. But she had never written. In six years, they'd had no contact at all.

A woman stood there, her hand over her heart, watching Millie with wide eyes.

Millie's heart broke into a thousand pieces as she forgot about her fears, her pain, and stared at her beloved sister. "Emmie."

That was all it took to free the dam for both of them. In the next instant, they were in the center of the room, crying and holding each other. Then laughing through their tears. Emmeline was taller, had a more mature figure, and her middle rounded with the promise of a baby. Her eyes were still a clear blue, her hair spun gold, and her smile bright and warm as the sun.

"Look at you," Emmie cooed, stepping back at last. She kept Millie's hands in hers. "Oh, Millie, you are so beautiful."

"I am still red-headed and freckled," Millie countered. "And you are stunning."

"Mama?" a voice asked from the doorway. A little boy stood there, no more than four or five years old, shyly looking around the doorframe. He had red hair, and freckles.

"Oh." Millie's eyes filled with tears. "I have a nephew."

Emmie laughed and wiped at her cheeks. She went to the door

and gently pulled the little boy around it. Then Millie saw the boy held the hand of a little girl, who was the exact image of her mother, only in miniature.

"And a niece," Emmie said softly. "Millie, these are my children. This is Aeron and Wren. Sweetlings, this is my sister, your Aunt Millie."

Bursting into tears again would likely terrify the children, so Millie gulped back her emotion and smiled warmly at them. "I am pleased to meet you both."

It was then that Emmie remembered her place as hostess. She began scurrying about the room, offering Millie a chair, asking the children to sit on the couch. The maid who had answered the door reappeared and took Sarah with her to the kitchen to fetch food and drink. Millie sat quietly, watching her sister, with a sense of familiarity.

When the burst of energy ended with Emmie sitting between her son and daughter on the sofa, her arms around them, she gave Millie another brilliant smile.

"I cannot believe you are here. I did not know when I would see you again." Her smile weakened. "Mother and Father do not know you came, do they?"

Millie slowly shook her head. "Though they will when my letter reaches them. I was in Suffolk. I found out where you were, and I had to come. Emmie. Why did you not write to me?"

Emmie's blue eyes clouded over. "I did. I sent a letter last month."

The truth finally hit Millie, hard enough that the breath left her lungs. Her parents—one or both, it did not matter—had kept her sister's letters from her. Which meant they had always known where Emmie was, but they had never told.

"My dear Millie, you are so grown up." Her sister's words were bright, the message in her expression clear. They had been apart too long. "What were you doing in Suffolk?"

They talked. About everything. The children eventually left the sofa to play on the floor between the sisters, after dragging a box of wooden animals from beneath a chair. Millie told her sister of London, of her time in Suffolk, though only of the happy moments. Then Emmie spoke of the children, of her life as a solicitor's wife. Her eyes glowed with life and warmth, especially when she mentioned her husband.

"Cadoc is a wonderful solicitor, of course, but he is an even better husband and father. He will be home soon, and so glad to see you."

"I hope so." Millie lowered her gaze to her lap. "He has made you very happy."

The maid appeared with tea, and she offered to take the children to their dinner. The boy and girl kissed their mother, bowed to Millie, and scampered off to their meal.

"They are perfect," Millie said as soon as the door shut behind them.

Her sister's eyes glowed with motherly pride. "I certainly think they are. Even when they get into mischief."

With the children gone, Millie had to ask the question burning in her mind and heart. Everything depended on her sister's answer. "Emmie. Are you truly happy? Is your life what you would have it be?" She leaned forward in her chair, clutching her hands together.

Emmie's gaze captured Millie's. The elder sister's expression softened, and when she spoke it was with great deliberateness. "My life is not perfect, but I am happy, and I find joy in the choice I made. I love my husband. He loves me. Our children bring greater light and love into our marriage. If I went back again, all those years ago, I would choose the same. Always."

Millie's eyes filled with tears, and she thought of Isaac. When he had stood before her, begging her to come away with him, all she could think upon was Emmeline's choice.

Before Isaac's confession, Millie's thoughts had shaken loose. Shifted. At last, with the evidence of her sister's happiness before her, surrounded by love, things fell into place.

"I fear I have made an awful mistake." Millie hadn't meant to speak her confession aloud, but she teetered on the edge of her thoughts and a decision.

"Tell me." Emmie opened her arms in invitation, and Millie rose from her chair and went to her sister's embrace. An embrace she had yearned to feel again for six long years. "Tell me everything."

Chapter Twenty-Eight

Two glorious days in the Powell home nearly put Millie to rights. Her heart lightened, and her fears receded in the shelter of her sister's love. The children did an excellent job of distracting her, too. Millie had started painting their little wooden animals, creating stripes on a horse to turn it into a zebra, and swirls of flowers on a wolf to make Wren love it all the more.

She sat at the breakfast table the third morning, listening to Cadoc as he teased her sister. Thankfully, even his reception of Millie had been kind. He had immediately called her "little sister" and thanked her for coming at last.

Millie's thoughts repeated themselves as she watched him brush a kiss upon Emmie's cheek when he rose to leave the table. *I would have come sooner, had I known what a paradise this place is.*

Amid the turmoil of her mind, of Lady Olivia's schemes and threats, Millie had found sanctuary. But how long could it last?

A loud knock at the front door reverberated through the house, causing Cadoc to pause in the doorway. He looked over his shoulder at his wife.

"A bit early for guests, love?" He had a lilt to his voice Millie had always liked, up until the moment he ran away with her sister. She found she rather enjoyed it again.

"A bit. But we do seem to be lucky in our unexpected guests just now." She smiled warmly at Millie. Cadoc waved the maid away and went to answer the door himself. The house was not especially large, but no one could call it cramped, either. They had a maid, a cook, and a man-of-all-work. Emmie ruled them all with kindness.

The sound of Cadoc's greeting traveled back to the ladies, who sat quietly, listening.

"Please forgive the intrusion. I am Isaac Fox. I was told I might find Miss Wedgewood at this house."

Millie covered her mouth and exchanged a look with Emmie. For her part, Emmie's entire countenance changed, her eyes widening and her mouth parting in a gasp. Millie's stomach fluttered. Her sister grabbed her hand and tugged her up.

"Go to him, you ninny," she whispered, hands on Millie's shoulders to propel her from the room. "This very moment. Go."

Millie's feet finally caught up with her sister's commands. She stumbled out of the dining room, into the main corridor. Cadoc still stood beside the open front door, and there, holding his hat beneath his arm and wearing an uncertain expression, was Sir Isaac Fox.

He caught her gaze with his, and they stared at one another. Millie's heart thudded like a hammer against her ribs. Vaguely, she heard Cadoc say her name. But it was Isaac's look that unbound her at last. The light in his eyes softened, one corner of his mouth came up almost sheepishly, hopefully.

She stepped forward, slowly, but then her feet flew, and her arms reached for him.

Isaac dropped his hat—What other choice did he have, really?—and scooped her up with his arm, holding her tightly against his chest. Millie kept her face buried in his cravat, hardly believing it was him. He had come looking for her. How had he known where to find her? She kept her arms around his waist, drinking in his scent, allowing the warmth from his body to seep into hers.

Isaac's lips brushed her forehead, his arm not loosening its hold upon her, and he breathed deeply. Content.

"I take it you know the gentleman." Cadoc's lilting words made Millie laugh as she leaned back, only enough to face her brother-in-law.

"This is Isaac." She lifted her gaze to the baronet's again. "I am going to marry him."

Isaac stared at her, his shock at her pronouncement quickly replaced by a grin. "Are you?"

Cadoc chuckled and stepped aside. "Perhaps you two ought to come inside. Settle the matter where the neighbors will not be privy to what you decide."

Millie felt her cheeks warm, but she tossed her head, uncaring. Isaac gave her waist one last squeeze before he bent to retrieve his hat and follow her through the door.

Cadoc bowed them into the front sitting room. "We will worry over introductions later," he told them, giving Millie a wink before he left them alone. Door open.

Isaac put his hat down on a table and held his hand out to her, and Millie did not need more of an invitation. She stepped back into his embrace. He kept it gentle, his arm looser, but no less full of his adoration. She laid her cheek against his chest.

"Isaac. How did you find me?"

⊱⋅⋆⋅⊰

Isaac parted from Millie enough to stare down at her, incredulous. "The box." She blinked at him, uncomprehending. "You left a letter in the box, and the direction for this house. I hoped you would be here when I arrived, but I was not certain—"

"The box was empty," she said softly. "I wanted to write to you, but I could not. I sent the box instead."

Somewhat reluctantly, Isaac released her, much to her disappointment judging by the tiny frown that appeared. He withdrew a well-worn piece of paper from his coat. Millie accepted it from him and unfolded it. After a brief glance at the words, she raised her gaze back to his.

"I did write this." A pretty pink stained her cheeks. "But then I left it, and Sarah—" She broke off and her eyebrows rose. "Sarah."

Isaac did not bother to hide his amusement. He quickly drew her to him again. "Your little maid is clever. She knows what you need better than you do. I would be willing to wager she left the paper with your destination, too." He glanced around the house. "Where are we, exactly? Whose home is this?"

"It belongs to my sister, Emmeline, and her husband." Millie took his arm and tugged him to the couch. "Oh, Isaac. I have so much to tell you. I am sorry, so terribly sorry, that I ran away before. But you see, it has all been for the best. Emmie has told me everything about how happy she is, how much she loves her husband, and they have two children." Millie beamed with genuine pride.

He listened, trying to pick out the bits that made the most sense to him. He had so many questions. But what did they matter? Millie was safe, happy, and had declared her intention to marry him. He could want for nothing more.

She broke off in her cheerful prattle and squeezed his hand. "Isaac. Why did you come? You do still care for me, do you not?"

He lifted her hand to his lips and brushed a kiss across her skin. "Always, my heart. I will always care for you. I love you."

Millie leaned into him, keeping her gaze upon his. "I love you, too." She drew in a shaky breath. "My parents will disown me, I am certain. Lady Olivia and Lord Carning will make our lives as miserable as they can. It is their nature to be vindictive. But if you can overlook those things, if you do not mind them, and if you still want me—"

He cut her words off with a kiss. A deeply felt, passionately given kiss. She returned his ardor as she had on both the previous occasions. Any doubt she had, he kissed it away.

When they finally parted, both breathing more heavily than normal, Isaac's heart pounded against his chest. He spoke over the sound thrumming in his ears. "You do not need to worry about Lady Olivia. Perhaps not even Carning. I have spoken to the Marquess of Alderton about his daughter's schemes. And her behavior."

Millie jerked back from him, her mouth open wide. "No. And that worked?" She narrowed her eyes at him. "Lady Olivia will never let that stand. She is conniving, devious, unprincipled—"

He interrupted her with a laugh and a gentle squeeze of her hand. "All true. Her father's displeasure will restrain her for a time. Well enough to keep Lady Olivia from daring to so much as whisper your name for the foreseeable future." Isaac grimaced. "The man is a hypocrite. He would silence his daughter for acting as she has seen him act. But it is done. Carning will not say much, unless he wishes to hurt his own standing, because Lady Inglewood will sponsor your introduction to the Crown, as her sister."

"Introduction?" Millie's eyebrows drew down. "Isaac, I know you detest London. We need not ever return to that wretched place."

He leaned back into the couch, retaining her hand in his. "Too late for that, love. I have come to a decision. It will be difficult. I cannot find the confidence—not yet—to move about as freely as I once did. But I cannot bury myself in my house like a hermit."

Millie slowly leaned into him, keeping her gaze upon him. "What do you intend to do?"

"Make a difference," he answered, lifting his left shoulder. "Speak to politicians as you suggested, like my brother-in-law, about the fate of men returning from war. Help them. Somehow. I cannot do much on my own. But with the help from the right people, and with you at my side for courage and care, perhaps I can improve things for men who live without the support I have had from my friends. And you."

Her eyes glowed up at him, admiration clear and bright within them. "That is a beautiful idea, Isaac. I will support you however you wish, however I am able. I promise."

"I promise the same for you, darling. I will protect you, I will defend you, and I will make you the queen of my life." He watched her, noting everything from the light dusting of freckles across her cheeks to the way her eyes glowed amber in the light. "You said you will marry me?"

She blushed. "I am certain we both know that is what comes next."

"Then I had better return you to your parents. With or without their blessing, we need to do the honorable thing."

She pouted. "I would rather elope as Emmeline and Cadoc did."

A woman who could only be Millie's sister rounded the doorway, eyes narrowed, hands upon her hips. "Absolutely not. I eloped because I was betrothed to a snake with the power of a duke behind him. You, dear sister, have no such dangers to keep you from an honorable marriage in a church."

Cadoc—the man who answered the door—put his head barely around the corner. "Do forgive us. We only started eavesdropping a moment ago."

Millie blushed furiously, but Isaac only laughed. He had a feeling his friends at home would have done the same. What did it matter who heard their confessions of love or their plans for the future?

Whatever anyone else thought, Millie and Isaac belonged together. Somehow, it would all turn out as it should. As it had. With the two of them in love.

Epilogue

Millie walked along Inglewood's beach, her arm through her husband's, her face lifted toward the breeze. "I will miss this." She leaned her head against Isaac's shoulder and released a sigh. "Must we really go to London this Season?"

Her husband did not laugh at her reluctance, but she could *feel* his amusement. "I remember a time when all you wanted was a long winter in Town."

"Thought I wanted." She snorted and pulled back, looking up at him with one eyebrow raised. She had studied Esther's ability to appear imperious. "But it really is such a horrid heap of political maneuvering."

She looked behind them to see Silas and Esther walking several feet back, each holding one of little Isaac's hands. They counted to three and swung the small boy forward, and he shrieked in delight.

Isaac drew her back to their conversation. "You will get to spend time with your parents."

"And Emmeline." Millie's heart lifted. When her parents had been confronted with the loss of a second daughter to a less-than-advantageous marriage, Millie had been certain they would cut her off as they had Emmeline. Instead, they had packed their London household up and went directly to Warwickshire, to meet their grandchildren.

Cadoc had welcomed them, Emmeline had forgiven them. Things were not easy, not all the time. Millie's mother still made occasional comments meant to slight her sons-in-law, but the family did their best to ignore her when she behaved that way. And their father—he was happier than his daughters had ever seen him, declaring there was nothing so wonderful as having grand-children.

What a change a year could bring.

"Very well," Millie conceded at last. "But we will not stay for the whole of the Season. I should much rather be home in the spring. I think our first child ought to be born at Woodsbridge."

Isaac stopped walking abruptly and turned to look down at her. "Our first—Lady Fox. What did you say?"

She grinned and stood on her toes to give him a kiss upon his jaw—the only thing she could reach unless he bent to give her greater access. "Our first child should be born at home. Surrounded by the people who love us most."

Isaac wrapped his arm about her, pulling her close enough to lift her from the ground and twirl her about. He was laughing, the sound joyful and bright. Then he hastily set her back upon her feet, his eyes widening with alarm. "I am terribly sorry. Are you well? Dizzy? Perhaps the walk has fatigued you. Come. Let me get you home to rest."

Millie laughed, and Isaac stared at her, with an expression that bordered on panic.

"My love, are you going to be so overly protective the entire time?"

Esther and Silas had come up close enough to hear that question. Silas had little Isaac in his arms and a smirk upon his face. Esther came up to Millie and shared a commiserating look with her. "Told him, did you?"

Isaac glared at her, then his expression immediately softened when he looked back down at Millie. "Essie knew?"

Millie grinned at him and shrugged. "She guessed."

Millie kept walking, smiling to herself. Isaac looped his arm around her waist, holding her close as they walked.

"A child," he whispered, barely loud enough to be heard over the waves. "I hoped—"

"As did I." Millie snuggled closer. "And we will come home for the birth."

"Whatever you wish, my dear."

It was as Emmeline had said. Not perfect. Isaac had nightmares still, but Millie was there to soothe him when he woke. The marquess's family made it a point to avoid Silas, Esther, Isaac, and Millie. But her reputation, as insignificant as it was, remained intact.

And they were happy. There was joy in the laughter they shared, gentleness in the sorrow, and hope for what was to come.

"I love you, Sir Isaac."

"And I love you, Lady Fox."

While she had begun as the villain in her own love story, Millie had ended the happiest of heroines.

≈

If you enjoyed this story, and if you're just as confused by Lord Neil's behavior as Sir Isaac, you might want to check out Reforming Lord Neil, the fifth book in the series. Do you think Lord Neil could ever be someone's hero?

Acknowledgments & Notes

Writing isn't easy. No matter how hard an author tries, they can never be perfect. I have yet to publish a book completely devoid of typos or minor mistakes - even the largest publishing houses in the world usually have what they call "an acceptable error rate." No book is perfect, because no author, editor, or proofreader, is perfect, either. So I am all the more grateful for the wonderful people on my team who help me polish my drafts until they shine.

Thank you to Jenny Proctor, an incredible editor, and Carri Flores, my proofreader and assistant. Thank you to Shaela Kay, a dear friend, my designer, and my favorite sounding board for all my author struggles.

I must express my gratitude to my wonderful readers! There are so many of you who reach out through email and messenger to let me know what you think of my books. I do this for you, and I'm grateful my stories have touched your hearts. Thank you especially to those who are part of my Sweet Romance Fans on Facebook.

My darling husband is my greatest support, my hero, and the man who makes certain I have the time and emotional energy to write. My children are understanding, kind, and they will never know how much I need their sweet hugs and encouragement.

My favorite people in the world, after my family, are all my author friends. Thank you to Joanna, Arlem, Heidi, Megan, Jen, Mindy, Ashtyn, Sarah, Martha, Jennie, Deborah, Jess, Kasey, and ALL the authors who consider themselves Obstinate, Headstrong Girls.

Also by Sally Britton

The Inglewood Series:

Book #1, *Rescuing Lord Inglewood*

Book #2, *Discovering Grace*

Book #3, *Saving Miss Everly*

Book #4, *Engaging Sir Isaac*

Book #5, *Reforming Lord Neil*

The Branches of Love Series:

Prequel Novella, *Martha's Patience*

Book #1, *The Social Tutor*

Book #2, *The Gentleman Physician*

Book #3, *His Bluestocking Bride*

Book #4, *The Earl and His Lady*

Book #5, *Miss Devon's Choice*

Book #6, *Courting the Vicar's Daughter*

Book #7, *Penny's Yuletide Wish (A Novella)*

Forever After:

The Captain and Miss Winter

Timeless Romance:

An Evening at Almack's, Regency Collection 12

Entangled Inheritances:

His Unexpected Heiress

About the Author

Sally Britton no longer lives in the desert with her husband and four children. Instead, she calls Texas home no matter where her adventures take her.

Sally started writing her first story on her mother's electric typewriter, when she was fourteen years old. Reading her way through Jane Austen, Louisa May Alcott, and Lucy Maud Montgomery, Sally decided to write about the elegant, complex world of centuries past.

Sally graduated from Brigham Young University in 2007 with a bachelor's in English, her emphasis on British literature. She met and married her husband not long after and they've been building their happily ever after since that day.

Vincent Van Gogh is attributed with the quote, "What is done in love is done well." Sally has taken that as her motto, for herself and her characters, writing stories where love is a choice.

All of Sally's published works are available on Amazon.com and you can connect with Sally and sign up for her newsletter on her website, AuthorSallyBritton.com.

Made in the USA
Las Vegas, NV
31 March 2023

69976065R10166